A
Thrilling
Novel
by

PROJECT KYLE

Protect your sanity at all costs.

ISBN-13: 978-0692169278
ISBN-10: 069216927X
[1. Science-Fiction 2. Mystery 3. Suspense 4. Phycological 5. Thriller]

Photos of Sophia Nelson-E.A. Catania.

Cover art © Project Kyle.

Book art © Project Kyle.

Note from the author

⚠ Warning. Although this book is intended to reach a wide audience and does not contain explicit material, *Deep Cosmos* is a sci-fi series that contains content that is susp-enseful, intense, and sometimes scary. It tackles several serious issues and dives deep into the psychiatric mind. If you are easily terrified, sensitive to eerie content, or overwhelmed when stories contain psychological elements, I would not recommend reading this book until you are familiar with material that features suspense. This has been your warning.

With that being said, sit back, relax, and enjoy your experience as you embark on your journey…into the Deep Cosmos.

Table of Contents

The Galactic Times

After a long session, the galactic court has found Dr. David Bell guilty of spearheading the human laboratory experiments of Cosmic 5. David Bell has been charged with genocide and given the death penalty!

Documents supplied by Dr. Crimson show that David Bell ordered the mutilation of at least 685 subjects, including men, women, and children. The experiments were inhumane and highly illegal. Thankfully, the inhabitants of our galaxy can sleep soundly tonight, as David Bell will be executed by tomorrow. He will no longer be around to cause any more grief.

We at the *Galactic Times* would like to express our gratitude to the galactic court for taking such strong action against this despicable human being. May the human race continue to prosper, and may better times come our way.

Earth date: March 12th, 2009

Missing!
Sophia Nelson

AGE: 21

HEIGHT: 5'4"

WEIGHT: 120 LBS

EYES: SILVER

LAST SEEN AT THE HOT SPRINGS OF KETHAR
IF YOU HAVE ANY INFO OR HAVE SEEN SOPHIA
PLEASE CONTACT DR. CRIMSON IMMEDIATELY

CHAPTER 1 SOPHIA

Earth date: February 4th, 2010

Time: 1200

Location: Underground Lair, Zentar

Sophia groaned. The sound of dripping water surrounded her. She had no idea how long she was out, let alone who had attacked her, putting her in this state. Her vision was blurry, and at first she was unable to identify where she was. All she knew was that she was no longer sitting by the hot springs of Kethar where she had been anxiously waiting for her boy-friend, Dr. Crimson, to arrive. Her former location was warm, fresh, and had a sweet aroma. Her new location was cold, the air was stale, and the stench of mold was so bad that it made Sophia feel sick.

As time passed, she was slowly able to regain her vision. There was only one light in the room, and it revealed a horrid

3

sight. Rusty machines stood all around her: a giant saw to her right, a large drill to her left, and a three-pronged claw with a razor welded onto each tip lurking above her face. She knew she was in danger and needed to escape immediately. She attempted to prop herself up but was unable to do so.

Her heart began to race as her eyes shifted downward, informing her that she was strapped to an operating table. Her arms, legs, neck, feet, and wrists were shackled. There was a belt wrapped tightly around her waist and another wrapped around her forehead, making it impossible for her to shift her position. She was totally paralyzed and unable to escape.

Afraid for her life, she attempted to let out a scream, with hopes that someone would hear her cry for help. She was unable to, as her mouth had been muzzled shut. There was no escape, no way out for her, meaning she would be at the mercy of her captor, and there was nothing she could do.

Sophia's vision cleared some more, and she was able to make out the silhouette of a man about ten feet in front of her. He was sharpening a large Bowie knife, which was visible due to the light reflecting off it.

"Hello, Sophia," a soft, calm, yet disturbingly familiar voice called. "It's time to find out what makes you so… special."

The shadow man stepped forward into the light. Sophia felt her heart sink as her captor's identity was revealed.

Dr. Crimson? She thought to herself. The man she had been dating for well over a month. *No…no!* She refused to believe it; this had to be a misunderstanding. Crimson would never try to hurt her. He would never try to hurt anyone; she was certain of it. But something was different about him this time. The last time she saw him, his face was vibrant and full of life. Now, his face seemed to be grim, emotionless, and dead. There was no feeling, no sign of life or energy. He was an empty shell with no substance inside. It was terrifying, and it was evident that he was not the same man that she knew.

Sadly, whatever faith she had left in him was quickly shattered when he responded to the startled look on her face.

"Don't look so surprised, my love," he said to her. "Surely you must've known I was way out of your league. What would a famous doctor ever want with someone like you? The facts were right in front of you. You were a disappointment to your family and a failure as a person. You confided this to me many times, so you must have known that you never had a chance. But you allowed your human emotions to take control. You fell for me, even though you knew I could never love someone as low as you, and because of this, you will pay."

A dull numbness began to fill Sophia. Her racing heart began to slow down, and an ache began to grow within it. The man who claimed to be her true love had taken advantage of her, and through his actions he had dug up every mental scar she had fought so hard to bury. Her silver eyes began to fill with tears, which only seemed to amuse the monstrous human being in front of her.

"Oh, don't cry, little one," Dr. Crimson taunted. "It's your fault that you're in this mess. You were stupid enough to trust me, and now you have become my next victim. Although you may be worthless, your organs are very much needed right now for my next experiment. I'm afraid I must remove them from you, piece by piece."

Dr. Crimson slowly ran his fingers through Sophia's soft red hair and gazed deeply into her eyes. She felt her skin crawl as he did so, but then she realized that things were about to get a lot worse. Crimson's cold, calm state began to shift, morphing into a lust for human life. He had trapped his victim, and now he was ready to devour his prey.

A psychotic smile spread across Crimson's once emotionless face. He placed the Bowie knife above Sophia's shoulder, ready to cut her open. He laughed vigorously as he savored his moment of glory. However, right as he was about to begin, a blue light flashed from the back of the room. Crimson instantly lost focus and turned to face what was behind him.

"You!" He shouted in rage. "I told you what would happen if you ever stood in my way again. Do you really have a death wish? Have you really fallen that low?"

The mysterious man slowly walked into the light. Like Crimson, he was wearing a white lab coat with a button-up shirt underneath, accompanied by a pair of long black leather gloves that covered his bare hands and a third of his sleeves. He had dark hair and round, oversized glasses. He stood at about 5'9" and weighed no more than 160 pounds. His skin was very pale, and his face was straight, firm, but far from emotionless. Overall, the man looked to be quite the geek, and he would've been the last person Sophia could see standing up to Crimson, who was tall, strong, and robust. However, as the mysterious stranger started talking, she began to realize that there was more to him than his appearance gave him credit for.

"Because of you, I lost everything," the man responded. "My life is not what's important, the life you're trying to take right now is. So why would I hesitate to risk a life that doesn't matter to save a life that does? But a man like you would never understand. Your mind is just too small to grasp the more complex things this universe has to offer. That's why you feed on the innocent. It's the only way someone like you could ever have a sense of self-worth."

Crimson's right hand started to shake. He gritted his teeth, and for the first time since he and Sophia had met, he seemed to be frustrated and angry.

"Your senseless preaching bores me!" Crimson said to the man. "I no longer have any use for you. If you want to die so badly, then die!"

Suddenly, Crimson darted towards the man, swinging his knife back and forth at a speed that seemed to challenge the sound barrier. The man quickly walked backwards, matching Crimson's speed, and miraculously managed to dodge every thrust Crimson made with his blade. Sophia was stunned; both men showed tremendous speed and skill. However, a great deal of frustration overcame her as well, as an old flame started to burn deep inside.

After a few seconds, the mysterious man led Crimson towards the light. He was so focused on killing the man, Crimson paid no attention to what was behind him as he took a swing at the man's head. He missed and drove his blade straight into the light. A bright flash filled the room, and darkness soon followed.

For a brief second, all went silent. So much so that the room seemed to be empty. After a moment had passed, however, it was evident that the mysterious man had planned this all along as Sophia felt her restraints unhinge. She was swept off the operating table and carried across the pitch-black room.

Twenty seconds had now passed since the battle had started, and it wasn't soon to finish. Crimson had found a flashlight and was able to spot the two individuals running out of the hall.

"Well played!" Dr. Crimson shouted across the room. "It took you long enough, but you have learned how to give me the rush I need. Let the hunt begin!"

Crimson's eyes began to fill with excitement. He started prowling like a lion stalking his prey. As soon as the moment felt right to him, he charged at his two victims, with his large knife still flashing in his hand. The man carrying Sophia stopped as soon as Crimson started running. He turned around to face Crimson and fearlessly confronted the raging monster that was charging at them. Sophia attempted to scream at the man and urge him to continue running, but the muzzle was still wrapped around her mouth, as the man did not have the time to remove it.

The man reached into his pocket and pulled out a comm-unicator. Sophia looked up at the man's face. He had exch-anged his glasses for night vision goggles, which explained why he was able to maneuver through the dark so easily. Sophia lowered her gaze to the ground, noticing that they were standing on a teleport pad. It was the only good news she could find in the situation, given the fact that Crimson was only ten feet away from them, ready to carve them both up like a turkey. Sophia closed her eyes, preparing herself for the worst, as Crimson swiftly approached.

CHAPTER 2 NERD

Dr. Crimson continued to close in, his eyes heavily focused on Sophia's position. Things looked grim, but the mysterious man had timed everything perfectly, and he betrayed only a little fear in his voice as he spoke into his device.

"Away team to *Iron Heart*. Two to beam up, now!"

Crimson was now only three feet from them and had lunged forward in an attempt to reach them before either could be transported. In a courageous move, the mysterious man turned his back towards Crimson, putting his body in bet-ween Sophia and Crimson's blade. This told Sophia that he was indeed more interested in protecting her than himself. However, the move was unnecessary, as a flow of energy surrounded them both.

White light seemed to cover the two of them, and a weightless feeling soon followed. The light then faded, and thankfully, both individuals were now in a new location. The man quickly put her down, ripped off his night vision goggles, and ran towards a set of stairs leading upward, dropping his goggles next to Sophia in the process.

Sophia sat on the ground, attempting to process everything that had just happened to her. Her eyes were still red and puffy from the crying she had done earlier, and she was still weighted down by shock and heartache due to what had just taken place. She was in the dark as to what had happened between Dr. Crimson and the mysterious man. But it was evident that the two held a deep-seated grudge against each other, and somehow, her being kidnapped had ignited it. It was powerful, even a little scary. Still, she felt a level of gratitude to the man who had just risked his life to save her, even if he did look like a goober.

Sophia attempted to chuckle at the thought of the appearance of her hero but realized she couldn't, as the muzzle was still forcing her mouth shut. She wanted it off and wanted it off now. So, she picked herself up and followed the man up the stairway and into a large room, which seemed to be the main deck. The starship began to shake, and a loud warp sound could be heard, giving her the impression that they had just entered hyperspace.

Upon gaining her footing, Sophia looked ahead and noticed a doorway, where she could faintly hear the man's voice. She walked towards it, hoping she could get some answers.

The door automatically opened, and she was easily able to walk through. She was now in a long hallway that led to another door. The room was lit by a long row of lights that were located on either side of the floor. She now knew what type of ship she was in: it was a J2 Dragon-class spacecraft, which had been extinct for years due to the fall of the Zecarah family. Somehow, this man had gotten his hands on one, which told her that he had connections with the upper class.

Sophia made her way down the long hallway, her footsteps echoing through the metal room with each step she took. When she finally reached the door at the end, it opened automatically, revealing what was on the other side.

Sure enough, she was on the bridge of the small spacecraft. The man was sitting in the pilot's seat and chomping on a bag of cheese puffs. She looked around the room and noticed bags of chips and empty soda cans covering the entire bridge. It was a pigsty, and clearly the man didn't care. It was evident that he was aware she was in the room, as he spoke to her with half-chewed cheese puffs still rolling around in his mouth.

"That was quite a close call, wasn't it? A second later and you would've been missing your right arm at the very least. Good thing I was there to get you out of that mess, eh?"

Sophia was unable to respond. The man swallowed what was in his mouth and tried to talk to her a little bit more seriously than before.

"I was just kidding. What he tried to do to you, it was horrible. I'm just grateful that I was able to stop him before it was too late. I wasn't always able to do so with him in the past. I'm glad I was at least able to save one life, compared to the thousands that he slaughtered."

Sophia was still unable to respond. The man was concerned, and he quickly turned around to face Sophia. Cheese puff crumbs covered his shirt, pants, and lab coat.

"Look! I know I'm not a charmer by any means, but you could at least..." Suddenly, the man noticed the muzzle around Sophia's jaw. A panicked look covered his face, and he reached into his lab coat to pull out what looked like some sort of key. "Aaaaaah!" he shouted. "Sorry, sorry, so sorry! That was very insensitive of me. Please hold still, I'll get that off ya."

The man placed the key in one of the muzzle's slots. The muzzle unhinged, and Sophia was finally free to speak. She rubbed her jawline with both her hands. A sudden jolt of pain shot through her jaw. She sharply inhaled through her teeth and swiftly retracted her hands. The muzzle was strapped so tight that it had bruised the lower part of her face. Sophia was not thrilled about this, but she was relieved that the stupid thing was finally off her.

The man noticed, and concern could be seen in his eyes as he examined the bruises, but after noticing that Sophia was attempting to hide her face, his eyes diverted from the bruises to her. She was very self-conscious of how she looked, especially right now, and he seemed to notice. Yet he didn't seem to know how to respond, so he simply put the key back in his pocket, smiled, and continued talking to her like nothing had happened.

"Welcome aboard, my friend! Don't worry about that mean old doctor; he has been trying to find me for the last year. The only way he will ever see me is if I come to him, but I guess that's not important right now. What is important is you! Obviously, you had to be special for him to build an operating room underground just to…operate on you. Which makes me feel very curious as to who you are. What is your name? Where do you come from? Why was Dr. Crimson so obsessed with dissecting you?"

Sophia's mind was still catching up to all the talking the man was doing, so there was a pause in her response. However, it seemed like, through all the scattered words, he simply wanted to know who she was and reassure her that she was safe. She felt that this was very sweet of him, even if his methods of expressing it were primitive at best.

She took a deep breath and answered him with a soft, timid voice.

"My name is Sophia Nelson. I am a warrior from the V.T.C... Or I was. Vincent Taylor didn't trust me, and I had to leave, fearful that he would set up a court-martial to have me executed for a crime he staged. It was a common practice against warriors that either advanced in rank too quickly or simply made him paranoid. So, I decided to step down and I asked if they would cut me free. Vincent, thankfully, was relieved that I wanted out and accepted my request. Since then, I've been searching the galaxy for work and traveled to the planet Zentar. I was hoping to get a job as a simple care-taker. However, I was distracted by...him."

Sadness seemed to cover the man's face at Sophia's response. It was evident that he knew Dr. Crimson all too well and that she was not the first girl he had deceived or tried to kill. It was troubling him greatly, and Sophia knew he was lost in thought.

Sophia took a deep breath and gently grabbed the man's hands, which were starting to tremble.

"I didn't have a chance with that stupid muzzle locked around my jaw," Sophia started. "So, now that I have the chance, I just want to say thank you for saving my life. That was a very noble thing for you to do for me. But goodness, I was greatly impressed with how swiftly you were able to dodge Crimson's attacks. I've seen him with a blade before, and he's insanely good. As an ex-warrior, I want you to know that I am deeply impressed, and I can tell you that I do not impress easily."

The man instantly snapped out of his little phase of sadness. A huge smile covered his face, and he spoke so quickly and so loudly that Sophia was startled at his change in attitude.

"Of course! Why would I not help such a nice girl like you? It was my honor."

Sophia let go of his hands and paused again, as she needed a moment to get her bearings. But the man seemed to understand her need for a little time to respond; it was like he expected it. So, she didn't feel rushed to speak, which was nice, considering how awkward the situation was becoming. But there was one question she still needed an answer to, one that should've been asked earlier in their conversation but had been forgotten, given the wild roller coaster ride she had been through. But it was time nonetheless, and Sophia finally asked the question that, unknown to her, would change her life forever.

"What is your name? Certainly, I must know the name of the man who saved my life."

The man gave her a dorky grin.

"My name is irrelevant. Just call me Nerd. Supreme human intelligence and sole human agent of the organization known as Deep Cosmos."

Sophia laughed at his response and was clearly amused. "Nerd? You had all the names to pick from and you picked Nerd?"

"I felt it was fitting!" Nerd responded. "I'm smart, witty, deep, but not much of a social butterfly, as you can see by the way I talk and converse with others. Besides, it was the code name of the former agent who…used to own this starship."

Nerd began to lose focus again. The mention of the former ship's owner had saddened him, but he was fighting it with everything he had. This was another puzzle piece to her hero's backstory: it wasn't Nerd who had originally owned the spacecraft. Obviously, he was close to someone who had connections. This didn't mean much at the moment, but if she learned more about him, maybe it would give her some more insight into who he was.

Now Sophia was very intrigued. There was a lot going on within this strange man, and although he was socially awkward, he seemed to care about others a lot. He seemed to care about her a lot, even though they had just met that day.

Nerd regained his focus. He felt it was best to change the subject. He didn't want to have a meltdown in front of his new guest like he did the last time.

"So!" he started. "You wanted to be a caretaker. I'm quite intrigued that you would go from a warrior to someone who preserves life. We kind of need more people like that nowadays!"

"I suppose so," Sophia responded. "I was hoping that connecting with nature would help me to recover."

"Recover?" he asked.

"Yeah, it's a long story. Can I ask you a question?"

"Shoot!"

"Are you a doctor? You carry yourself like one."

"I am indeed! I do more research than attending patients, but I can prescribe medication, diagnose illness, and I've been trained to be a therapist if I need to be."

"I have always felt safe around doctors. I don't know why, but I always have. But today, I saw one attempt to do something that was completely inhumane. You seem to know Dr. Crimson well, obviously better than I did. I just...I just want to know why he would do that to me. Why would he try to hurt me? I've never tried to hurt him."

Nerd took a deep breath and answered Sophia's question the same way he did to the others before her who had escaped from Crimson's clutches.

"Dr. Crimson suffers from a mental condition known as antisocial personality disorder. Most of humanity recognizes those with the disorder as psychopaths. Someone who does not have the capability to feel compassion or remorse. In fact, with the exception of emotions that run on adrenaline and dopamine, he really can't feel emotion at all. Still, he is a master at mimicking human emotion, especially if someone has something he wants. He can appear to be a perfect angel, a gentle-natured man who loves everyone. Believe me, as a friend, I fell for it too. But when he gets bored with you, or if you don't see eye to eye with his twisted view of human life, that angel literally shuts off, and a cold, empty killing machine takes its place. One that longs to devour any trace of light that can be found in this galaxy... I'm sorry, Sophia, I really am. I was able to save you from the physical damage, but knowing him, he attempted to cut more deeply than his literal blade ever could."

Sophia suddenly felt something break inside her. She wasn't at all ready to reveal her secrets or insecurities to a man she had just met, especially after what just happened with Crimson. It didn't matter if Nerd was a doctor, or that he had even saved her life, she didn't want to be that vulnerable again; but, the cold state of shock was starting to wear off and reality was rearing its ugly head. Despite her desperate attempts to keep her emotions to herself, Sophia felt her grip on control slip as words and emotions spilled out without letting up.

"He ripped open everything!" Sophia shouted as her emotions came to life. "My childhood, my teen years, all the pain and disappointment I went through; it's all been brought back to me! He reminded me of how worthless I am, how unloved I am. No one loves me, and for a moment I thought that he did... I was wrong."

"You're not worthless, Sophia," he said to her. "I have known you for precisely one hour and 9.4 seconds, and even I can see you have many qualities that make you valuable."

"But that's not how I feel," Sophia responded. "He used me, and I can't get that out of my head!"

"Let me guess. You were his one true love, an angel in his eyes, a glimmer of light in a dark reality, a gift, and one he would cherish with his life. Then, when his little show was over, you were worthless, beyond hope, a disappointment that would be better off dead, and he used that twisted logic to justify what he was about to do to you."

"Yes," Sophia responded, "that is exactly what he said...and what he did."

Nerd closed his eyes and began flicking his fingers into his chest like he was typing. He started mumbling and was again lost in thought. Sophia was at least touched that Crimson's actions against her upset him. But she was also a little creeped out, as her savior seemed to be a little off. He was far from normal, and although he showed extreme intelligence, he was really struggling to carry on a normal conversation with her. Everything had to be advanced, intense, or quirky. Even the simplest of things were complicated, and it made her feel a little uncomfortable at times. She didn't know why she trusted him so quickly and opened up to him after knowing him for only an hour. It was like he had abilities normal humans just didn't have. It was beautiful, yet very unsettling.

While all this was going through Sophia's head, the silence was broken as Nerd began to speak again.

"Sophia," he continued. "Why don't I show you to your room? It's been a rough day, and I think we both need some time to ourselves. Just tell me where you need to go, and I will make sure to take you there. I will have to make a stop before I drop you off. After that, I'll make sure to set you free. Remember, you're not a prisoner here. No one is ever a prisoner here…not on my ship, not ever…"

Sophia let out a sigh. She began to tear up again, as her current situation was brought to mind.

"I have nowhere to go," she said to him. "I'm not safe on Zentar, and I have nothing on my home world Zecarah… especially with what's happening there right now. My parents disowned me, and every friend I've ever had abandoned me. You can drop me off wherever you wish. I have no home to return to."

Nerd seemed to be drawn into Sophia's story. He removed his glasses, giving Sophia a clear view of his hazy blue eyes. They were focused on her, which was unusual considering how he had struggled to make eye contact before.

"You're…alone," he said to her in a very calm yet sadd-ened voice.

"Yes," Sophia responded. "I am alone. I'm the one that no one wants in their life, and no one ever will."

Nerd let out a huge sigh. He maintained eye contact, but this time in a way that was not creepy. It was clear that he understood what she was feeling, even though he was unable to put it into words. It was there, buried underneath his geeky shell. He closed his eyes and rubbed his forehead, grimacing, before seeming to come to a temporary solution with a slight nod.

"I need time to think this through. Please go upstairs into the top section of the ship. The room is small, but it contains everything you will need. Try to rest up…you're going to need it."

Sophia could not think of a response, so she didn't say anything. She simply nodded her head and left the bridge. She walked through the long hallway, entered the main dock, and made her way upstairs until she reached the room Nerd had asked her to go to. It was indeed small, but there was food, along with a refrigerator full of drinks. There was a TV with a game console plugged into it. There was a sleeping bag on the floor and next to it was what looked to be a tablet. Sophia wasn't in the mood to eat or drink; she was very depressed and still shaken over everything that had happened. But she figured she would at least try to keep her mind active enough to keep it off of Dr. Crimson. She sat on the sleeping bag, picked up the tablet, and turned it on.

There was no password, so she had no problem getting to the main screen. There were many apps on it: games, news, social media, photos, and galactic livestream, the number one video streaming site in the galaxy. *I guess I can binge watch my favorite shows,* she thought to herself. *At least until Nerd finds me a new home.*

She crawled under the sleeping bag and held the device upward. She was about to view the movies and videos on galactic livestream when she noticed that someone had sent a text to the device. It wasn't in her nature to snoop; however, her curiosity got the better of her. She pressed the message and was stunned when a video popped up.

She let out a yelp at the sight that appeared in front of her. A strange creature wearing a double-breasted gray suit and a gray fedora was looking back at her. It wouldn't have been so frightening if it wasn't for the fact that the creature's face was simply one giant eyeball, bloodshot and angry-looking. The creature began to speak. It didn't take long for Sophia to realize that the creature was not evil at all. In fact, the message was pre-recorded, intended for her. It was about Nerd, and the creature was speaking about him as a concerned friend. Sophia listened to every word, eager to hear what the creature had to say.

"Greetings, young human. I am known as the Observer. If you are receiving this message, then Nerd's little disobedience to orders paid off. He was able to save you from the second most wanted man on the Deep Cosmos criminal list, Dr. Crimson.

"First, I want to offer my condolences, because I know how much pain that man can inflict on others. I know how much pain he inflicted on Nerd, and it broke my hearts to watch. The kid has done well, filling the shoes of the former legend and living up to our expectations as Aiden's successor. But as hard as the kid has tried, he is still very much lost. Crimson messed him up good and used his mask as a means to incriminate Nerd. Yes, you are in the starship of the most wanted criminal in the galactic government. Nerd's real name is David Bell. He is the one who was found guilty in the Cosmic 5 tragedy of illegal human experimentation."

Sophia felt her joints lock as her heart accelerated. She had read about David Bell in the *Galactic Times* and learned what he had done to people. Thousands were mutilated against their will, and many of them died within the laboratories walls. The papers were only able to report a small fraction of the things he had done, but the small fraction that was revealed was enough to spread fear and terror throughout the galaxy. She began trembling, realizing that she had simply switched hands from one psychopath to the other.

"I know you probably feel scared right now." *That was the understatement of the year!* "But I can reassure you that you have no reason to be. David did not kill those people; that has been proven. Dr. Crimson killed those people and paid off the judges to support his story. David took the fall, Crimson got away with murder, and he continues to murder down to this very day.

"Now that I have revealed the truth, I have a favor to ask of you that may decide whether this galaxy survives or not. We need David if we're going to survive the things that are about to come.

"As you know, David Bell is a hated man. This is why he hides behind his glasses and nerdy exterior. It's built up in him over this last year, and although I am proud of the progress he has made as an agent, I fear that this man is at the end of his rope. It's going to get worse now, considering he disobeyed the central commander's orders not to get involved with Dr. Crimson. To put it mildly, he may have sacrificed his future in Deep Cosmos for you. Your life was more important to him than his own, and the amazing thing about that is, he never even knew you. He never knew who you were, yet he sacrificed everything to save you. That's the kind of man I've grown to know and love—the man who would sacrifice everything to save the life of a stranger. And now, I want you to do the same. I beg you to do the same.

"I want you to save the one person he is incapable of saving. I want you to help the one person he could never upbuild, encourage, or protect. Sophia, I want you to save David Bell. He is the only source of light this galaxy has to offer. Please, please save David Bell."

The video message ended, and Sophia felt all her emotions fade away. She had been on such an emotional roller coaster ride that day, and finally it had become too much for her heart to handle. She no longer knew who to trust, for it seemed that everyone who promised to take care of her was eager to stab her in the back as soon as she let her guard down.

She wanted to believe what the Observer was saying; she wanted to believe that David was framed by the same man who tried to take her life. At least then she could know her life wasn't still in danger. But could she really trust the words of a creature she had never met? Could she believe that a man she had feared for a good year was just an innocent victim, incriminated by someone who was far worse? She didn't know, and her mind couldn't handle it right now.

Sophia crawled further into her sleeping bag and pulled it over her face. Her body and mind had finally had enough and shut down for the rest of the night. She faded away into a dream, a faraway place, a reality where she could escape from the grim existence she was trapped in.

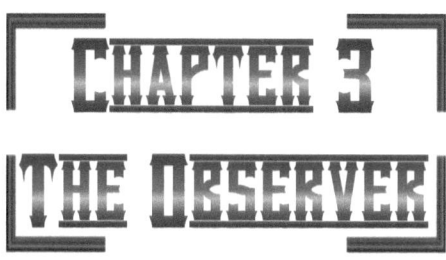

CHAPTER 3

THE OBSERVER

Earth date: February 5th, 2010

Time: 1400

Location: Central Core, the gap between realities

The Observer made his way into the airlift, deathly nervous over what he was about to do. It was not every day the supreme commander would listen to an appeal, especially before the court-martial even took place, but it had to be done. If he did nothing, his friend would be removed from the Deep Cosmos ranks, shattering any hope of Crimson ever being brought to justice.

The airlift door closed and the structure shot up like a cannon.

Only moments separated the Observer from his greatest fear, a meeting with the one person he was unable to monitor, predict, or understand. A person who many avoided approaching at all costs. For although the Supreme Commander oversaw an organization devoted to doing good, he was not known for his ability to tolerate the imperfections of those working underneath him.

Within seconds, the top floor was reached, and the airlift door slowly opened. The room was dark and lit with dim blue and purple neon lights. It was huge, with enough space for a large house to sit comfortably inside it. There were monitors everywhere, each one displaying a different person or territory in the SC's command.

At first, the Observer did not know what to do. He was too nervous to make a move. The supreme commander, however, wasn't going to waste much time with him and commanded him to walk over to his desk.

"You said this meeting was urgent," the supreme commander stated.

"Yes," the Observer replied as he hesitantly made his way toward the commander's desk, shrinking in the commander's presence.

No one had ever seen the supreme commander's true identity, as he was somehow able to hide behind a shadow. No one knew how he did this, and no one knew what race he was or where he came from, let alone how he was ever granted the authority that was bestowed upon him. All they knew was to never question the supreme commander's logic. Those who did were often fired or mysteriously disappeared

26

from existence. Still, there was too much on the line for the Observer to be worried about his own safety. The Observer spoke up and began to plead his case.

"David Bell is returning from his away mission. On his return, he will most likely be court-martialed for disobeying your orders."

"Ah yes!" The supreme commander replied. "The human agent. Such a tragedy; honestly, I rather liked that one. He was most entertaining, I must say."

"Entertaining, sir?"

"Oh, come now. When you have been cramped up in here for as long as I have, watching every agent under your command, you begin to pick your favorites over time. David is one of mine. To be honest, I had great faith that he would never stand in Dr. Crimson's way until his time came. Pity he let me down."

"Dr. Crimson was going to kill an innocent person, Commander! He was going to cut her up and bleed her out. I know David may have put his identity in jeopardy, which could potentially cost more lives in the long run, but I do know a thing or two about humans. I don't feel that this is something that David will make a habit of. He saw an innocent girl in danger, and he wasn't cold enough to hold back and do nothing. That's not a sign of weakness, Commander; that's a sign of strength, and we want people like him roaming the universe! Trust me, the galaxy he was assigned to protect needs it right now."

The supreme commander let out a sigh. It was clear that he was not angered at the Observer's straightforward words. Still, there were concerns he had with the situation.

"I'm a perfectionist," he continued. "Those who disobey orders are either dismissed from Deep Cosmos or executed. I can reassure you that David will not be executed. His actions were not evil, and although I don't understand human compassion, that doesn't mean I don't appreciate it; however, there are great concerns about what could happen if we allow David to keep doing this. I may keep a close eye on my agents, but you…you're called the Observer for a reason. Your insight goes well beyond the agents of Deep Cosmos. So, tell me, does Crimson know that it was David Bell who interfered with his plans?"

The Observer took a moment to refresh his memory. He searched through the vast files that comprised his seemingly endless knowledge of the people he kept an eye on.

He remembered seeing Crimson after David and Sophia had escaped. After diving head first into the basement wall behind the transporter, Crimson howled in rage, letting out the words that revealed where his empty heart was.

"Curse you, Nerd! I won't rest until you ▓▓▓▓▓▓▓ ▓▓▓▓▓▓▓▓▓▓▓▓▓▓▓▓▓▓▓▓▓▓▓ *for what you have done!"*

The Observer breathed a sigh of relief.

"No, he thought it was Nerd, the same Nerd who retrieved all the evidence from Cosmic 5."

In a rare moment unseen to most, the supreme commander began to laugh. He was greatly amused at the Observer's words, and it was clear that things were starting to skew in David's favor.

"Very well, I'll order the central commander to call off the court-martial. Honestly, it's kind of nice to watch David toy with Crimson like this. I wish it could be like this more often, but both you and I know it can't. So, although he will not be court-martialed, I want you to lecture the boy so hard that he dreads the thought of ever doing it again until his orders come. Understood?"

The Observer felt a huge weight lift off his chest. David was still in, and he could not have been any happier about it.

"Yes, sir!" he said with relief. The supreme commander dismissed him, and the Observer walked out of the room, knowing that his time had been well spent. The airlift doors closed, and he made his way back down to the lobby, where he would soon meet David to tell him the news, and then give him a good whack across the head to remind him of what an idiot he was. It was this that the Observer looked forward to the most.

CHAPTER 4 THE GAP

Earth date: February 6th, 2010

Time: 360

Location: The *Iron Heart*

Sophia was sipping her coffee as Nerd frantically searched the starship for the things he needed. She was uncertain why he was so nervous, considering he would not tell her why the stop they were making today was so important, but it was distracting him on a level that she had not seen in him before.

She had only really been able to spend one day observing him, not including the night that he saved her life. It took all the will and strength she had left to act like she wasn't terrified whenever he was around, but somehow, she had man-aged to pull it off. He suspected nothing, and that was a good thing.

At the moment, her observations were the same as when she first met him. He was off, but thankfully he didn't show any signs of ill intent. It was evident that underneath his geeky exterior lurked something much more intense. She could always sense the gears turning and the brain calculating, with no difference between his doing an incredibly detailed task or doing nothing at all.

She quickly got used to waiting for him to respond when-ever she spoke to him. It wasn't so bad, considering he was willing to do the same for her. Still, it got a little irritating at times, as it was so constant, even though he could be reached at any given time.

Today was a day where Nerd was unreachable. So, she didn't bother trying to start any small talk. She let him do his thing, hoping that he would be more receptive once he accomplished his task.

Although she had trust issues with her host, Sophia's stay on the *Iron Heart* was far from miserable. Nerd was obsessed with collecting electronics; there were stockpiles of food, enough to last them for a few years. There were even a few board games and decks of cards stored away. Nerd even offered to play a game of chess with her, a game that she would never play with him again, since he slaughtered her without mercy.

He was also a decent cook and worked hard to perfect whatever meal he was making. However, his recipe list was very limited. Already he had made the same breakfast for her twice and admitted that he only knew how to cook a few other dishes for lunch and dinner. This meant that Sophia would have to cook if she wanted variety, which was something V.T.C. warriors were not known for.

But now was not the time to be thinking too far ahead. Coffee was Sophia's friend, and it was easily making her day a lot better.

Nerd, on the other hand, was not doing so hot. He had obviously misplaced something and was ripping apart the main level to find it, making the starship even more of a mess than it was before. Sophia couldn't understand why Nerd would constantly obsess like this. She felt bad for him, as he seemed to be a slave to his own mind.

Finally, Nerd stopped. He remembered something and ran to a pile of clothes that he'd left lying around next to his bed, which was located at the end of the main level. He reached into an old pair of pants and pulled out a photograph.

"Yes!" He shouted. "I found it!"

"What is it?" Sophia asked. Nerd quickly put the photograph in his lab coat pocket.

"Nothing!" he said. "Just something I needed to get through today." Sophia was not in the mood to argue. She had only just woken up about 30 minutes ago and she didn't want to get into a confrontation with someone as intense as Nerd. She simply finished her coffee and enjoyed the brief moment of silence that followed Nerd's diabolical victory over his lost object. The silence didn't last long, however, as the ship's computer alerted them both they had arrived at their destination.

Nervous and excited, Nerd urged Sophia to follow him to the main bridge. Sophia finished off her coffee and chose to follow him…and was very much underwhelmed when all she could see out the front window was empty space. No planet, no space station, just space. Sophia shot Nerd an unimpressed glare.

"It's…amazing," she said in a sarcastic voice. Nerd laughed at Sophia's response. It was obvious he didn't pick up on her sarcasm at all.

"Oh, this?" Nerd replied. "This is nothing. However, if you're so fascinated by empty space, I'm sure you're going to love what comes next!"

Nerd entered a code into the control panel located at the front of the ship. Both of them waited for a few seconds, and suddenly, a large scanning beam appeared out of the blackness of space. It scanned the ship and ran across both Nerd and Sophia. Without warning, Sophia began to glow red. Several balls of purple energy entered the ship and slowly started to move towards Sophia. Sophia screamed and grabbed Nerd's arm.

"Oops…" Nerd said. "Hold on a second."

He typed in another code with the hand not being restrained by Sophia, who refused to let go. As soon as the code was entered, the red balls of energy turned green and then vanished. Everything was safe again.

"Those were Owl Eyes," Nerd said to Sophia. "They are security drones that vaporize anyone they touch. Sorry about that; I forgot to notify them that I had a guest with me."

Sophia punched Nerd in the shoulder with a scowl. Nerd, however, just laughed and refocused his attention on what was about to take place outside the starship. Surprisingly, Nerd did not disappoint, as a massive wormhole opened in front of them. Sophia was stunned; she had never seen one before. In fact, until now, she wasn't even sure if they existed. But here one was, right in front of them. Nerd turned to Sophia and smiled.

"Are you ready?"

Sophia was too stunned to answer. She simply nodded her head. Nerd activated the thrusters, and the ship entered the wormhole. As soon as the ship entered, it began shaking like an airplane flying through heavy turbulence. The ride was bumpy and a little intimidating, but the calm way in which Nerd handled the controls set Sophia's initial worry to rest.

After 30 seconds, the blue energy surrounding them vanished, and the starship appeared to be in what looked like a purple nebula. The visible space was very narrow, but the length of it seemed to go on forever. Sophia was excited at what was a new discovery for her and asked where he had taken her. Nerd smiled and responded.

"A place where only a few humans have the honor of visiting," he stated. "Welcome to the gap between realities."

"What?" Sophia responded incredulously. "That's impossible; there is no such thing." "You'd be surprised at how much you can discover in this universe. It's been a humbling experience for me to realize how small I am compared to what's out there; but I can assure you, I'm not lying. We are in between every universe that exists—a narrow hallway that leads into eternity. From here, we can travel to any part of the universe we wish. Everything is accessible to us, with the exception of the one thing the gap cannot control, and that's time. It continues to move forward; that is one thing we cannot change."

Sophia only heard half of Nerd's speech as she caught sight of a space station in the distance. It was a dark, pyramid-shaped structure that was about the size of Earth's moon. There were thousands of spacecrafts swarming around it like bees around a hive; large, small, primitive, and advanced, but all of them moved together as a single unit, making the sight all that more fascinating.

"What's that?" she asked.

"That is the headquarters of Deep Cosmos," Nerd responded. "Get a good look at it, because this may be the first and last time you ever come here, depending on what happens to me."

Sophia turned to Nerd with a concerned look in her eyes. She could tell he was in trouble, but he refused to answer what was going on. She remembered the Observer telling her he may have sacrificed his future, and this upset her, because whether he was a killer or not, she didn't feel that it was fair for him to take the fall.

"Nerd," she said to him, "if you are in trouble, please let me help. It's the least I could do for you."

"I appreciate the offer," Nerd responded, "but these people will not acknowledge you as one of their own. Trust me, I know them well. Please stay here while I take care of this. If things don't go well, I can assure you that they will return you to your own reality and find you a home where you'll be taken care of. It is the way of Deep Cosmos, and the reason I chose to join them in my time of need; but, if you become a threat or give them the impression of being a threat, things will only get worse, so I need to ask you to stay here. It is the only way we can get out of this in one piece."

Sophia was deeply bothered by what Nerd said, and although she knew that none of this was her fault, her conscience niggled at the back of her mind uneasily. The situation felt heavy, and she felt helpless to make things better. Nerd noticed she was upset, so he walked up and patted her on the shoulder.

"It's going to be okay, Sophia," he said to her. "They won't kill me or execute me or anything like that. They only do that to people who threaten them or the galaxies they protect, and I have never once done anything that could give them that impression. I just need to explain a few things to them, and hopefully they will understand. Their viewpoint of life on the whole is good, but their understanding of a single individual life is bad. Maybe I can use this time to speak up and help them understand. If they don't, then hopefully they'll at least allow me to keep the ship so I can still explore the galaxy without their protection. Though I doubt they will be so generous. Regardless, it's time for me to go. Take care of yourself, my friend. If a strange mutated alien beams into the ship instead of me, don't be scared. Just do as he says, and you will be able to enjoy a normal life soon enough."

Nerd left the bridge and made his way downstairs into the transporter room. Sophia followed him to wave him good-bye. Nerd stepped on the transporter and smiled.

"Farewell, Sophia!" He said to her. "It was an honor to get to know you."

As soon as the words left his mouth, the transporter activated, and Nerd vanished from the room. Sophia was now alone, something she was very much used to. She had gotten exactly what she needed. With Nerd off the ship, she now had a chance to investigate without him looking over her shoulder.

Sophia took a deep breath and slowly clasped her hands together. It was time to find out what kind of person David Bell truly was.

CHAPTER 5 LAYERS

Sophia made her way upstairs and looked around the main room. She gazed at the three pictures mounted on the wall next to David's bed. One was a picture of a scientist with red hair, the second was of a ten-year-old girl with blonde pig-tails, and the third was of a man that looked exactly like Nerd, only his hair was light brown and his eyes were emerald green, which was different from Nerd's dark hair and blue eyes. He never talked about any of them, and when Sophia had asked about them, Nerd ignored her and tried to change the subject. The thing that really stood out to her was the state of the picture frames. Nerd was no doubt a slob—the spacecraft's floors were covered with soda cans and empty bags of chips, and dust lay everywhere, even on the walls. But these photographs were completely spotless. Not a single speck of dust could be found on them, meaning that Nerd was very obsessive about keeping them clean.

Sophia decided to start digging through some of the clutter, as that was where Nerd had hidden the picture that he was looking for. She thoroughly went through his clothes and made sure to explore every pocket or compartment she could find. In the end, however, all she could find was some loose change, an expired invite to the yearly formal held at space station 1529, and a blob of gum which had welded a pocket shut when Nerd had apparently put the article of clothing carelessly through the wash without checking it. There was nothing to be found here, nothing of importance anyway.

Sophia then looked through his wardrobe and carefully removed everything from it. She examined each item she could find before she examined the wardrobe itself. Again, nothing.

Focusing her attention on the bed next, Sophia pulled off the sheets and checked under the mattress. She found a letter under Nerd's mattress, written to him from a young boy who thanked him for saving his family from a Kelson swarm. This was encouraging, as Nerd had clearly done a good deed for them, but Sophia needed more than this, as his heroic shell may only have been a mask to hide something much darker inside. Sophia had learned this much from her experience with Dr. Crimson.

After putting everything back where she had found it, Sophia looked at the table next to his bed. There was a shelf underneath that Sophia had missed, which looked very promising. She opened the shelf and dug through its contents.

"Bingo!" She said as she pulled out Nerd's diary.

This was a huge find, as she could now find out what was going on within the mind of the ship's commander. Her conscience was bothering her, because she would never look through someone's diary under normal circumstances, but in this situation it had to be done. Besides, Nerd only gave her two rules. One was to never touch any of the Rubik's cubes that could be found scattered across the *Iron Heart*, and the second was to stay on the starship until someone came back. He had said nothing about his diary.

Sophia took a deep breath, opened it up with her trembling hands, and began to read the thoughts and feelings her host had seen fit to write down. "The diary of David Bell." The diary began with a long, poetic entry about how excited he was to be joining Cosmic 5.

She read on and learned that David had been the victim of bullying. He didn't know how to retaliate, as he hated violence, and this made him an easy target for the Cosmic staff. The only person that protected him was, regrettably, Dr. Crimson, who had pretended to be his best friend. David opened up very strongly about how much he admired Crimson and wanted to be more like him. Deeper into the diary, he expressed paranoia. He was catching on to what Cosmic 5's true motives were and suspected that they were doing something horrible behind his back.

As she got deeper into his entries, she learned about two of the people in the photographs that she had seen—the assistant with red hair and the little girl with blonde pigtails. The little girl's name was Amelia and she was the daughter of Cosmic 5's president; she had been nearly murdered by a stalker known as Experiment-1. David spoke very highly of her and expressed frustration, because he didn't know how to treat her kindly and was often a jerk to her as a result, and yet, she never stopped being kind to him. This reached him and motivated him to save her life twice from the same stalker that lived on Cosmic 5.

The redheaded scientist was his lab assistant, Ronald. He was very nerdy, like David, and the two understood each other pretty well. Ronald wanted to be just like David, and David did his best to take him under his wing, but Ronald tragically disappeared after being called to take part in an experiment, which was the last straw for David. It drove him to take immediate action to get to the bottom of what was going on in Cosmic 5.

Next, she began to read about his new friend, Nerd, the only human agent in Deep Cosmos. The two teamed up and discovered many horrific things that were going on within the company. David was so determined to expose Cosmic 5 that he stupidly sent Amelia to spy on her father. She was discovered by Dr. Crimson and was almost murdered by him. She then ran into a monster that was created in one of the labs and had every limb in her body broken. The staff took her away to receive medical treatment. David never saw her again; he was informed that Amelia had died while in surgery.

The story continued, with David expressing how lonely he felt. He had either lost or been betrayed by everyone he loved, and his only friend was Nerd, a human he had only met a few days ago. The two worked hard and gathered enough evidence to overthrow Cosmic 5, but Nerd was tragically killed when the station was about to release a weapon on the planet below, which would've killed everyone on that world. Without any time to really think, Nerd took a detonator, activated it, and threw himself into the weapon. He died along with everyone within a 50-foot radius of the explosion.

David took his evidence to Nerd's starship. He escaped with his own life and was confident he could finish what the two of them had started. Later on, Sophia read about how Dr. Crimson had paid off the judges in the galactic court, which was why in spite all the evidence, David Bell was found guilty of the Cosmic 5 tragedy, and Dr. Crimson appeared to be the hero of the situation instead of the murderous psychopath he really was.

The remaining logs were very dark and depressing. Sophia began to tear up after realizing that David had gone through emotions very similar to her own. He was alone, and he often felt worthless and beyond hope. However, one entry got her attention more than any of the others before it. It read:

David Bell's log. Earth date: January 7th, 2010.

Today I unintentionally killed a man who attacked me while I was treating a patient at the Galactic Asylum. He had broken out of his room and attempted to kill the first person he saw, which was me. I turned around to face him and drove my fist into his nose, driving it upwards between his eyes. He dropped dead from the impact, never to face another living moment again.

I am horrified at what I'm experiencing right now, and I need to write it down before fear and panic overtake me.

When it happened, when the life faded from my attacker's eyes, I felt—

Those were the words written on the left page. Sophia then moved her eyes to read the right.

—and that is why I will never intentionally kill someone. That is why violence will always be a last resort. Because the memories of what I experienced will forever stay with me, and I don't ever want to go through that again! Never... never.

Sophia was very confused. It was as if there was a huge gap between the left and right page. But as she examined the book, she noticed a thin torn paper line in between the two sections. Nerd had ripped the page out that explained his feelings. But why? Why would he do that? It was obvious that he felt terrible about what he had done, even though it was unintentional and clearly in self-defense. Why would he remove two pages worth of his feelings?

Sophia was a little frustrated at the missing puzzle piece that had been removed, but it didn't really matter. She knew David felt remorse for what he did, which meant that she could trust him. Finally, something had gone right for her.

After breathing a huge sigh of relief, Sofia continued and finally got to the end of his diary. She was stunned to read what he expressed in his Final Log.

David Bell's log. Earth date: February 5th, 2010.

Yesterday, while on a Deep Cosmos training mission, I was tipped off by a Zentar barkeeper about Crimson's next victim, a young human girl named Sophia. Although I was ordered not to get involved with Dr. Crimson until our moment to strike comes, I decided to disobey the supreme commander's orders and save the life that Dr. Crimson so desperately wanted to take. I will most likely lose my job for this, but I'm okay with that, because it was worth it. Sophia is an amazing person. She's very kind-hearted and has displayed a great deal of patience with me in dealing with my quirkiness. I appreciate her gentle nature, but I also admire her strength and determination to keep fighting despite all the disappointments she's had in her lifetime.

To have known her is an honor that I wouldn't have traded for anything, and knowing that I had a part in helping her stay alive means more to me than anyone will ever know. Sadly, I am who I am. I don't know how to express that I care about her, and although she's been very patient, I know I make her feel uncomfortable at times. For that, I don't blame her, because I truly am a wreck of a man. But with what little time I have left with her, I will try to be a better person. I've already learned a lot from watching her, and maybe…just maybe, she will be able to look past all my imperfections and learn to tolerate me. I don't expect that, but I hope she can bring herself to trust me in that way. Because whether she knows it or not, she has been a huge inspiration to me over the last day and a half.

Time will be short, however, as we will probably be separated after my court-martial. I made my decision. I had to decide whether a human's life was more important to me than being a member of the Deep Cosmos team, and in the end, I chose human life. I will always choose a human's life. It's who I am and who I will forever be.

End of log

Sophia froze, completely stunned by what she had just read. She didn't cry, though tears were starting to build up in her eyes. For so long, Sophia had felt like an object with no value, as her parents, friends, and even her lover Dr. Crimson had driven her to feel that way; now, for the first time in her life, it was clear to her not everyone saw her like that. David expressed his thoughts on the matter very strongly, and the fact she was an inspiration to him helped her to remember all the good qualities that she still had. She was strong...even though the people she had loved had made her feel weak.

She closed the diary and walked up to her room. She lay on her sleeping bag and processed everything she had just read. It was going to be difficult existing with David, considering he was an emotional wreck. There was something very off about him, and she was scared to ask about it because she didn't want him to take it personally, but she wanted to help him. That's why she became a warrior, after all—to fight for the innocent and to save people who could not save themselves. So, with the issue of David's intentions out of the way, she had to accept the Observer's request. She had to find a way to save David Bell, or at least encourage him long enough to get him to a point where he could save himself.

An hour passed, and Sophia heard the sound of the transporter downstairs. She anxiously stood up and darted down the stairway as fast as she could. She felt a huge wave of relief when she saw that the visitor was indeed Nerd. He was holding what looked like shopping bags in each hand, which was very unusual considering he had just come back from Deep Cosmos HQ.

"Hey!" he said to her. "Guess what? I..." Sophia walked up to him and gave him a hug. Nerd froze and clearly did not know how to respond. "...Ah...okay, that was unexpected. You actually seem somewhat happy to see me... But anyway, I need to tell you something!"

Sophia let go of David and stepped back.

"Go ahead," she said to him. "What do you need to tell me?"

"Well! I realize I don't wear makeup and jewelry and stuff. You're probably missing that here. So, the Observer and I sent a few others out and had some agents find a few things for you across the universes. It wasn't cheap, but I figured it would make your brief stay here a little more manageable."

"Wait, you told me you were about to be court-martialed. That was why you came here, right? What happened? Are you still a member of Deep Cosmos?"

David dropped his bags and put his hand on his forehead.

"Ah, yes!" He responded. "I completely forgot about that. Sorry, I probably should have contacted you through the ship's communication system. The supreme commander decided to drop the charges! The Observer made an appeal and won before anything even had to take place, so I'm good! Well, other than the huge lump I have on the back of my head that was given to me by the Observer. The guy's got a good swing, no doubt about that. But other than that, I'm good! Sorry it took so long for me to get back. I wanted to have lunch with the Observer, as I don't get to see him that often, and then we paid a few agents to get your little gifts, which took some time for them to retrieve, so yeah, everything is golden! Now the only thing I have left to do is to take you home."

Sophia paused for a moment. She was unable to comprehend how Nerd could forget something like a court-martial. Though at this point, she shouldn't have been surprised. It was going to take time for her to understand him.

She smiled and told him what she had spent the last few hours thinking about.

"Nerd," she told him. "I want to be part of your crew for a little while…at least until I can get back on my feet again. I have nowhere to go, and I need some time to recover from the damage that Crimson did to me before I can decide on where I want to live. Can I stay here with you for a bit? Maybe we can find a few more people to join up with us? You don't have to be alone like this forever, and your ship is big enough to house a few crew members if you choose. What do you think? Would you accept me? I would love to see the galaxy, you know?"

To Sophia's surprise, Nerd's expression went from being very goofy to very serious, and even a little guilty. He turned his back to her and removed his glasses. He let out a sigh and was obviously very troubled.

"What's wrong?" Sophia asked. "Do you not want me around?"

"No, no, no," Nerd responded. "It's not that, trust me. You are very much wanted. But there's something about me that I haven't told you about…my real name. There's a reason I don't reveal it to anyone."

"David Bell? The most wanted man in the galaxy? I already know about that. You don't have to hide it from me. The Observer was concerned about me finding out on my own. So, he sent a message to the notepad you let me use. I know you're not responsible for what happened on Cosmic 5. You were used just as I was…by the same person, sadly."

David turned around to face Sophia. He was completely stunned and did not know how to respond.

"You knew this all along?" He asked her. Sophia nodded her head. "Great!" he exclaimed, his face instantly turning back to the goofy look he had before. "You can stay here as long as you want!"

Without hesitating, he quickly started walking to the stairway leading to the main deck. But Sophia grabbed him by the collar of his lab coat.

"Not so fast!" She said to him.

"Oh, great." He sighed. "A catch, why does there always have to be a catch!"

"I want to know a little more about you. You're hiding so much from me, and I would trust you a lot more if you could tell me a bit about yourself. Don't do it in one sitting, because my mind can only handle so much, but give me little segments I can understand. We're going to be spending a lot more time together, so the less you keep from me, the more I will trust you."

David snapped both of his fingers and gave her a thumbs-up.

"You got it!" he agreed.

"Also," Sophia continued, "I want you to try to keep the main deck and bridge a little cleaner than you do. I'm a little OCD, so it would make things easier on me. I will help you keep things clean, but I need you to do a little better. Can you do that for me?"

David lifted both his eyebrows. He wasn't completely impressed, but he realized this was an opportunity to connect with his new crew member.

"I will try," he said to her.

"And one more thing," Sophia continued, "be a gentleman and carry my bags up to my room."

She gently punched David in the shoulder and chuckled. Then she gave him another hug and thanked him for the gifts and for allowing her to stay on board. She walked up the stairs and left the transporter room. David Bell looked at the bags he had gotten for her. He walked over, picked them up, and shook his head.

"What...have I gotten myself into," he said with a concerned look on his face. Then he smiled and made his way upstairs, laughing so hard that he shook.

CHAPTER 6 STONE COLD

Earth date: February 7th, 2010

Time: 600

Location: Cosmic 5

Drake Robinson, one of the most feared bounty hunters in the galaxy, was shaking in fear at the horrid scene that surrounded him. Cosmic 5 was once a happy, cheerful place to be. However, ever since the David Bell incident, the caretakers had let the station go. No one wanted to visit anymore because of the rumors that illegal human experimentation was still taking place, and the terrifying sight he could never un-see proved the rumors true.

The staff didn't bother keeping it secret anymore. Operation pillars were located everywhere through the station, and to get victims for their inhumane experiments they resorted to kidnapping, because volunteers were at this point unheard of.

Drake's two companions—Manic, his sniper and personal hitman; and Jungle Boy, a rogue Zentar warrior—were both disturbed by the sight. This was a feeling that was often a stranger to the members of Menace, as it was usually them putting fear into the minds of their opponents; but the palace of the dreaded psychopath was a gruesome facility, and even they felt it.

The three men were accompanied by five cosmic staff members, who guided them to an elevator that would lead them to their destination. The eight men walked into the elevator and turned around to face the horrid experiments that were going on. The doors slowly closed, and Drake breathed a sigh of relief; he no longer wanted to witness what was happening.

The elevator slowly made its way towards its destination, moving upwards, side to side, downwards, back and forth, followed by a loud creaking sound filling the elevator as it moved. Drake turned to his men, signaling them to stay alert in case the Cosmic staff got any ideas. Both men nodded their heads and prepared themselves for the worst.

The doors slowly opened to reveal the old VIP room, which used to house only the highest-ranking staff members of Cosmic 5. Now even more operating pillars were being set up and worked on, as again, there was no reason to hide what was going on anymore.

Thankfully, this time, no operations were taking place in this particular room, meaning the men didn't have to witness any more mind-scarring sights.

The men made their way to a doorway that was located at the end of the transporter room. Drake looked over his shoulder at one of the air vents and swore he could see two glowing green eyes staring back at him. He closed his eyes, shook his head, and re-opened them. The eyes were now gone. Presumably it was just paranoia setting in, given the circumstances. Drake refocused on the situation at hand. They had reached the doorway leading to Dr. Crimson's lair, and it was evident from the smile on the lead staff member's face that they were in for a rough ride.

"Are you ready?" He said to them.

"Just get this over with!" Drake responded in his strong Australian accent.

The doorway opened, and all eight of the men entered the room. There, sitting at his desk, was arguably the worst human being ever to set foot in the galaxy: Dr. Crimson, the president of Cosmic 5. His appearance was just as the rumors depicted him. He had a face that seemed to be crafted by perfection itself, complemented by brown shoulder-length hair that brought his chiseled features to life. His vibrant blue eyes were almost angelic and had the power to lure anyone in. Although he was wearing a lab coat, it was evident that he was very strong and muscular. According to rumors, he stood at about 6'2", which Drake could not determine for himself as Crimson was sitting down. Regardless of his height, he was one of the few pretty boys you would never want to get in a fight with, especially considering the monster that lurked beneath his angelic eyes. The same eyes were fixed on the human experimentations that he was able to witness live through a tablet. He was clearly thrilled, as the dopamine rushed through his brain at a level no human could understand, but his focus was broken as soon as he noticed that Drake Robinson had arrived.

He regained his composure and put the tablet down.

"Welcome, my friend," Dr. Crimson said in a disturbingly calm voice. "Welcome to Cosmic 5, where only humane and legal human experimentation is permitted." Crimson then started laughing psychotically. "Ah, they fall for that one every time!"

Drake felt uneasy, as the rumors were again proven true. As normal and down-to-earth as the good doctor appeared to be, a cold monster lurked beneath his exterior, ready to strike at anyone who he saw as weak or defenseless. Thankfully for Drake, the legendary bounty hunter was neither, meaning that Crimson would have to work hard if he had any plans to stab Drake in the back.

Bravely, Drake swallowed his fear and took a step towards Crimson.

"I hear you want to hire us to track down a young Sheila that used to be in your possession," Drake stated. "I also heard you're willing to pay a small fortune for her, yeah?"

Crimson was not impressed with Drake's get-to-the-point attitude. His face went completely emotionless, and it was clear that he was very much bored with his new ally, which was often the kiss of death for anyone cursed enough to know the twisted doctor. Nevertheless, Crimson still had use for Drake; he knew he had to keep it together if he wanted his prize back again.

"Yes," he acknowledged. "The girl named Sophia Nelson. She is…important to me, and to my research. Bring her to me alive. If you kill her, I swear I will hunt you down! But if you bring her back alive, I will make you and your little band of bounty hunters the richest men in the galaxy; this I promise you."

"Where will we find her?" Drake asked. "Any leads on where she could be?"

Dr. Crimson slowly leaned back in his chair and smiled. He closed his eyes and spoke with a voice even softer and more bone chilling than before.

"Have you ever heard of the legend known as…Nerd?" Crimson asked.

"That little bloke who teamed up with the most wanted man in the galaxy to overthrow your operation? Yeah, I've heard of him. Don't know why he picked such a weak name …but I must admit, his intelligence is indeed legendary."

"He is the one that took her from me, and knowing Sophia, she has nowhere else to go. She will stay with him for a while, given her current circumstances. As for finding Nerd, he has a weak heart that cares deeply for others. Use his compassion to lure him in."

Drake gave a rare smile and nodded his head.

"It would be my honor to hunt down such a worthy opponent. I…take it you have nothing special in mind for him?"

"No, he's been a fun little rival for me, but I know his type. I will get bored with him soon. You may do with him as you wish; all I want is Sophia. Honestly, a day doesn't go by when I don't think about her. I long to gaze upon the sight of life slowly fading from her helpless eyes and to witness her pain-stricken cry burn within the rhythm of her last breath. Nerd took that away from me, and I need that feeling back. I need her to be released from this life! It's the only way I can redeem myself for what happened."

Drake slowly started walking backward. He was beginning to have second thoughts about bringing this poor girl to such a horrid and monstrous human being. Assuming he even qualified to be called a human anymore. But Drake's crew had not been paid in well over a year, and he needed to reward them for their patience and loyalty. Loyalty was profitable to Drake, so it was a principle he was willing to pay for.

"I will bring her back in one piece," Drake said. "Don't worry about that. Just make sure you pay us what you promised when we hold up our end of the deal. I respect you, but I will not hesitate to make you my next prisoner if you try to stab us in the back."

"Amusing, but pointless considering I have no plans to betray you. Bring me the girl, and I will see to it that you get paid. You have my word."

Crimson was about to dismiss the three men when suddenly the sound of what seemed to be an animal moving through the station's air vents could be heard. Dr. Crimson opened his desk drawer, swiftly pulled out a laser gun, and aimed it at the vent where the sound was coming from.

The mad doctor broke out in a sweat, his eyes became focused, and the hand that was holding the gun trembled violently. Drake was confused, as it was reported that Dr. Crimson was incapable of experiencing fear. But somehow, someway, the dreaded psychopath was clearly disturbed by this apparently trivial issue.

"You all right, mate?" Drake asked.

"Its...him," Dr. Crimson replied in a very intense voice.

"Him? What do you mean, him?"

Dr. Crimson slowly lowered his gun. He wiped the sweat off his forehead and regained his composure.

"It's nothing, just a little job for pest control to take care of. You may leave. I have said all I need to say to you."

The three men saw no reason to argue. They left the room and returned to the elevator. As soon as the door closed, Manic instantly voiced his concern.

"This doesn't feel right, boss," he whispered into Drake's ear, hoping that the staff wouldn't overhear him. "This man clearly has no honor. What makes you think that he will follow through with his end of the deal?"

"Not now, Manic," Drake whispered back. "I have it all figured out. I just need you to trust me. If Crimson attempts to stab us in the back, I swear it will be him who lives in fear of me. Even a psychopath will have nightmares of the great Drake Robinson; this I swear…"

CHAPTER 7 DECEIVED

"David. Why are you so sad?"

"...I'm just having a bad day. That's all."

"Are you sure? I have seen you have bad days before...this is different."

"...Yes...yes, it is..."

"David. I know I'm only nine years old. Maybe I can't handle your adult problems. But...I want you to know, I'm always here for you. Always!"

"...I have been such a jerk to you. Why, Amelia, why are you being so...nice to me?"

"Because I don't think you're a grumpy old man. I think you're a nice man who is scared to be nice because someone hurt him. Not because you want to be mean. I know you will learn to be nice, David. I have always known. Because under the grumpiness, you have a soft, loving heart that will always move you to do the right thing."

"...That's deep for a nine-year-old."

"I have my gifts."

"Gifts… Oh, that reminds me! Here, I want you to have this. It's a music box that I found in the abandoned labs."

"Aww! Thank you, David. See, you're not such a bad guy after all. Here, let me wind it up."

"…On second thought, why don't I give you something else?"

"No! I love this. Thank you so much."

"But the melody… It's so creepy. I should've thought to test it out before I gave it to you."

"It's not creepy, it's just a little different. Kind of like you."

"Are you sure you want it?"

"I see light where many are scared to look, and given time, David, I know you will learn to do the same. You just need time."

"…Amelia…"

David Bell was awoken by the sound of the ship's alarm system and the stench of burnt pancakes. He opened his dusty eyes, looked at the time, and groaned in irritation. The space time was 480, which was equivalent to 8:00 AM, at least three hours before he was used to waking up.

He turned his head to face the commotion and noticed Sophia franticly trying to control the mess she had created by the stove. He realized that it was a mistake to place his bed on the main deck, considering the kitchen was located on the same level. But alas, David had never planned for anyone to join him on his spacecraft. As it was, there were no other rooms designed for individuals. The only one that was even close was the small fourth level that he gave to Sophia, which had previously been used as David's personal man cave.

David was not used to waking up early unless he had to, but Sophia was on a different sleep schedule than him. It was going to take some time to get used to…unless of course he moved his room onto the bridge, in which case he could shut the door and lock Sophia out anytime he wanted. He chuckled at the thought but kept it as nothing more than a thought, as David was genuinely grateful to have her around.

He got out of bed and put a ball cap over his hair, which looked like it had just been struck by lightning. He pulled on a flannel coat and walked over to Sophia, who had managed to set the stove on fire. He grabbed an extinguisher and put out the flames.

"Well then!" he said to her. "At least I was not the only one who destroyed everything the first time I tried to cook."

"I have to learn!" Sophia replied. "I like bacon and eggs…just not every morning."

David laughed at Sophia's response. He knew he was very limited in his cooking. But up until this point, he had no reason to try anything new. David was used to routine, and up until now, he saw no reason to change. He walked over to the table located in the center of the room and sat down, coffee in his hand. It was the one thing Sophia had managed to perfect.

"I have been working on recruiting some new people," David said. "But it's difficult given that my true identity is a wanted criminal…so I've actually been looking at the escaped convict list. Turns out there are a few I think we could go after!"

Sophia at first laughed at David's response, then went silent after she realized that he wasn't kidding.

"David…" she ventured, "…no. No, no, a thousand times no!"

"These are desperate times, Sophia," David stated. "We need to think outside the box."

"David! I am not staying on the same spacecraft as a wanted criminal!"

"I'm a wanted criminal, and you've done just fine."

"You're different. You didn't actually commit the crime that you were convicted of. That kind of makes me feel a little less terrified than if we invited someone who did."

"I'm not gonna take in a murderer or anything. I was thinking more a thief, or a thug, or both!"

"David! I'm not—"

Suddenly their little disagreement was interrupted by an alert. David lost focus on what Sophia was telling him and quickly ran to the bridge. There was a red light flashing by the intercom. He activated it, and a transmission began to play.

"This is a distress call to all nearby ships. Please help us! We were attacked by a Kelson fleet. Most of our crew is dead; the rest of us are injured and need medical assistance."

Sophia walked onto the bridge with an irritated look on her face. David was too distracted to notice it. However, her punch in the shoulder was a lot harder than usual. That he did notice as he grabbed his shoulder in pain.

Sophia listened to the transmission as it repeated the same words. She was very concerned and knew that they were in trouble.

"What do we do?" Sophia asked.

"We do our job," David responded. "I'm a doctor; that comes before my responsibility as an agent. We must help these people."

"Are we able to respond to them, to let them know help is on the way?"

"I can send a long-range message, but it will take time to reach them. As it is, it will take us a few hours to arrive at hyper-speed. Normally, at this distance, I would call in another ship. However, I know the location their ship is at. It is on the very edge of Kelson territory. Not many non-hostile ships in that area would be willing to help them."

David set the coordinates and activated the hyperdrive. The ship took off and entered hyperspace. Sophia was ready and eager to take on her first mission. She waited, waited, and…her eagerness fled from her.

"In the movies," she said to David, "they always cut this part and go straight to the next scene. It's so epic and in the moment. This feels more like a long family vacation car ride."

"Isn't it boring!" David said as he opened a bag of cheese puffs as a substitution for his breakfast. "If you have anything you want to do to pass the time, go right ahead! We've only been in hyperspace for 30 minutes. We have at least two and a half hours more to go."

Sophia left the room and David was left to eat his cheese puffs by himself, just like old times. About 40 minutes later, Sophia returned. She had done her makeup and dressed in the attire she had worn when the two had met. Her red hair was braided into a ponytail, which was common for a woman in the V.T.C. Her attire, on the other hand, was very unique, telling him that she was from one of the western tribes of

Zecarah. Sophia wore a black tank top, which was comp-lemented by a strip of blue fabric resting on her right shoulder. She had a dark blue battle skirt with leggings underneath, and for reasons unknown to David, she always wore high heels when she was in her favored attire. She was obsessed with them, and she even ran in them when David introduced her to the virtual reality room. She was fast, and very agile, but she never removed her high heels. It was like they were part of her, a part she couldn't live without.

Sophia was definitely a lovely woman, and David was at times mesmerized by her appearance, but he knew he had to keep his heart in check. Sophia was a beautiful girl, but she needed him to be her friend right now, nothing more. She couldn't handle anything more, not after all she had just been through.

David was so busy processing Sophia's wellbeing that he hadn't noticed she had brought his notepad with her and was lifting it in front of David's face.

"Smile!" she said as she took a picture. David was quite concerned when she showed him the pic.

"…I'm not usually the one saying this," he said nervously, "but please don't post that…"

David's response gave Sophia an idea. She became drawn in to her notepad and was obviously up to something. David felt his communicator vibrate. He quickly reached into his pocket and noticed he had a friend request on Spacetime. He turned to Sophia with a concerned look. Sophia laughed at David's expression.

"I promise I didn't post your picture!" she said while still laughing. "But I figured I would create an account."

David breathed a sigh of relief. He accepted Sophia's friend request and then left the room himself to change into his lab coat. He returned with his glasses in his hands, obviously needing them to disguise himself as Nerd. He sat back down in his chair and watched the energy of hyperspace flow by his starship.

"How much longer now?" Sophia asked.

"At least two hours," David responded. Sophia groaned, clearly bored out of her mind.

"Do you mind if I watch a romantic comedy on your notepad?" she asked.

"Go ahead!" David invited.

Sophia walked up to David, sat on the floor next to him, and made him watch it with her. David's face became mortified as the images of a low-budget, brainless film flashed before his eyes.

As soon as the movie was done, David breathed a huge sigh of relief. It was the longest two hours he had ever spent in his life. However, it put Sophia in a good mood, and that almost made the agonizing torment and pain worth it.

David looked at his dash monitor and was thrilled to see that they were only a few minutes away.

"We're almost there," David said. "Are you ready?"

"I've been ready!" Sophia responded. "Let's get this show on the road."

David deactivated the hyperdrive, and the ship reentered normal space. An old cargo ship was visible in front of them. It was huge and had a very boxy look to it. There were two hyperdrive engines on the right and left side of it, and a massive cargo bay door in the front that could easily swallow the *Iron Heart* whole. The ship was ugly and evidently damaged from battle.

David attempted to hail the ship, but there was no response. So, he then decided to scan the ship, and he breathed a sigh of relief when a few weak life signs were detected. That was the good news; the bad news was that no transporter pads were showing up on his scans, meaning there was no way to beam to the ship. David groaned, obviously frustrated at the news.

"What do we do now?" Sophia asked.

"Something I really don't want to do," David grumbled.

He activated the thrusters and navigated the *Iron Heart* into the ship's cargo bay. Sophia was not liking this idea at all, but she understood that it was the only way to get inside the massive spacecraft.

David activated the landing procedure and slowly managed to land the *Iron Heart* inside the cargo bay. A harmless beam of energy hit them as they entered the main door, and Sophia was at first very confused about what had happened.

"We just passed through an air bubble," David told her as he landed the ship. "It keeps a breathable atmosphere inside so that oxygen doesn't escape. But it's a weak force field that allows ships to pass through. That means we will not need environmental suits as we enter."

David left the bridge and headed to the main bay. He gathered all the medical devices he needed and stuffed them in his lab coat pockets. He then grabbed a Rubik's cube and stuffed it in his pocket as well. Sophia was a little concerned about David's priorities upon seeing this.

"Is that really necessary?" she asked.

"We may need it," David explained. "Trust me." David then slipped on the black laboratory gloves that he always wore outside his ship, put on his big round glasses, and smiled. "Remember! My name is Nerd, supreme human intelligence. You can't call me David while we're outside the *Iron Heart*. If anyone else finds out, I'm finished." Sophia nodded her head. "Sweet! Then let's go find us some patients."

Nerd gave Sophia a thumbs-up and activated the ship's docking bay door. The door slowly opened, and the gloomy interior of the freighter was revealed. Sophia was a little hesitant to walk out, as the interior of the ship reminded her of the basement where Dr. Crimson had attempted to take her life. Nerd, however, had no negative memory on the matter. He ran out without giving it a second thought before quickly turning to Sophia, signaling her to come out. Sophia took a breath, pushing past her fear and making her way outside. She kept her eyes fixed on Nerd to block out the triggering sight that surrounded her.

Nerd pulled out his communication device and activated the scanner mode. The remaining life signs were all in the same room, making their job a whole lot easier. He turned to Sophia and smiled.

"Follow me!" he said to her.

He then darted ahead, and Sophia did her best to keep up. Despite her training, Nerd was a little faster than her, which took her off guard, given the fact that all he seemed to do to stay in shape was sit in a chair and eat junk food all day. Still, it had been a long time since her speed had been challenged like this, which was feeding the competitive side of her she'd lost after leaving the V.T.C. It felt good, and she was hoping that after this mission, maybe, just maybe, she could become the warrior she used to be long ago.

The two found an elevator, and Nerd wasted no time running inside and waiting for Sophia to catch up. As soon as Sophia entered the elevator, Nerd pressed one of the buttons, which had a symbol on it Sophia didn't recognize. The doors closed, and the elevator made its way upward. Sophia smiled upon hearing Nerd's heavy breathing. Although he was faster, his lack of training was catching up to him, and he was already winded. Sophia, on the other hand, could run at her more consistent pace all day without tiring out. This increased her confidence even further; she was ready for anything. Whatever challenge came their way, she would overcome it.

The elevator doors opened, and the two made their way out. Bodies lay across the floor. It was evident a fight had taken place, and it had taken a heavy toll on the crew members. Nerd ran to one of them and scanned the body. Sophia looked around and noticed they were on the ship's bridge. She saw a tablet on the captain's chair, similar to the one that Nerd had on his ship. She picked it up and noticed that it contained the captain's logs, which included one the captain had posted today. Opening it up, she was stunned to see the word "*Gotcha!*" written on the tablet. Nerd, on the other hand, had just finished scanning the body. The crew member was at full health. No signs of a fight, no signs of trauma, not even a common cold could be found in this crew member.

"Sophia!" Nerd shouted. "We've been had!"

Nerd leaped up and turned to face Sophia. He gasped upon seeing a man holding a laser gun, pointing it right at her, in the process of pulling the trigger.

Immediately, Nerd went into analysis mode. Time seemed to slow to a crawl as his brain calculated all the possibilities. Sophia was precisely six feet from him. The man holding the gun was precisely 15.8 feet from him. He first calculated the time it would take for him to run over and neutralize the man before he could pull the trigger. He calculated the quickest path to get to him, but it would take too much time. Nerd could easily save himself, but the man would shoot Sophia by the time he got to his target, which would be a real problem considering he was aiming at her head. He analyzed the room from his memory and from what he saw with his eyes at the moment. There was nothing strong enough he could pick up to use to deflect the blast. He considered the option of grabbing Sophia and dragging her down to the ground before she was shot. But alas, by the time gravity kicked in, she would already be dead.

There was no possible way that both of them were going to survive. That gave Nerd only one option if he wanted to save Sophia. Nerd calculated how long it would take for him to run in front of Sophia to shield her from the blast. There was just enough time for him to do this, but he would have to jump in front of her to get that extra boost to make it.

With all other options off the table, Nerd now had to decide whether he or Sophia would go on living. He needed no time to calculate and process that decision, as it was the easiest decision he could make in this scenario. He ran towards Sophia and began to jump in front of her. The man pulled the trigger, and a blue beam of energy flowed from his gun. He had set the laser to stun.

Crud! David could've let Sophia take the blast. He could've easily picked up Sophia upon her being hit and run out of the room, into the elevator, and back onto their ship before the man caught up. However, Nerd was now airborne, and there was no way to stop his momentum. So, he stuck with the plan. His body absorbed the blast, and he fell to the ground. With his consciousness slowly fading away, he watched as the man took a second shot at Sophia. She also fell to the ground, making any plan of escape impossible.

Three of the men who had pretended to be hurt stood up and walked towards Nerd. Nerd was so groggy that he couldn't make out the men's faces. They appeared as shadows...staring through his weary soul.

Nerd took one final breath as his consciousness faded away. A bright light filled the darkest parts of his mind, and swiftly, the light faded as everything went black.

CHAPTER 8 MENACE

Earth date: February 9th, 2010
Time: 120
Location: The freighter *Wrath*

Nerd felt reality return to him. He was unsure how long he had been out, but the fact that he was blindsided told him that he and his friend were in danger. He couldn't do anything about it until his senses fully returned. Still, with what little sight he had, he was able to make out the shadows of seven men standing about 20 feet from him.

His sight returned a little more, and Nerd noticed there were iron bars separating him from them, which gave Nerd the impression that he was in a jail cell. He groaned and closed his eyes, hoping that the groggy feeling would soon wear off.

"That was quite a move, mate!" one of the shadow men said. "But pathetically predictable! I knew you'd try to save the Sheila rather than escaping with your own life, and in the end, your compassion was your downfall."

Nerd's vision began to fully clear up, and the image of the man who was talking slowly began to take form. He was a gruff, gritty-looking man, with long black hair and a ninja sweatband wrapped around his forehead. He had a black, painted-on mask that went across both his eyes, making him look fierce and a bit on the creepy side. He had a laser gun in his hand, which Nerd was easily able to identify as the same gun that was used to neutralize him and Sophia. The man was wearing a gray military vest that had a ridiculous amount of ammo attached to it. He had a pistol on his belt and a hunting knife sheathed on his left thigh. Nerd had never seen this man in person, but he had read up on him many times before.

"Drake Robinson," he said in a groggy voice. "The most feared bounty hunter in the galaxy. I actually respected what others said about your combat ability and wit, even though you only use them for whoever has the deepest pockets. Pity you had to resort to such a weak method of capturing me. I must admit that I am quite disappointed."

"Oh! It's not you we were after. We just want the Sheila! A former…friend of hers wants her back. A very powerful friend."

Nerd's groggy eyes busted open. He stood up and charged at Drake. Drake backed up and just barely missed having his throat grabbed by Nerd's hand. The other six men were about to open the cell door to beat him up for attacking their boss, but Drake ordered them to stand down.

"If you open the cell door now," Drake warned, "he will have a chance to escape. Trust me, he's good at breaking out of things. Besides, the bloke's little outburst is understandable, considering what we're about to do."

Nerd was panting in rage. He knew his friend's life was in grave danger, and that struck a deep chord with him. Still, Drake's tone had expressed a mild vibe of remorse. So, Nerd held back his anger as best he could and attempted to reason with him.

"Drake," he said. "Please don't do this! I know Dr. Crimson hired you to bring her back, but you know what he will do to her if she returns. That man has no compassion for others, and if he gets his hands on her, he will dissect her alive! Drake, if there is any humanity left within you…please let her go. There is no honor in any of this."

Drake hesitated for a second; he was obviously uncomfortable with what he was about to do, but not enough to stop him from going through with it.

"Mate…" he said. "I'm sorry…but I made a deal with Mr. Crimson, and I never go back on a deal. Loyalty is profitable; that is one principle that I will never break."

Nerd stepped away from the jail bars. He ran his hands frantically through his hair as his eyes began to twitch. Drake could see Nerd's frustration. So, the bounty hunter decided to change the subject, making a desperate attempt to earn Nerd's respect.

"I want to introduce you to my band of misfits," he started. "This is my lieutenant, sniper, and personal hitman, Manic Blackheart."

Nerd looked over at the man that Drake was signaling to. He was very tall and, like Drake, had long black hair. He had a leather vest with no shirt underneath. The vest was open, revealing his chiseled abs and broad, toned chest. Manic was wearing a bandanna over his mouth that had a skeleton jaw on it, giving him the appearance of being quite vicious. He was wearing dark shades, even though the room was already very dark, and also wore a large leather top hat, which also had a skull and crossbones on the front of it. His top hat was a little quirky, but Nerd could see the eyes of a cold, calculated killer hiding behind his tinted shades. This one posed a serious threat. Nerd would have to be on the lookout for that one if he succeeded in escaping his prison.

Drake continued by introducing the man on his left.

"My assault-class soldier!" He announced. "His name is unpronounceable to the human vocabulary, so we like to call him Jungle Boy. He is a Zentar warrior who went rogue. He is lightning fast and definitely someone I am grateful to have on my side."

Jungle Boy looked like a child compared to Manic. Manic stood somewhere between 6'8" and 6'10". Jungle Boy stood no taller than 5'2", which was normal for a Zentar warrior. Still, that did not change the fact his appearance was just as intimidating as the former menace thug's. His face was completely covered with a helmet that had a large, monster-looking jaw carved on the front of it. It was showing its razor-sharp teeth like a dog ready to attack. The top part of the helmet, located where the eyes were supposed to be, had multiple lenses on it. There were at least five, and it was uncertain what they were used for, given the fact that a Zentar only had two eyes. The rest of his body was covered in green armor. It looked tough on the outside, but there was a reason his full body needed to be covered. Nerd knew what this reason was, and although Jungle Boy would be a difficult opponent, he concerned Nerd the least out of the seven men.

Drake then turned to the fourth man in the room.

"This is my demolitions expert, Smiley. Though he is a shoot-now-ask-questions-later type, he's saved my life more than once and is definitely a valuable member of this here team."

The man that Drake was referring to was quite disturbing. He was wearing white face paint and had green hair and red paint on his nose. He had a giant smiling mouth painted on his face, with razor-sharp teeth painted inside of it. He was obviously trying to make himself look like a creepy clown and pulled it off perfectly. His armor was a color mix of yellow and red, with a flamethrower mounted on his right hand and a rocket launcher mounted on his left. He also had a rifle strapped to his back. His armor was covered in spikes and was very Gothic-looking, with the exception of the unappealing color pattern. The image gave Nerd an unpleasant flashback to an adversary he had met long ago…but now was not the time to get caught up in that. He refocused and continue to analyze.

He had read up on Smiley before. He was psychotic, unpredictable, and had a killer instinct that motivated him in a way that was inhuman. Smiley presented a challenge for him, as Nerd would not be able to predict any of his moves, which made him the greatest threat of all.

Drake continued to the fifth man.

"This is my tank, Star-Creeper. He used to be a solo, and quite successful, bounty hunter, but he joined up with me when his personal job was no longer paying like it used to.

He can take a hit from a laser cannon with ease and has been an excellent frontline unit when taking on multiple targets."

This man was still a little scary, but not as scary as the others prior to him. He wore a steel mask and had a soldier's helmet with a spike on top. The mask was connected to the helmet and obviously provided a level of protection. The rest of his body armor was blue, and he was clearly a force to be reckoned with. He was huge, standing around 6'10", and was made up of at least 320 pounds of pure, rugged muscle. He carried a large laser cannon around like it was a rifle, and his size made most of the other men look small, but Nerd had been watching him very carefully. He was slow-witted and carried himself in a lazy way. It was obvious that he relied on his strength for everything, making him a much easier target than he appeared at first glance.

Drake continued to his sixth crew member. "This is my special operations force, Unit 1587. Even I'm not sure what he—or she—is, as it has never told us. But it does its job, collects its money, and never asks any questions...just the way I like it!"

This man, or woman, was the most bizarre of the group. It had what looked like a welder's mask, with a smile spray-painted on the front. Its armor was dark gray and orange. It had a tank filled with some type of fluid mounted on the back, which Nerd suspected to be harmful. There was a hose that went from the tank to a gun that it had in its holster, meaning that it most likely used the fluid to thrust out at its opponents. Other than that, there was very little to go off of with this one. But Nerd would continue to analyze it, hoping to find a weakness down the road.

Drake now signaled to his final team member.

"And finally, my medic, Jake Roberts. He's pretty good at both technology and human physiology…kind of like someone else I know. He reminds me that the team I command is still a team of people, not objects. He has saved more lives in Menace than I have been able to take. Without him, most of us blokes would be dead!"

This man was the least scary of the seven. He had a robotic mask on his face, dark skin, and spiky yellow hair that went in all directions. He seemed to be smart but didn't look like much of a threat in hand-to-hand combat. This made him a great guy to have around, but not the most dangerous opponent to be facing.

Nerd took the information he had learned and began processing all of it. This was going to be difficult, but he knew he could find a way to overthrow this little gang and get his friend home safe. Nerd smiled at Drake, and Drake began to sweat.

"You're looking at me like a carnivore ready to devour his prey," he said to Nerd. "You're already calculating how you'll escape, aren't you?"

Nerd shrugged his shoulders and didn't reply to Drake's speech. He wanted to get into Drake's head a little, hoping that Drake would have a change of heart and let them go. Sadly, this did not happen.

Drake knew it was time to head back to the bridge. He ordered his men to head up and told them he would be close behind. The men left the room. Drake made one final attempt to let David know he had the upper hand.

"I removed every item that could help you escape from your lab coat. So, if you're thinking of escaping, it's going to be difficult! The only object I left with you was your

Rubik's cube… You're going to be here for a long time, so I want you to at least have something to keep your mind entertained." Drake turned around and began to make his way out of the prison room. "Farewell, Nerd. May your stay with us be…most miserable indeed."

Drake left the room and closed the door behind him. Nerd looked at the cell ahead of him; inside was Sophia. She had been crying, which was evident from her red, puffy eyes— the same eyes he saw when he saved her life less than a week ago.

"Sophia!" he breathed a sigh of relief. "I'm glad you're okay."

"I wish I was dead right now," Sophia responded. "I overheard your entire conversation. They want to take me back…to him."

"Sophia, listen to me. I'm going to get you out of this, but I need you to be strong right now. I know you can do it. I know deep down you have a warrior's spirit. So, please try to keep yourself together, because I have a plan to get us out of here. You know my true identity; this isn't the first jail cell that I've needed to escape from. Drake has no idea what he's in for."

Sophia was still in rough shape, but she trusted that Nerd had a plan. Taking a deep breath, she tried her best to calm down. Nerd walked over to the back wall of the cell and sat down. He pulled out his Rubik's cube and started working on it with his right hand, slowly but efficiently.

"Really, bro?" a voice said from Nerd's left. "That's not going to help you escape."

Nerd was startled. He had been so caught up in trying to think of how to beat the Menace team that he had not noticed there was indeed another man in the cell with him, sitting by one of the cell beds. The man was very tall, had black skin, and was wearing shorts, a white tank top, and a black do-rag on his head. He was wearing large tinted sunglasses, and Nerd was a little concerned as he could not read the man's eyes. He was slouched over, and his stance gave off the impression that he had an attitude. He was a little shady-looking, but somehow Nerd was not getting a bad vibe from him.

Nerd turned his head so it was facing forward again, still focusing on the task at hand, but he acknowledged the man's question, saying, "This is critical to my plans. Trust me, I know what I'm doing."

The man laughed at Nerd's response. He clearly did not believe him and thought he was crazy with the way he was going about his escape plan.

"You're obviously delusional, my brother," the man said. "Still, I like how you nearly broke Drake's neck. That would've been so cool, man! What's your name?"

"I cannot tell you my real name," Nerd replied. "Just call me Nerd, supreme human intelligence... Also, I wasn't going to break Drake's neck. I was just going to give it a little squeeze."

"Nerd? Come on, man! You could've picked something better than that."

"It works for me, trust me. What about you? What might your name be?"

"The name's Smith, Henry Smith! I'm a wanted space thug, one that made a lot of profit from looting spacecrafts. The authorities couldn't lay a finger on me, so they hired these guys to come hunt me down. Sadly, they succeeded."

Nerd smiled. He had heard the man's name before in the galactic news. He was slick, athletic, and witty. He was known for being very charismatic and was likable despite his criminal deeds. However, he was also quite the wreck of a man and did not have his priorities straight. Still, Henry's background may prove useful in his plan of escaping, giving Nerd more confidence that his plan would work.

He continued slowly moving the slots on his Rubik's cube. It was starting to come together, but Nerd still wanted a little more time to talk to Henry before he finished it.

"Tell me, Mr. Henry Smith," he said. "If you were given the chance to be a space explorer rather than a space thug, would you take that chance?"

Henry gave an arrogant smirk in response to Nerd's question.

"Are you making me an offer?" he asked.

"Maybe," Nerd continued.

"How much would you pay me to be an explorer?"

"Standard salary. I get a paycheck from Deep Cosmos every Earth month. It pays well, as they know I may need crew members to help me in my little quests. I could definitely use someone like you...however, you'd have to give up on your criminal pursuits if you want to stay on my ship."

"Blah! What fun is there in that? Besides, I make much more through robbing and plundering. So, I think I'll stick to the thug business. It's what I do, and it's what I do best."

"Pity you cannot be made to see reason."

"Hey, hey, I'm Henry Smith! Whaddaya expect?"

Nerd smiled. He knew what he had to do now to reel Henry in. It was risky, but he had seen his type before. He knew what he was doing.

Nerd was nearly finished with his Rubik's cube and knew it was time to act.

"Sophia!" He yelled out. "Please flip your bed over onto its side and hide behind it." Sophia acknowledged Nerd and did so. "You too, Henry," he added.

"Since when did I start taking orders from you?" Henry asked in a sarcastic voice.

"It wasn't an order," Nerd responded. "In about 15 seconds, these iron bars are about to be thrown across the room! I would rather you not die, I'm just saying."

Henry did not believe Nerd. He put his hands behind his head and relaxed. Nerd knew he had to pull out his ace card if he was going to get Henry's respect. He smiled again and said the one thing that he knew would get Henry's attention.

"You wanted to know my real name," he said. "I guess I have no choice but to tell you. Obviously, Nerd is just a code name that I use as a front to hide behind. My real name…is David Bell."

Henry's face dropped. He instantly stood up and did as Nerd had asked. Nerd laughed and knew that everything was set.

Nerd was one move away from solving the Rubik's cube. He pushed the part of the cube that needed to be moved slowly into its place. As soon as the cube was completed, a click was heard. The cube lit up, and Nerd wasted no time. He chucked the cube over to the edge of the iron bars, stood up, and ran behind the bed shelter that Henry had made.

Suddenly, the cube exploded and completely shattered the iron bars that were keeping them locked in. Thankfully, the beds were made of steel, as Drake didn't really care about his prisoners' comfort. So, both men were protected from the hot iron as it shot across the room.

The intruder alarms instantly went off, and Nerd wasted no time in standing up.

"Game on!" He said as he darted outside.

Henry was in shock; he could not believe that this pale, skinny man was truly the most wanted criminal in the galaxy. So, he followed Nerd, hoping to get answers to the questions that were now plaguing his mind.

Nerd examined the keyhole that opened the doorway to Sophia's cell. He was clearly frustrated, as he did not have the tools that he needed to get the job done.

"Curse you, Drake!" Nerd yelled. "He took my universal key, and I only brought one Rubik's cube, considering that I expected this to be a peaceful mission."

"Dude!" Henry responded. "They keep everyone's items in a locker at the edge of the jail room. Let's get our stuff, save your friend, and go!"

"What? That's a stupid design…but good for us, I guess. Let's go!"

The two men ran to the lockers and got all their possessions before they ran back to Sophia's cell. Nerd put the key in the lock and smiled as it swung open. He opened the cell, and Sophia kissed Nerd on the cheek. Nerd did not know how to respond, so he didn't.

The three were about to leave when Nerd saw a security camera in the room. It was looking right at him. Nerd walked over to it and spoke to it.

"Drake!" he said. "I'm going to come find you, and when I do, I'm going to break you in a way you've never been broken before!"

Nerd then grabbed the security camera and ripped it out of the wall. He threw it across the room as hard as he could.

Sophia had never seen Nerd this intense before, and she was worried that he was going to do something on this mission that he would forever regret. But there was no time to reason with him, as they all knew they'd be having company soon.

The three left the prison room and desperately searched the halls, hoping to find the cargo bay where the *Iron Heart* was kept. They ran until they came across a room that appeared to be useful. "*Armory*" was written next to the doorway.

"Now we're talking!" Henry said as the doorway opened automatically. He walked inside, followed closely by Nerd and Sophia. The room was filled with weapons of all kinds: alien, human, and medieval from multiple societies. The discovery thrilled Henry and even made him a little giddy.

"You gonna take anything, my bro?" he asked Nerd.

"Nope!" Nerd said. "I'm a lover, not a fighter."

Henry pretended he didn't hear Nerd's response and turned his attention to Sophia, who was eyeing a bow and a quiver full of arrows. There was a note tied to it that read:

The bow of Dugan of Shadows

Sophia excitedly grabbed it. She pressed a button on the side and was amazed to see the bow compact itself. Though its weight stayed the same, it was just small enough to fit in Sophia's skirt pocket, which she had cleverly included when she crafted the skirt.

After placing it in her pocket, Sophia looked for another weapon to get her hands on. She noticed another medieval-looking weapon. It was a lightweight sword, held within a black sheath. There was a note that read:

The sword of Karla Nelson

Sophia gasped. She had heard stories of her ancestor before but did not expect to ever find anything that belonged to her. She quickly ripped off the tag before the other two could see it. She then took the sword. Henry was not at all impressed by Sophia's choice of weaponry and had no problem expressing it.

"Low-tech girl!" he chided as he picked up a large laser cannon.

Although Henry was fit and toned, Nerd and Sophia were both impressed at how he was able to carry the large cannon with ease. He was clearly strong, and hopefully this would help them out in combat.

After observing Henry's strength, Nerd's focus shifted to what looked like the handle of a shield. Its only feature was a single button located in the middle. He picked it up and stuffed it in one of his lab coat pockets.

"We got everything we need!" he said. "Let's go!"

The three ran out of the armory…only to come face-to-face with the dreaded heavyweight, Star-Creeper! He grabbed his communication device and contacted Drake.

"Star-Creeper to Drake," he said. "I found them! They're in the…"

Star-Creeper's conversation was cut short as an arrow went straight through his communicator. Both men were in shock and looked back to see that Sophia had activated her bow and taken the shot herself. She desperately reached for a second arrow, but she was not able to get it in time. Star-Creeper had pulled out his laser cannon and was firing it up. The three of them spread out, Sophia going left, Henry and Nerd going right.

Nerd turned around and was relieved to see that Star-Creeper was following the two of them. He quickly pulled out the metal handle he had found in the armory. He pressed the button on it, and an energy shield that was as big as him appeared in front of them. It absorbed all the blasts that Star-Creeper's gun was delivering.

Henry was about to step in front of David in an attempt to use his cannon against Star-Creeper, but David stopped him.

"No!" he said. "You will be dead before you can even get a shot in."

"Well, what do we do then!" Henry demanded. "Your shield isn't gonna last forever. Especially considering it's being hit by a GIANT LASER CANNON!"

"Just be patient. He is so focused on killing us right now that he forgot about someone who is kind of important—and kind of behind him at the moment."

As soon as the words fell from Nerd's mouth, Star-Creeper lit up with red electricity. He hollered in pain as the energy roasted his flesh, bones, and vital organs. He fell forward and collapsed on the floor. An arrow was sticking out of his back, and Sophia was standing behind the fallen corpse.

Nerd was very grateful, as the energy from his shield had just depleted and could no longer be used in action. He dropped it and ran to Star-Creeper to scan for life signs. He was only moments away from dying, so Nerd took a stimulant shot from his lab coat and injected it into Star Creeper's bloodstream.

"What are you doing?" Henry asked.

"Saving a patient," Nerd responded.

"What!? Why? He was trying to kill us!"

"I am a doctor. I don't care who the patient is or what they tried to do. Besides, he will be out for a long time, even with the stimulant in his bloodstream." Nerd turned to Sophia and gave her a thumbs-up. "Well done! You just brought down the great Star-Creeper with a bow and arrow."

Sophia was still frozen from shock. She did not know that the arrow was electric, as the first one she used was just a normal arrow. Nerd could see her confusion, so he looked through her quiver and noticed that several of the arrows were labeled.

"You, my friend, picked a shadow archer's weapon," he said to Sophia. "Make sure you know what you're firing. If the legend is true, some of these can do astronomical damage!"

"Yeah…" Sophia said dryly. "I'll keep that in mind."

After laughing at Sophia's sarcasm, Nerd urged the two to follow him to where he thought the cargo bay was. They headed to the left of the armory, traveling deeper and deeper into the hallways of the massive freighter, not paying any attention to a hostile force following close behind them.

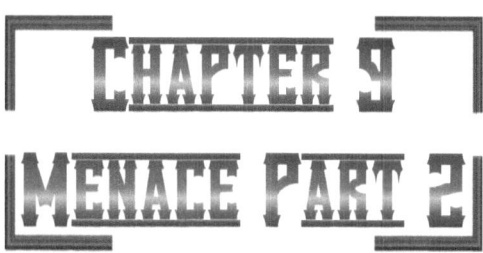

CHAPTER 9
MENACE PART 2

Nerd felt an overwhelming sense of discouragement when he realized that he had led his troops in the exact opposite direction he had intended. The three were now in the engine room, which was quite an intimidating sight.

It was five stories high and had a perimeter of at least half a mile. There were five platforms on each story, which encircled the perimeter of the room. The engine was a massive yellow star-like ball of fire, which was contained within a spherical cage.

It was the last thing that any of them wanted to see given the fact that the cargo bay was on the opposite side of the ship. Sophia and Henry each gave Nerd a dirty look.

"That is the last time we ever turn to you for directions," Sophia said.

The three of them began to turn around to exit the room, when suddenly, Unit 1587 charged toward the engine room from the hallway they had entered through. Nerd ran over to the automatic doorway and pulled out a USB card from his lab coat. He inserted it into the panel next to the doorway, and instantly the door locked shut. He removed the USB card and turned around to face Henry and Sophia.

"Don't worry, guys," he said cheerfully. "I have a bunch of these pre-programmed for a multitude of different tasks. It won't be getting to us any time soon."

Henry and Sophia stared at Nerd with very concerned and identical expressions, which was soon followed by them urging Nerd to get out of the way! Nerd looked behind him and noticed that the door was burning orange. He leaped out of the way just as the door exploded and a wave of orange acid fell from it.

Unit 1587 walked in with its acid gun in hand, aiming it at Nerd. Sophia instantly ran in front of him, which concerned Nerd greatly.

"What are you doing!" He shouted in a panicked voice.

"Both of you guys stay close to me!" She ordered. "Obviously they're getting paid a lot to deliver me to Dr. Crimson alive. This guy's weapon has a wide spread, and I doubt he'd risk harming me to get to one of you."

Henry wasted no time and stood near Sophia. Her theory appeared to be correct, as Unit 1587 seemed to be frustrated and refused to fire its only weapon.

Henry gave an arrogant smirk and fired up his cannon. He was eager to see the energy vaporize his nemesis…but nothing happened. The front of the cannon spun around, but no ammunition came out. Nerd glared at Henry upon realizing what had happened.

"You did remember to check if there was ammunition in that thing," he asked sarcastically. "Right?"

Henry did not respond. He simply hurled the giant cannon at Unit 1587's head. Unit 1587 fell to the ground, and Henry urged the other two to run to the upper levels, since the exit on the first level was still burning with acid.

The three made their way up to the second level and were greeted by Jungle Boy, who darted at Nerd upon seeing him. He activated the claws on his armored suit and went in for the kill. Nerd smiled and jogged backward the same way he did with Dr. Crimson, dodging every swift attack that Jungle Boy could make.

"Go to the third level," he said. "I got this!"

Henry and Sophia rushed up to the third level. There was no exit, meaning they would have to travel up to the fourth. Upon reaching the fourth level, they noticed they were in the repair section of the engine room. There was a bridge that led to the top of the cage, which was a breathtaking sight for the two. However, even more exciting to see was the exit doorway on the opposite side—escape was possible.

The two began to make their way to the exit, when suddenly, a clown-like figure appeared out of the dark hallway. A huge blast of fire was hurled between the two of them. Sophia was able to dodge most of it, but Henry was picked up off his feet, sent flying past the platform that they were standing on, and fell down the four-story drop. Henry reached out just in the nick of time to grab the ledge of the platform on the second story, a sharp burst of pain overwhelmed him as his shoulder violently dislocated from his arm.

The room was filled with the sound of Henry howling in pain. He grabbed the ledge with his left hand as well and attempted to prop himself up, but his strength with one arm was sorely lacking and he was unable to gather the leverage he needed to hoist himself up to safety. He considered letting go, as it was only a one-floor drop, but rejected the idea upon realizing that Unit 1587 was stalking him from below, his gun pointed right at him, waiting for him to fall.

Nerd could hear the scream of his new friend, which nearly caused him to lose focus. After almost getting sliced up, he realized he needed to make his finishing move. He took a step forward while dodging a few swipes, and grabbed the switch which unlocked Jungle Boy's helmet. His helmet came flying off, leaving Jungle Boy's head vulnerable.

Jungle Boy took another swing at Nerd. Nerd dodged it again, but this time he clenched his fist and punched Jungle Boy square in the face. Jungle Boy was sent careening backwards and was knocked out cold from Nerd's punch.

Nerd ran to the second level and noticed Henry, who was hanging from the ledge. He ran up to him and helped him up to the platform. Henry was stunned to see Nerd outwit a Zentar warrior, given their inhuman speed.

"How did you—" he started to ask.

"Zentar warriors are very fast and have a strong offense," Nerd interrupted. "But their physical defense against attacks is relatively weak. They are easily a one-hit KO if they don't have their armor."

Nerd very much wanted to continue geeking out about the physiology of the Zentar, but was cut short upon the sight of

Unit 1587 making its way up the ramp leading to the second level.

The two men darted up to the third level and were stunned to see Smiley slowly walking towards Sophia on the fourth level. Psychotic laughter was echoing through the room, revealing that Smiley was very much enjoying himself.

"You realize what will happen if you kill me," Sophia stated. "You won't get a dime from Dr. Crimson, and your boss is going to want to kill you for that!"

Smiley was unfazed by Sophia's warning. He drew two short swords from his large arsenal of weapons and continued to laugh, with a murderous look radiating from his eyes.

"You think I care about money?" he said to her. "Or, for that matter, my own wellbeing? Think again!"

Smiley lumbered towards Sophia; she knew she had only moments to respond. She reached for her sword and drew it just in the nick of time. She was able to deflect Smiley's first attack with ease, but she realized how skilled of a fighter her opponent was as Smiley continued to swing both his blades at an intimidating speed. This was a challenge, and Sophia felt a burst of adrenalin that she had not received in a long time.

Nerd noticed Sophia engaging in combat, so he ran towards the ramp leading to the fourth level to aid his crewman. But Smiley caught sight of Nerd, activated his rocket launcher, and blew the ramp to smithereens. Sophia took advantage of the switch in Smiley's focus and attempted to strike him from behind. But Smiley's bloodshot eye caught sight of Sophia's move, and deflected her attack with the blade in his right hand. He quickly swung around and sliced Sophia's midsection with the blade in his left hand. Sophia screamed in pain, but thankfully the blow was not deep enough to be fatal.

Nerd now had no way to get to the fourth level, and Sophia realized that she would have to attack Smiley at full force if she wanted to defeat her opponent alone.

She blocked out the pain, pushed herself forward, and started focusing on the offensive. Sophia attacked with her sword with passion and strength, moving Smiley backwards, towards the rooms exit. But Smiley was not intimidated by Sophia's sudden adrenaline burst. If anything, he seemed excited to have a stronger challenge. He deflected the blows and continued to fight.

Meanwhile, Nerd and Henry were busy with Unit 1587. It was making its way up to the third level, and both men realized they would have to neutralize their enemy if they were going to continue living, as it would not hesitate to kill them with Sophia out of the picture.

Henry turned to Nerd and asked him to relocate his shoulder back into its socket. Nerd did so, and a loud, disturbing cracking sound filled the room.

Rolling his shoulder and grinning, Henry found himself back in the game and ready to play. He charged toward Unit 1587. Unit 1587 aimed its acid gun at Henry and fired. Henry leapt over both the attack and Unit 1587 itself. Following the curve of Henry's lunge, the unit found itself disoriented, gravity working against it as the trail of acid fell on it instead of hitting the thug. While the units armor protected it from the worst, the caustic acid hissed and devoured the lens of its welding mask. It was blind.

Henry flung himself back up the ramp, lunged towards Unit 1587's gun, feet first, and grabbed the gun between his legs. Gravity pulled his hands to the floor, and as soon as Henry's hands hit the floor, he pulled his legs back and ripped the gun right out of Unit 1587's hand. He then did a somersault backward, disconnecting the hose that fed the acid to the gun.

Henry did a barrel roll all the way down to the second floor, springing to his feet at the base and realizing with nervousness that acid was still spewing everywhere like water from an out of control fireman's hose. So Henry ran to a spot where he felt safe. He smiled as a hole burned through the platform that Unit 1587 was standing on. It fell through to the second level, which also dissolved. Then it fell through to the first. Finally, Unit 1587's acid depleted. The last fall knocked it unconscious, and it lay there in a pool of its own acid. Henry felt a rush of adrenaline fill his brain as it sank in that he had defeated his menace without the aid of a weapon.

Sophia, on the other hand, was starting to ware down. Though she had started strong, the battle had taken a turn in Smiley's favor, and Sophia was now the one being pushed back across the long bridge leading to the ship's engine. She was tiring out, while Smiley seemed to gain more and more energy the longer he fought.

Now she had been pushed all the way back to the ship's engine, and Smiley forcefully pushed her as close as he could to the burning ball of fire. Sophia could feel the heat behind her. Her skin was starting to burn, and she knew she did not have much time left. Smiley laughed at Sophia's hopeless state.

"You are such a disappointment!" he said to her. "And here I thought you were going to give me a fight worth remembering. But in the end, you let me down just as all my other victims did. You are WORTHLESS. Do you hear me? WORTHLESS!"

A chord deep within Sophia was struck as her unpleasant flashback faded away. That word, it was the same word her dad used on her after her parents disowned her from their family. She looked at the sword in her hand, then lifted her line of vision to gaze into the eyes of the insane madman that wanted to kill her. He was trying to manipulate her emotions, he was trying to get her angry, and up until now, Sophia had played right into his hands. Smiley was physically a stronger opponent then her, he was fearless, vigilant, and never tired out. Yet, he was also unorganized and didn't strategize his attacks. It seemed his only strategy was to wear his opponent down and kill them when their energy had depleted. Meaning the last thing he wanted was Sophia to pace herself and fight smart.

Her memories of all the people who had let her down flowed through her mind. Was this why they picked her apart? Did they really feel that she was such a disappointment? Or…were they afraid? Terrified over how strong she would become. Discouraging her so she would become too frustrated and angry to ever reach her full potential?

Things began to fall into place, and the hurtful words she had to endure through her life began to burn within her like wild fire. But this time, she did not crumble. This time, she did not break down or give in… She was focused.

Sophia caught her second wind, and an overwhelming sense of peace flowed through her mind. She was ready to finish the job.

Smiley was still attempting to push her into the fiery engine, but his opponents' tactics had changed. She was shifting her weight, searching for Smileys center point of gravity, and eventually, she found it. Sophia shifted to her right, causing Smiley to lose his balance, and then pushed off from her opponent, driving Smiley to stumble back. Sophia was now free and ready to fight. She went back on the offensive and began attacking with her sword, but it was different this time. Her attacks were not as near as aggressive, they were controlled, and even a little graceful. Her stance became poised, and her movements were very calculated. Her training as a warrior had come back to her, and not a moment too soon.

Smiley desperately deflected her blows, but Sophia now was planning her attacks, something Smileys damaged mind struggled to comprehend. It was now him who was being driven back. Sparks were starting to fly from the blades meeting, and Smiley knew that he had made a horrible mistake in taunting Sophia. But he got what he wanted—a fight worth remembering. So, he continued laughing as Sophia dominated him in battle.

Sophia delivered an attack that met Smiley's face. He laughed again as the sharp pain from the slice began to burn. Sophia took another shot at his leg. Again, Smiley failed to deflect it. He fell against the railing of the bridge, leaning over it. The railing was weak and rusty and was starting to break apart under his bulk. Again, Smiley was laughing, knowing that he could've fallen four stories to the ground. He was clearly winded and was helpless to defend himself. Sophia seized the opportunity, as she did not want him to catch his second wind. She delivered a kick to Smiley's stomach. The railing broke, and Smiley was sent plummeting downward to the hard metal floor four stories below him. But he was not done. He pressed a button on his rocket launcher; there was a grappling hook built into it. It launched and attached itself to the room's ceiling, and Smiley was able to save himself. However, his momentum caused him to swing headfirst into the ledge of the second level.

Disoriented, Smiley did not realize Nerd and Henry were waiting for him. Henry walked over to Smiley and detached the wrist device that contained his flamethrower. He strapped it to his left wrist and was thrilled to see there was another grappling hook build into it. Then he calmly detached the device on Smiley's other wrist that contained the rocket launcher and grappling hook. Smiley went tumbling to the ground, landing hard following the two-story drop. He blacked out and was no longer a threat.

Henry attached the device to his right wrist and told Nerd to grab onto him. Nerd did so, and the two were lifted to the fourth level.

Upon reaching the level, Nerd caught sight of Sophia, who was panting in the distance. He let go of Henry and walked up to her. In a rare moment, Nerd hugged Sophia, but very awkwardly and distantly, given the fact that he still hated hugs.

"You're amazing!" he said to her.

"I told you I was a fighter." she responded with a grin.

"That clown is going to feel it when he wakes up."

Henry lifted both his hands. Nerd laughed upon seeing his response.

"Yes, Henry," Nerd acknowledged. "You were amazing too, and now you have both of Smiley's lead weapons. I think our chances of escaping have just gone up!"

"Yeah, bro!" he shouted. "But who else do we have to worry about?"

Nerd calculated who their final opponents were and groaned when he realized that there were still three opponents left, one of them being the team's leader.

"Jake Roberts," he started. "He will be the easiest out of all of them. However, the other two pose a deadly challenge. Manic is a well-known sniper; he could be anywhere right now, and we wouldn't know until it was too late. But Drake…Drake is the sneaky one. He will be a little easier to beat now that half his team has been neutralized. But until he's out of the picture, we're going to need to keep our guard up." Nerd looked towards the room's exit and smiled. "It's time for us to go."

The three left the room and navigated themselves through the long hallways of the giant spacecraft, staying alert, hoping that none of the Menace team would catch them off guard.

Finally, after a few minutes of running, the three found the docking bay. The doors were now closed, but the *Iron Heart* was visible in the large room. This was encouraging. What was discouraging was what stood between them and their chance of escaping.

Drake Robinson and Jake Roberts stood side by side. They knew where the three were headed and had decided to guard the area, knowing it would only be a matter of time before they would meet.

"Well done, mate!" Drake stated. "But I'm afraid your little escape ends here. In about ten minutes, Dr. Crimson's ship will be meeting us, and your pretty little friend there is going to be his. I would recommend surrendering now. If you do so, I'll offer you two blokes a spot on my team. You've earned it today, and you have proven to me that—"

Henry had grown tired of Drake's speech. He aimed his rocket launcher at the two men; it still had one rocket left in it. He fired, and both men seemed to be vaporized by the explosion that consumed the two of them. But as the dust settled, he realized he had made a huge mistake. An energy field was covering the two of them, one that was activated from a device on Jake's armor—the same Jake they initially thought wouldn't be much of a threat.

"Guess you blokes like doing things the hard way," Drake continued. "Very well. Game on!"

As soon as Drake got the words out of his mouth, a red dot became visible on the top of Henry's head. Nerd turned in the direction the dot was coming from and caught a glimpse of Manic sniping Henry from the cargo bay's top level.

Nerd again went into analysis mode and calculated his options. Henry was precisely 6'4". Nerd was 5'9". Manic had just pulled the trigger, but the two men were close enough for Nerd to make a move. Nerd quickly made his decision and ran into Henry Smith with all his body weight. He took Henry's place, standing where the sniper shot was headed. Nerd smiled as the shot just barely went over his head, saving Henry Smith, and not sacrificing himself in the process.

"Everyone spread out!" Nerd ordered.

He ran around and did his best to distract Manic, yelling out several cunning remarks about his top hat, thinking maybe Manic would try to kill him rather than Henry and Sofia. It worked, and Nerd was able to dodge the attacks of Manic Blackheart. Henry seized the opportunity and active-eated his grappling hook. He carried himself to the ledge Manic was sniping from and closed in to make his attack.

Sophia, on the other hand, ignored Nerd's command. She drew her sword, ready to attack the shield with it. Knowing that Manic would not go after her, Drake used his weapon's stun setting against her. He fired a shot, and in a futile attempt to defend herself, Sophia raised her sword, hoping that it would protect her from the attack. Oddly enough, it did. The sword absorbed the blast of energy and began to glow blue. Drake kept firing on her, but she continued to deflect the shots. Her sword glowed brighter and brighter with blue energy. It was now getting to the point of being lethal, as many shots on stun could easily do damage to a human being.

Meanwhile, Henry had made his way up to the top level. He detached the grappling hook and aimed his flamethrower at Manic. Manic caught sight of him, swiveled and ran up, grabbing Henry's left arm and forcing it upward. A huge ball of fire went soaring through the air.

Nerd realized that the sniper shots had stopped. He was now able to focus on Drake and Jake, who were still trying to stun Sophia.

Nerd took note of Sophia's sword and how it was radiating blue energy. He remembered the note that had been attached to the sword, claiming it had belonged to Karla Nelson. Who was one of the founders when the humans discovered Zecarah. *Could Sophia be of her family's dissent?* There was only one way to find out.

The blue energy was now starting to get blinding, and Sophia was worried that her vision would be impaired. Nerd called out to her and revealed something about the sword that she had not considered.

"Thrust it out like a sling at their shield!" he shouted. "The energy will leave your sword!"

Sophia did so, and the energy crashed into the shield that was protecting the two men. The energy overloaded the device on Jake's armor, and the shield dropped. Nerd ran towards his opponent and took a swing at Drake. He made contact with Drake's rib cage and managed to break three of Drake's ribs. Drake howled in pain and dropped his gun. Nerd was ready to take another shot at him but noticed that Jake had equipped himself with what looked like a small laser cannon. A beam of energy flowed from the cannon to Drake, and Drake's ribs immediately started healing themselves. Drake was now at full health, and he took a swing at Nerd, decking him in the face. Nerd took the hit surprisingly well, and the two men began fighting each other hand to hand.

"Jake!" Drake yelled out. "Go get the other men; we're gonna need 'em!"

With blinding speed, Jake left the room, and Nerd realized they needed to act fast.

Sophia was tempted to shoot an arrow at Drake, but she caught sight of Henry and Manic struggling on the top level. Manic had managed to aim the flamethrower towards Henry's face.

Manic was reaching for the trigger, and Sophia knew that her new ally was in danger. She reached for an arrow and drew her bow, and the tip of the arrow burst into flames. She realized she had activated another special arrow. She released it, and the arrow flew through the air and embedded itself in Manic's shoulder.

Manic was now on fire. He panicked and lost his footing, falling off the edge and plummeting five stories down to the ground. He landed hard on the metal floor, but amazingly, he was still breathing after he hit the ground. The man was tough, certainly tougher than the average human, as even a fall from five stories would not kill him.

Sophia turned her attention to Drake, who had just knocked Nerd to the ground. Drake noticed she had her bow and arrows in her hand. He charged at her, hoping to get to her before she could fire another shot or draw her sword. Sophia responded by dropping her bow and took a swing with her fist right at Drake's nose. Drake cried out in pain again as his nose broke. Sophia wasted no time and continued to attack Drake. He was unable to get his fists up in time and she delivered several hard blows to his head.

He was now disoriented, so much so that he didn't even know where he was, and Sophia knew it. She took one final shot at Drake's face, and the blow knocked him clean out.

He lay on the ground, defeated by his own prey. Sophia stood over him, the roaring of adrenalin shouting in her ears. She turned to face Nerd. The innocent look in her eyes had faded, and a vicious look of hostility overcame them. It was as if she was about to attack him. Nerd was not intimidated however, as this gaze had met him many times in his field of expertise. He smiled, walked over to her, and gently put his hand on her right shoulder.

"You really are an amazing fighter." he said to her in a calm, reassuring voice. "But please, don't ever lose sight of the things that truly make you strong."

Sophia didn't understand what Nerd meant by that, but the tone of his voice was soothing to her. She took a deep breath and regained her composer.

Using his new grappling hook to reach the bottom floor, Henry ran toward Nerd and Sophia, jerking his thumb at the ship.

"We gonna go now or what?"

Nerd nodded his head in agreement. The three ran over to the *Iron Heart*, and Nerd pressed an icon on the screen of his communicator. The platform used to enter the ship opened, and the three ran up the ramp and into the starship. Nerd closed the ramp and headed straight to the bridge. He approached the science station, which Sophia had never seen him use, since he always piloted the ship.

"What are you doing?" she asked.

"Downloading a virus into the freighter's database," Nerd responded. "And it will be ready right…about…now."

Suddenly the freighter's lights started flashing on and off, the massive cargo bay door started to open, and the freighter's computer began mouthing off announcements at random. Nerd activated his ship's engine and fired up the thrusters. As soon as the door was open wide enough for them to escape, he flew the ship out. He panicked when he caught sight of a Cosmic 5 science ship in the distance. He quickly set a course for the nearest space station and acti-veated the hyperdrive.

The *Iron Heart* vanished into the depths of hyperspace. Just like that, it was over. He and his friends had won; they had gotten home safe.

Nerd reclined back in his pilot's chair as his mind aggressively processed everything that had happened to him in just one day.

Dr. Crimson made his way out of his starship. He noticed Drake and Manic lying on the ground and ordered his men to examine them.

"He is still alive!" the man examining Drake answered.

"So is he!" the man examining Manic added. Dr. Crimson smiled at the news, pleased to find they were still alive.

"Well then," he said. "It looks like Nerd got the best of them! Oh well, I was going to sedate and capture Drake as soon as he delivered Sophia anyways. He will make a fine specimen to experiment on. At least this makes half my job a little easier now."

Dr. Crimson started laughing and ordered his men to carry the mercenary crew to his starship…but as soon as the men began to do so, a wave of laser fire came flooding through the room. It hit Crimson's starship, and the starship blew up, destroying Crimson's opportunity to escape. He looked over and noticed Star-Creeper holding a laser cannon. It was he who had fired the shots and destroyed his spacecraft. Dr. Crimson gritted his teeth and held his fist up at Star-Creeper.

"Men!" he ordered his remaining staff members. "Attack!" The remaining five men charged at Star-Creeper. However, they were overtaken by the remaining members of Menace. First came Unit 1578, which had just repaired its acid gun. He fired upon the first member of Crimson's band. The man screamed as he was slowly dissolved by the orange acid that came out of Unit 1578's gun.

Next came Jungle Boy, who was running in a fury. He picked off the second member of Crimson's band and diced him into little tiny pieces within seconds.

Third to enter was Smiley, who had reequipped himself with a new flamethrower. He activated it and set the remainning three members on fire, laughing as he did so.

They vaporized within the flames, leaving Dr. Crimson to defend himself.

Being a psychopath, Dr. Crimson was unable to comprehend fear the way a normal human would; he was the predator, not the prey, and he needed to take control before that changed. He drew his Bowie knife and was about to charge at Smiley, who had just defeated three of his men, but he was knocked off his feet by a kick to the rib cage.

Dr. Crimson fell hard on the ground and noticed Jake had revived the Menace leader, Drake Robinson. Drake was furious when his men explained that Crimson had attempted to betray them. He walked over to Dr. Crimson, who was lying on the ground, and lifted his foot over Crimson's head.

"No!" Crimson shouted as Drake drove his armored boot into Crimson's skull.

Crimson began to lose consciousness after taking such a strong blow to the head, but he could still make out what Drake was saying to his men.

"Well, mates!" Drake said. "It looks like we got ourselves a new prisoner to use for target practice. We're gonna have fun with this one!"

These were the last words that Crimson heard before the light faded away and everything went black.

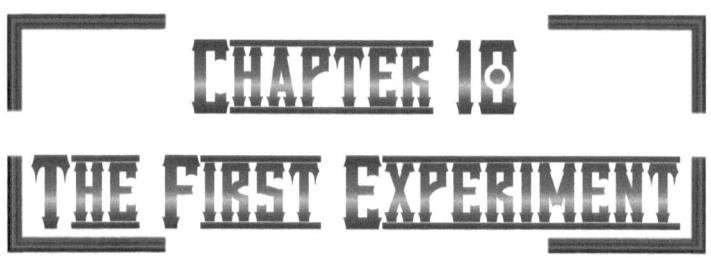

CHAPTER 10
THE FIRST EXPERIMENT

Earth date: February 10th, 2010
Location: Cosmic 5
Time: 600

The Little Warrior made his way through the ventilation shafts, his heart pounding the closer he got. It was true that his master had saved him from a formerly miserable existence, even putting his own life on the line to do so. For this he was very grateful. Still, woe to the fool who chose to cross him, for those who did usually ended up with a fate worse than death. This earned him both a deep sense of respect and a morbid feeling of terror from his henchmen.

He knew if there was anyone that could get the Cosmic experiments leader to listen to reason, it was the Little Warrior himself, but even this was no guarantee and that was enough to put even him in a state of fear.

He had now reached his master's room. He opened the ventilation cover and made his way inside. There his master lay, at the far end of the room. He was bedridden, for his depression had gotten worse since they finished exploring the western wing of the station.

There was still no sign of the Invader Project, which his master had been trying to find for well over a year. It was his only hope of getting to the heavily guarded core of the station, let alone freeing the rest of the experiments who were being tortured in the laboratories of Cosmic 5. The news was very grim to them all, but it hit his master a lot deeper than it did the rest, as there was something in the core his heart longed for on a level that surpassed the Little Worriers understanding.

The room was dark, so dark his master's face looked more like a shadow. His mask was on the table next to his bed. But even so, his identity was unrecognizable due to the lighting.

The Little Warrior took a deep breath and spoke to his master, hoping it would snap him out of the daze he was in.

"I have an update on David Bell," he said. His distorted voice crackled through the small room. "I have written out all the details on my communicator. I can send them to you if you wish."

"Send it to me," his master replied in a calm, soft voice. "Then leave. I do not want to be bothered right now."

The Little Warrior began to walk over to his master's bed, but he stopped dead in his tracks when his master sat up. His eyes began to glow with green energy, which radiated from his retinas whenever he was angry. It was blinding, given how dark the rest of the room was, and this reminded the Little Warrior of how powerless the rest of the Cosmic experiments were compared to him.

"Did you not hear me!?" His master snarled in a much harsher voice.

The Little Warrior bit down on his fear. He was scared for his life, but he cared too much about his master to let him self-destruct. He needed to know that he was endangering himself, and this motivated the Little Warrior to continue speaking.

"You've been stuck here for too long!" the Little Warrior ventured. "We need you back. The other experiments have lost their will to fight."

The light dimmed in his master's eyes, revealing that his anger had subsided. He lay back down and returned to his state of sadness. "So have I…"

"You can't! If you do, you will never get back what you lost."

"Without the Invader Project, it's hopeless. Dr. Crimson is a monster…but I have to give credit where credit is due; he has worked hard to keep us from taking control of the station and has trained his staff to put up a good fight. We won't last long unless we know precisely where to look, and the only way to get that information is to bleed it out of the one who hid it from us, the one known as David Bell. David currently has nothing to lose, and he cares too much about the weak to ever betray them into my hands. I don't see any reason to fight anymore; we are only delaying the inevitable.

Any attempt to change what we have been given is nothing more than a waste of time."

"Master! Please, at least look at the information I've sent to your tablet. You may feel a little differently when you see what your rival has done. Please trust me. Have I ever given you a reason to doubt my judgment?"

His master let out a deep sigh.

"No…no, you have not."

His master sat up yet again and picked up his tablet, which was next to his mask. He viewed the information that the Little Warrior had sent him, which explained the events that had taken place with David over the last week.

A long stretch of silence followed. He could not believe what he was reading. Once it sunk in, a demented smile began to form across his shadowy face, and a renewed sense of determination seemed to fill the very depths of his soul. He was ready to hunt his rival down, only this time, he knew how to bleed the information he needed out of him.

"A human friend…" he said. "David has become attached to a little human friend. Oh, David…I know how to break you now!"

The man stood up and got out of bed. He grabbed his pale mask and put it over his face, covering the identity lurking behind it.

"You're in charge until I get back," he said to the Little Warrior. "I will deal with this matter myself."

He vanished from the room. The Little Warrior smiled, for he knew the tide of their struggles had greatly turned in their favor.

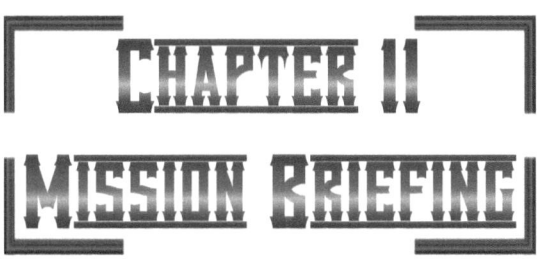

CHAPTER 11
MISSION BRIEFING

Earth date: February 21st, 2010
Time: 720
Location: The *Iron Heart*

David woke up to the sound of rap music blaring upstairs and groaned as an overpowering feeling of grogginess built up within him. He was unsure of how late he had stayed up, but he was paying for his obsessiveness towards re-creating the healing device Jake had used for his friends. There had to be a way—he saw it work. It was only a matter of researching how.

David had also been working on re-creating Sophia's shadow arrows, which again, had no results. Though the technology was hundreds of years old, it was still far more advanced than anything found in the known galaxy.

After giving himself a little time for his senses to return, David made his way upstairs to the main level. Sophia and Henry were both eating lunch, which notified David that it was already past 720, which would be noon in Earth time.

Henry gave David a slanted, arrogant smirk upon seeing him. "Look who finally decided to wake up!" Henry stated.

"I was up late working on a project," David responded in a grumpy voice.

"Someone didn't get their coffee today! Come join us, I made us some wraps. Sophia was getting a bit tired of hotdogs every lunchtime."

David chuckled a bit on being reminded of his inability to cook more than a handful of meals. It had only been a little over a week since the three of them had escaped the freighter Wrath, and all ready his companions seemed to have no problem picking apart his flaws, but as long as they did so with smiles on their faces, he didn't really care. As long as they didn't trigger any of his insecurities, he was content.

After asking Henry to turn his music down, he made himself some coffee and joined his companions for lunch. Socializing was something David had been without for nearly a full year, with the exception of the central commander and the Observer walking him through the ropes when he began his training as a Deep Cosmos agent. It was taking some time to get used to, especially considering he had never been the lead horse before, but oddly enough, David was starting to like it. He enjoyed seeing the goodness in others and helping them to reach their full potential. Even Henry seemed to have respect for him, though it took him a few days after David had revealed to him that he had not committed the crimes he was accused of. David chuckled at the memory and continued sipping his coffee…loudly, to his companions' discontent.

"So!" Sophia said in an attempt to drown out the sound of David's slurping. "Where to now? Our trip to space station 1529 was amazing! It was the size of a city…they had everything there."

"Ya, sista!" Henry enthused. "The bars and night clubs were pretty epic! Pity the two of you refused to join me."

"Really?" Nerd responded. "Could you ever see me at a nightclub? I would get beat up the moment I walked in! Besides, you got in a fight after your second visit. I asked you to lie low…that wasn't lying low!"

"You also asked me not to shoplift or rob anyone. Two out of three, baby! I would have to say that's pretty good!"

"Touché…I have to give you credit for that. You also returned an old lady's wallet, so that was cool, as you could have gotten easy money without pickpocketing. So yes, although your score wasn't perfect, you still passed. Although you blew your entire month's paycheck on weapons and alcohol…which seriously should not be put in the same sentence! So, it will be interesting to see if you can keep to that for the next month"

"Hey, hey, I'm Henry Smith. I make no promises!"

"You should've come with us to the indoor theme park!" Sophia added. "I actually got David to go on most of the rides!"

"More like brutally forced me against my will to go on them." David muttered. "And if I didn't, you made me hold your pocketbook for you while you went on the ride by yourself. If you only knew some of the looks I got. It was most…traumatizing."

"You were the one who chose to put the strap over your shoulder like it was your own! But thank you for being a gent. It was fun watching you scream your head off on the rides! Though I did think you were going to throw up when we went on that one that spun around. That would've been so awesome!"

"Yeah. I—"

The group's conversation was rudely cut off by the blaring alarm system and red flashing lights; just loud enough to be heard over the cacophonous noise of the alarm system, the computer warned on a loop, 'Message from the supreme commander. Priority one. Please report to the virtual reality deck immediately.' Henry and Sophia turned as one to look at David, whose eyes had widened in stunned surprise. It was clear that he was not expecting this at all, and he seemed nervous. Sophia gave him a worried look and asked him what was happening.

"It's a priority one alert from the supreme commander," David responded. "That means that there is a threat to the galaxy that they want me to neutralize… I've only been an agent for one year! Why are they asking me to take this!?"

"Calm down, bro!" Henry urged. "We got your back on this."

"I appreciate that…but sadly you're not going to be with me for the most difficult part of the mission."

"And that is?"

"Speaking to the supreme commander. That I have to do alone." David got off his chair and made his way downstairs.

Henry gave Sophia a puzzled look. "How is talking to the supreme commander the hardest part of a mission that threatens the entire galaxy?"

Sophia smiled at Henry's question. "That's David," she said to him. "He'll easily fight a psychopath without breaking a sweat, but will tremble in fear if he ever has to talk to one.

"That's wild, sista!"

"David is David," Sophia said as a smile formed from ear to ear.

David entered the virtual reality deck. He locked the door and ordered his computer to relay the message to him.

The ship's computer used the virtual reality deck to form a table in front of him. David sat down on a chair that his computer had also conveniently simulated. David then reached into his lab coat pocket and pulled out his large glasses. He donned them, and Nerd seemed to come alive as soon as the glasses were on. He was now ready to receive his mission.

A hologram appeared in the middle of the table. A dark, shadowy creature was visible within it. Nerd felt shivers run down his spine on a level he was not used to. It was true he felt nervous whenever talking to someone, even Henry and Sophia, whom he now saw every day. But there was something about the supreme commander that was very unsettling.

Nerd regained his composure and swallowed his fear as the supreme commander spoke to him.

"Nerd, a priority one situation has come up, and Deep Cosmos needs your assistance in a delicate matter. A rare disease known as I-417-248-79b has been released into our galaxy. The humans know it better as galactic plague. The disease can somehow survive and spread through space, it seems to only target a few select people within each location when it strikes. Zentar lost ten citizens, Zecarah lost six, and the space station Nebula recently lost one. Other locations have been infected. I will include the details in your mission briefing should you choose to accept. What I can tell you at this moment is that the targeted locations are random and have no pattern to them. It's impossible to detect and it is unknown how the virus spreads. The only reason we know of its existence is because of what happens after the virus infects its victims. I will warn you, it is extremely gruesome, and that is not a statement I often make. Your mission will be to discover the cause of the virus and incapacitate it before it devours our entire galaxy. Also, please keep in mind that if you or any of your crew members are infected with the disease, there is no known cure. If you succeed, however, your payment will be triple your yearly salary. Do you accept?"

A mission for a doctor. Now Nerd knew why he had been asked to take on this mission. He didn't give it a second thought.

"I accept, Commander!" he said confidently.

"Good! I am sending you your first priority one Deep Cosmos mission file! Do not show it to any of your crew, as the information in this file is classified. You may, however, bring your companions on the mission if you so choose. You may also inform them of the basic facts of this mission, such as the disease name and the mission location. Now get going! The fate of the galaxy rests in your hands."

The hologram of the supreme commander faded away. A long-range wormhole beam transported the file the supreme commander was talking about. It was the first time Nerd had ever received one and he grinned from excitement before remembering this was a serious case which required his most intense concentration.

Although it was shaped like a regular file, it was made of a strange material that was unknown to humanity; a material that was practically indestructible. The file had two locks on the top of it and a chain that was tied around the two locks. *Deep Cosmos* was scrawled across the top of the file in deep red, and each of the letters looked as if they had been gouged so deeply into the material that it bled the letters out, rather than having them painted or printed on. David felt a shiver go down his spine as he looked at the file, followed by a wave of goosebumps over his entire body; this was not going to be an easy mission.

Nerd pulled out his universal key and unlocked the two locks located on the top of the file. He pulled out the contents inside, and for the first time in his life, he saw a picture of one of the galactic plague victims. Nerd again felt shivers run down his spine, and a feeling of nausea filled his stomach at the horrid sight that lay in front of him.

CHAPTER 12
GALACTIC PLAGUE

Sophia and Henry were bored out of their minds. They didn't want to engage in anything until they heard from their commander, but he had been gone for almost two hours and there was no sign of his returning any time soon.

"Do you think he's dead?" Henry asked.

"He better be at this point," Sophia responded with her arms crossed and a matching look of irritation on her face.

Henry laughed at Sophia's moody state. "What's with the 'tude, girl? That's my job and the sarcasm is David's job."

"I'm just having one of those moments, I guess."

"Yeah, I get that… Do you think he will bring us on this mission?"

"I hope so."

"The last mission was pretty epic if I do say so myself. You were introduced to the most amazing human being in the galaxy—me!"

Sophia gave Henry a glare as she shook her head. Henry's self-obsession was definitely known to her and David at this point, but she had grown to appreciate him over the last week and a half. He was positive, funny, and very charismatic. She was also touched he didn't even consider selling her out when Drake made both him and David the offer to be part of his crew. Henry always claimed that money and fame were the only two things that kept him going, and other than those two motivations, he seemed like a basic guy, but even at his most basic, Henry had more layers than he was willing to admit. She felt much more relaxed with him on the crew, even if he was immature and rough around the edges, but she was certain his ego would be the death of him, or worse, it was going to be the death of her and David.

Ten minutes went by before they heard their commander making his way upstairs. He was wearing his glasses, meaning that they had to call him by his code name as he had requested.

"Nerd…" Sophia started sarcastically.

Nerd did not chuckle as he usually did at Sophia's sarcasm towards his code name. He was serious, stone cold serious. His crew members had never seen him this serious before, so much so that it was unsettling to them both.

"Dude," Henry said. "Lighten up, bro."

"We have an epidemic on our hands," Nerd said flatly. "We must head to the space station Nebula immediately."

"Then you're taking us with you?" Sophia asked excitedly.

"If you choose…I will explain on our way there."

Nerd ran to the cockpit and set a course for the space station Nebula. The ship entered hyperspace and the new journey began.

Sophia and Henry waited eagerly to hear what their mission was about. Nerd noticed his crew members' excitement and revealed to them what they were in for.

"What you are about to face is like nothing you have ever seen before," Nerd started. "It will feed on anything it can get its clutches on; it will kill without remorse; it will wipe out all life as we know it if we do not step in. It may take your lives in a horrible and gruesome fashion if you accept the mission…which is why I will give you the choice to opt out of this one."

"What?" Sophia exclaimed. "No way! Please tell us what we're going up against."

"A virus…the most deadly known to man…galactic plague."

Henry and Sofia both groaned at Nerd's words.

"Really?" Henry replied. "You got us all excited for a stupid virus?"

"…It's galactic plague, guys! The same virus that killed millions four years ago?"

"We were hoping for a mission where we would actually see some action," Sophia complained.

"…Ah," Nerd responded. "I see. Well, the good news is, we're only 30 minutes away from Nebula. So, we won't be in hyperspace for very long."

The three waited as they approached their destination. Sophia and Henry barely said one word, given their disappointment, and after a long 30 minutes, they finally arrived.

Nebula was nothing like space station 1529. Although it was still a good size, it was a lot smaller than the previous station and noticeably up there in years. The outside was starting to rust and looked like it could break apart at any given time. It had three rings, each ring a different variation of size, with the outer ring being the widest, tallest, and the inner ring being only three levels in total. In the very middle of all the rings was a tower about the size of a 30-story office building. The bridge was located at the very top, with a long antenna attached to it which was used to broadcast an emergency channel to all stations, colonies, and ships that belonged to humanity. The station was the center-point of the second human race and had a long history in the space wars that humanity fought in; however, time had taken its toll on this station, making it a now hideous sight for the crew to look at.

Nerd activated the intercom and asked the station for permission to dock. His request was granted, and he landed the ship within one of the station's four docking bays.

Nerd turned to his two companions and asked them if they still wanted to join. They reluctantly agreed, followed their commander out of the *Iron Heart*, and stepped foot on the space station Nebula.

Three men were waiting at the end of the ship's ramp to greet them. One was tall and skinny, with pale skin and short brown hair. The other was short, stocky, had dark skin, and was bald. The third was fit and robust, with tan skin and long blond hair. They were all in uniforms that were only worn by members of the galactic government, and Nerd became nervous, as he did not want his true identity to be discovered.

"Greetings!" said the short, stocky man who was located between the two other men. "My name is Captain Tim Baker. This is my lieutenant, Mr. Joe Collins." Baker signaled their attention to the tall, skinny man. "And this is my chief of security, Mr. Steven Howard." Baker signaled to the fit, robust man. "We are here to aid you and fill you in on the situation."

"I was not aware that Nebula was under galactic government control," Nerd said. "Beta Squadron commanded this station, the last I heard."

"Oh, we don't control this station," Baker dismissed. "We were called in due to the seriousness of this mission. The station belongs to the remaining members of Beta Squadron and is led by Commander Timothy Williams. We will make sure to introduce you to him."

"Oh good! Ah…good that the three of you are here to aid me… Can you take me to the body? I'm supposed to examine that first."

"Of course, please follow me." The three men led Nerd, Henry, and Sophia through the station. It was a bit of an eerie walk. The halls were rusty and strewn about with debris and cracks. The lights flickered off and on in several areas and some of the automatic doors were propped open, indicating that while repairs were desperately needed, there just weren't enough resources to do them. If there was anywhere that they were going to get stabbed by a random serial killer, it was here. There was, however, a large crew populating the station, which made the sight a little less frightening. But that didn't stop spirits from being very low. The fact that one of their crew members had just been infected with the horrid disease lay heavily on the minds of the space station occupants.

The six made their way to the spot where the crew member had been infected. To their surprise, the commander of the station had ordered for the location to be set up like a crime scene. There was caution tape around the area, and a chalk line of where the victim's body had been found. A few of the security officers were there, standing in the middle of the scene.

The six individuals were allowed inside the taped-off area and were instantly greeted by a blond haired, blue eyed man, who was wearing a uniform that revealed his authority.

"Greetings!" The man said, "My name is Timothy Williams, I'm the commander of the space station Nebula. I'm sorry I wasn't able to be down to greet you but, I'm sure you understand." He glanced back at the guards and chalk outline, a weary frown marking his face.

"Greetings, Commander," Nerd said politely. "My name is Nerd, supreme human intelligence. These are my associates, Sophia Nelson and Henry Smith." Henry walked over to the commander and gave the bewildered man a high five before shaking his hand with a broad grin. Nerd put his hand on his forehead and sighed. "Also, I would like to apologize for Henry's behavior in advance."

"Wait? Henry Smith? The wanted space thug? What is he doing here?"

"He's with me. Don't worry, he's on our side."

Commander Williams took a deep breath and let out a sigh. His instinct was to have Henry Smith arrested immediately, but even he would not dare challenge a Deep Cosmos agent. Those who did rarely lived to tell about it, and though Nerd was known for his mercy towards his opponents…he still didn't want to risk it. Nerd had already outsmarted many adversaries who were better equipped than he was.

Commander Williams regained his composure and directed their attention to where the victim had been infected.

"He was struck ten hours ago while attempting to fix a loose circuit. His name was Caleb Jones, one of the station's mechanics. He was 31 years of age and was in perfect health beforehand… None of us saw it coming."

"Did you get any camera footage of when he was struck?" Nerd asked.

"No…and despite the millions who have died from galactic plague, no one ever has. The virus has managed to evade observation."

"Were there any eyewitnesses?"

"Again, no. Most of the crew members were just waking up by the time he was struck. One person claimed to have seen him right beforehand. The next time they saw him…he was no longer human."

"I find that very bizarre. It's like the virus has a mind of its own. Is there anything that may connect the victims? Even the smallest of details?"

"No, trust me. An astronomical level of research was done when the virus was discovered four years ago, and now that it has returned, we are even more lost than we were back then. The victims were of different ages, genders, species, and health conditions. It struck at random points in the galaxy. The victims ate different food, originated from different planets, worked for different organizations… Then, we have a four-year period where the virus just seemed to die off, and now it's back again. Nothing about it makes sense! We can't research a cure, because the virus seems to leave the victim's body instantaneously. It swiftly alters the victim's DNA, and then it's gone. The bodies are not contagious and can be handled by pretty much anyone... well, at least once they're dead. One did react after it was touched by another person. I believe this happened a few days ago on the planet Zentar. Poor guy was ripped to shreds."

"What? What do you mean once they're dead?"

"Oh...you were never informed? It takes the victim about half a day to die. Their brain dies nearly instantaneously, but the virus doesn't kill the body right away. It alters the DNA to a decaying state, and after a period of time, the victim's body breaks down enough for them to die."

"Torture..."

"Sort of; they really have no concept of pain. As I mentioned, their brain is dead. They're just vegetables who can still physically harm whoever handles them. That is why contact is not recommended unless the victim is restrained."

Nerd yet again let out a sigh. He did not understand why the supreme commander did not inform them of this in his report. But it didn't matter; the information Nerd had received had gone nowhere. He was even further away from discovering the origin of the virus, and the feeling was very unsettling for him.

"Is the victim still alive?" he asked.

"Barely." Williams sighed. "We have him locked away in the med bay."

"Please take me to him."

"Of course. Just...just prepare yourself."

The seven were about to head to the medical bay when Sophia was startled by something. She had glanced up toward the ceiling, where an air vent could be seen, and gasped, grabbing Henry's arm.

"What's wrong, girl?" Henry asked.

"Nothing...nothing's wrong," Sophia responded, shaking her head with a frown. "I could've sworn I saw something, but the lights must be playing tricks on me, because it's gone now."

"Can you describe what you saw?" Nerd asked.

"No...it's nothing, really! I'm just paranoid right now. It's fine."

Nerd was concerned about Sophia's response, but on rare occasions he had seen her like this before, so he decided not to push the matter any further, as doing so would only upset her. Nevertheless, he filed her response within his memory, in case he needed to ask her again down the road.

The seven of them made their way to the medical bay. The room was creepy and primitive, which upset Nerd very deeply given his background in the medical field. There were several medical beds, medical tools that were out of date, and a very small medical staff, much smaller than what the station required given the crew population. Granted, good medics were hard to come by for the human race, which was how Nerd was able to get a license as a doctor, physician, and psychiatrist back when he was still in his adolescence. Still, it was concerning to see.

There was a research room located in the back of the medical room. The door had a tinted window and the area was locked off. The commander walked over to the door and unlocked it, turning to the others and explaining,

"Only myself and a few of the medical staff have a key to this room. It's safer that way."

Once inside, Nerd took a quick glance around. The room was dark and the sound of a monster softly growling could be heard near the center of the room, but couldn't be seen given how dimly lit the room was.

The commander closed the door behind them and locked it. He then put his hand on a switch and urged the others to prepare themselves. He took a deep breath and flipped the switch on. The lights in the room brightened, and Sophia screamed bloody murder at the grotesque sight in front of her. Even Henry, who was the least likely to be fazed, flinched and dropped his jaw at the sight of the victim's horrific state.

His skin had turned a sickly shade of dark green. His head was tilted awkwardly to the right, and his mouth was so widely open that it seemed to be unhinged. His teeth had all fallen out, leaving only a large, gaping black hole. Fangs were starting to protrude from his bleeding, empty gums, and his eyes were black and soulless. Wordless moaning and groaning came from his throat—he was obviously brain dead, just as the commander had informed them. But whatever was left of him was still hanging on for dear life.

To prevent him from hurting anyone, the creature was chained to a chair, and his arms were tied behind him. His mouth was, however, left open, as the staff wanted Nerd to get a clear view of what the virus had done.

Nerd let out yet another sigh upon seeing what had happened to this former human being. He walked over to examine it despite Commander Williams urging him nervously to proceed with caution.

Nerd looked the creature over for anything that could give him a lead on what had happened. But he was unable to find anything.

"I don't get it," he said. "This just doesn't make—"

Suddenly Nerd stopped. He became focused on something on the creature's neck. It was a very minor detail, but at this point he was willing to go off of anything. He walked over to the creature and touched his neck lightly, leaning in to examine it. It was a very small dot-shaped scar. This was not much, but it was an observation nevertheless. Sadly, that was all David could observe. The only way he could further investigate was to examine a second body, which would be bittersweet, given the fact that Nerd didn't want anyone else to die from this.

Nerd was about to ask the commander a few questions, when suddenly the creature reacted to Nerd's touch. It atempted to bite him! Thankfully it was unable to, as the rest of its body was chained to a chair. There was a monitor attached to the creature, and its heart rate was beating at an extreme level. The creature was going into shock, and Commander Williams urged Nerd to get away from it.

Nerd looked at the creature. It was clearly reacting in panic, and his caretaking nature began to kick in. He walked towards the creature and firmly cradled its head in his arms. The creature resisted, but Nerd spoke to the creature in a very calm, soft voice—a voice that Sophia and Henry had not heard come from him before. The creature began to calm down, and Nerd softened his grip. The creature's heart rate began to slow down. Slower, slower, and slower, until it stopped. The creature died in Nerd's arms.

Nerd let go of the creature and asked to be excused. Commander Williams granted his request and unlocked the door. Nerd let out a sigh, lowered his head, and walked out, determined to never step foot in that room again.

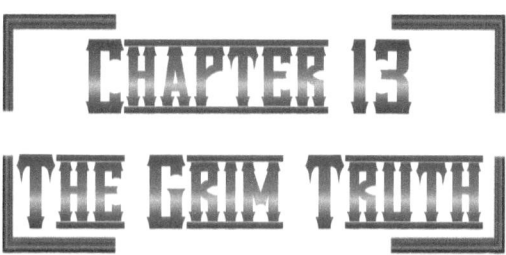

CHAPTER 13
THE GRIM TRUTH

Sophia and Henry gave each other a stunned look. It was difficult for their commander to be empathetic, but when he was, it was powerful and took them both off guard, as they did not expect to see such a reaction in that situation.

"I need to talk to him," she told Henry. "I…I don't think he's okay… Honestly, I don't think he's been okay for a while."

"Are you sure, girl?" Henry responded. "I think he needs a little space right now."

"I may not get another chance. Trust me, when his emotions come out, it's sometimes the only opportunity to talk to him about these things, but if he tells me to go away, I'll give him his space."

Sophia wiped the tears from her eyes, walked out of the room, and searched for Nerd within the small space station. She finally found him near a window, gazing out at the stars. He was deep in thought, and for a moment Sophia had second thoughts about talking to him; but she needed to work her way inside the mind that was still such a mystery to her. So, she walked over to Nerd and stood beside him.

She could sense the gears turning in his head, and it was intimidating. She was not sure if she could break in, given how deep in thought he was, but she had to try. She attempted to break the ice by focusing on another topic of conversation. Space was one thing that always fascinated Nerd, so she hoped that maybe she could reach him that way.

"They're beautiful," she said to him while gazing at the stars. "Aren't they?" Nerd did not respond. Still, she tried. "I always wanted to visit every single one. I know that's impossible…but thanks to you I have the chance to live out a part of my dream, and I'm grateful for that." Nerd still did not respond. She tried again. "Before I met you, I hated who I was…really! I was so insecure and convinced that I was worthless. But you saved me before it was too late. Not just from the clutches of Dr. Crimson, but from myself…and I just want to say thank you."

Nerd still did not respond. At this point, Sophia decided it was best to give him his space. She began to walk off, when suddenly, she felt a shift in Nerd's thinking. His attention seemed to turn, and he began to process the things she had told him.

"I did not save you," Nerd said.

"What?" Sophia asked. "What do you mean?"

"I did not save you from yourself. I don't do that for people…I can't. Yes, I saved you from Dr. Crimson. Yes, I save someone when I operate on them when they're dying, but I never saved you from yourself. From the beginning, I saw goodness within you. I knew you were unique and valuable…and no, I don't say that about everyone. When I saw that in you, I simply encouraged that goodness and helped support you in your time of need so that when you were strong enough, you could save yourself. That's all I did; everything else was you."

Sophia was stunned. She did not expect Nerd to respond that way at all. True, it was within his character—he was speaking in a way that sounded like he was analyzing—but he had opened her mind to a perspective she had not considered before. However, this was not the time to be dwelling on the subject. She wanted to know what was up with him. So, she shifted the conversation and attempted to break into Nerd's active mind.

"David…" she said, purposely calling him by his real name. "What's wrong? You seem to be deeply scarred by something…you always seem to be thinking about something, and…I just want you to know that I'm here for you. You can always tell me anything and trust that I won't overreact. I want to help you. Please…just let me in."

Nerd took a moment to process Sophia's words. After a few seconds of processing, he responded to her by saying,

"I feel sad about the plague victim, but because I'm me, I don't know how to express it. So, I just…go quiet and try to distance myself until my feelings ease. But it's hard because they're so powerful. Way more powerful than what is normal, and it's frustrating, because most people will never know…because I don't know how to let them know."

"In most cases, I've noticed you seem to struggle with empathy…but in other cases, I have seen you express it in a way that most humans can't. I was so terrified of that thing back in the medical bay; I didn't want to be anywhere near it. You looked past all of that and comforted it before it died…and now you're sad. That's sweet, and it's something that most humans would never even consider."

"I'm not like most humans…but I think you know that already."

"That's what I want to know… Is there any reason you're like this? It's not a bad thing, but from the moment I met you, I could tell that you were…different. At first it made me feel uncomfortable, but I'm starting to see things very differently. It's like you see things from a perspective that completes humanity. I'm always learning new things from you every day, and it's helping me to become better."

"I'm learning new things every day from you too. Things that I had never considered."

"So, what gives? Were you always like this? Or did something happen to you that drove you to become something that humanity needed?"

"Both." Nerd closed his eyes. He did not want Sophia to define him by what he was about to say, and he didn't want her to treat him any differently. He enjoyed their friendship the way it was. But she deserved to know; things would just get more complicated for her if she never knew. So, he decided to trust her. He felt it was the honorable thing to do. He felt that it was the human thing to do.

"Ever since I was a child, I knew I was different. I used to work on science experiments when I was a kid. My brain excelled at things that normal humans just couldn't do. I was very creative and visualized things in my own language. Even as a baby, I used to escape from my play pen by constructing a stairway with my toys. As a kid, my parents thought I was a little genius…but when I hit my teen years, things became a little more complicated. I began flapping my hands whenever I got excited or felt a strong emotion that I could not express. I became ultra-sensitive to textures and certain sounds. I began to hate socializing with people because they wanted me to be normal. So, I did whatever I could to stay away from other humans. Eventually, my hand flapping and emotional outbursts got so bad that my parents took me to a psychiatrist, and that was when I found out why I was the way I was.

Sophia, I have autism, specifically a mild case of Asperger's syndrome. I'm an ASPI, meaning that my mind works differently from that of most humans."

Sophia took a moment to process what Nerd had just told her. She was having trouble believing him at first, but the one thing about Nerd that was truly amazing was that he didn't know how to lie. Not that he wouldn't; he literally couldn't. She slowly nodded her head but maintained a very startled and disbelieving look in her eyes.

"You're autistic," she responded. "Oh…"

"You seem sad?"

"I am. Having autism is horrible. I can't even begin to imagine what that's like…"

"Having autism is not horrible! It's just been greatly misunderstood by humanity."

Sophia felt Nerd's tension starting to rise. She had unintentionally hit a nerve, but she wasn't sure how.

"Are you upset with me?" she asked.

"No," Nerd responded. "I'm just tired of people telling me that my gift is a curse. It would be like me telling a Zentar that it was horrible that they were a Zentar. Or a Zentar telling a human that it's horrible that they're human. Or if you want to go to the planet that we originated from, say that an American was told that it was horrible that he was American. Or someone that was British, that it was horrible that they were British, and so on and so forth. I know that may not make sense to you right now, but for me…it gets me very deep. I don't let my autism define me, just as where you were born or what race you are may not define you. But there's always going to be a little bit of affection towards what I view as my native roots…because despite what humans may believe, it's not a form of mental illness. It just means that I was born different than the rest of you."

Sophia again took a moment to let Nerd's words sink in. Her mind was starting to hurt, as there was definitely a lot to this, but she was getting the answers she needed, and at least her commander's character was starting to make sense. She took a few deep breaths and did her best to relax herself. She tried to hide the fact that she was starting to get a headache from all the information running through her mind.

"So, you're really smart, but you struggle on a few things."

"I am light years ahead of you in some ways but light years behind in others. I call myself Nerd, supreme human intelligence, because that's the title I was given as a Deep Cosmos agent. That and the fact that Nerd, slightly above average human intelligence doesn't quite have the same ring to it, so I have to play the part. I'm actually no more or less intelligent than you or anyone else. My mind just thinks a little differently, which through normal human eyes can be mistaken for either brilliance or primitiveness. That's all."

"And you have trouble expressing your emotions?"

"Yes. Although I have trouble expressing my feelings, I still have them, sometimes at a level that's way beyond human. As a result, I've had to learn how to act my emotions out. I used to spend hours in front of a mirror. I would think of an emotion, and when that emotion came, I would move my face to the position that it was supposed to be in, and then I had to memorize where my face muscles were when I thought of that emotion. It was a long process and took me forever to get right. I'm getting better now, but it still takes time."

"Okay! I can understand that. It makes sense. I want to talk to you more about this, but I need some time to chew on what you have just told me. But thank you! I think this will help me to understand you a little better."

"Of course! I'm always happy to—"

Nerd stopped for a moment and seemed to be distracted by something. He took off his glasses and started cleaning them with his lab coat. He was very confused, and it showed.

"What's wrong?" Sophia asked.

"Strange…" Nerd mused. "For second I could've sworn I saw some distortion out in space, like a cloaked starship, but I don't see anything right now."

The gears in Nerd's head began turning again, and this time, Sophia let him think. She needed time to think too, so in this case, silence was a good thing.

The two gazed at the stars together for almost ten minutes until they were interrupted by Henry Smith. He put his arms around them both and snapped them out of their thoughts with an enthusiastic voice.

"How're my brother and sister doing?" He said to them. "I was starting to worry about you; you were both gone for nearly half an hour."

Nerd's head was spinning. He never enjoyed being snapped out of it when he was deep in thought. To him, it was the equivalent of driving a car into a tree. However, he knew Henry's intentions were good, and his dynamic personality took the edge off whenever he distracted Nerd. Nerd rubbed his forehead and smirked.

"Your timing never ceases to amaze me," Nerd said to Henry.

"It's fantastic! I know, but enough about me. The commander wants to talk to you. He's eager to know if you have learned anything about the virus. All of us noticed you were observing something on the victim's neck. We were wondering if that was of any importance?"

Nerd did not say anything. He simply nodded his head and made his way over to the commander after noticing that he was standing a few feet behind him.

"Ah, Nerd!" Commander Williams said. "We were curious what your thoughts were about the victim. Have you made any discoveries?"

"I have a few theories…but I don't want to voice them until I have more facts. I hate to say it, but I will need to view another victim if I'm going to know for sure."

"I see…well, I just hope it doesn't happen again here. I don't want to lose any more of my crew members. This tragedy was devastating enough!"

Nerd was going to respond, but he was interrupted by the sound of his communicator alerting him that he was receiving a video call from the central commander. Nerd pulled out his communicator and responded to the commander's call.

"Greetings, Central Commander," he chirped. "I hope you bring good news?"

Sophia and Henry were both stunned to see the central commander's appearance. He was a jellyfish-like blob with transparent skin and was filled with a gel-like fluid. His muscles and nerves were visible, his brain was visible, and all of his internal organs were visible. The creature had four eyes, one on the front of his head, the other on the left, one to the right, and one behind him. This was obviously not the supreme commander that Nerd was so intimidated by; in fact, judging by the tone of Nerd's voice, he seemed to view the creature as a friend. But given the creature's name, he was still a high-ranking officer within the Deep Cosmos organization.

The creature responded in a voice that echoed and sounded a little like he was underwater. "Nerd!" The central commander responded. "There has been another strike on a citizen located on a nearby freighter, located only a few light years away. Their captain has just been struck with the galactic plague, and they're sending out a distress call."

"I see. I'll have my team investigate right away."

"Good. Central Commander out."

The video chat ended, and Nerd turned to Commander Williams. "I'm sorry, but I must investigate this matter, as this may give me the lead I need to solve this mystery."

"As you wish...but I'm going to send the three galactic agents with you. The government is going to want to know what's going on."

"What? No! I don't need anyone else's help; my two companions will do fine."

"Nerd," Captain Baker said, "we have our orders. The galactic government wishes no quarrel with the Deep Cosmos organization. But this mission has become serious. We just need to stay with you for a little while. If this turns out to be a wild goose chase, we will leave you in peace. You have my word."

Nerd groaned; he was clearly not impressed, but he needed to get on his way as soon as possible, and, considering how much trouble his true identity was in with the galactic government, he did not want his alter ego to suffer the same fate.

"Fine!" David said. "But if you cause me any trouble, I will eject all three of you into the nearest airlock I can find. Got it?"

Captain Baker nodded his head in agreement.

The six of them said their goodbyes to Commander Williams, then made their way towards the *Iron Heart*. Nerd activated the ship's engines, and within moments, they had left the space station Nebula. He set a course for the freighter coordinates that the central commander had sent him. He activated the hyperdrive, and the *Iron Heart* entered hyperspace. The jump only took ten minutes, and before they knew it, their destination had been reached.

The freighter was a lot smaller than the freighter *Wrath* and was thankfully in much better condition. Nerd scanned the ship and was grateful to see that there were indeed transporter pads located within it. He contacted the freighter and asked permission to beam aboard. He was swiftly given permission, and Nerd urged his crew to head downstairs to the transporter room. As soon as his crew left the bridge, he put the ship on autopilot and followed them downstairs.

Upon reaching the transporter room, he beamed each crew member on board, two at a time, until it was only him and Henry left.

"Wait!" Henry said. "How are we going to get back if all of us are beaming aboard?"

"The ship's computer will handle it," Nerd assured him. "Trust me! I had to do this all the time when I was by myself."

Nerd and Henry both stepped on their transporter pads, and Nerd asked the computer to beam them both aboard. A weightless feeling enveloped them both, and they were transported to the nearby space freighter.

As soon as they arrived at the scene, panic and fear surrounded them. The crew members were losing it, and the four members of Nerd's crew he had previously beamed aboard looked terrified.

"The plague is spreading!" One of the freighter's crew members yelled out. "Six more have been infected!" Nerd realized that they were not safe and urged the crew of the freighter to calm down. He was approached by the ship's lieutenant. Though he was less panicked than the others, it was evident that he was still upset and on the brink of losing his own sanity. But he was relieved to see Nerd, as he knew help was on the way.

"Nerd!" He said. "Thank goodness you are here. My name is Lieutenant Braxton. The galactic plague has infected multiple crew members. We're not sure if it's spreading…or what it's doing. But it's obviously taken a liking to our ship and our crew!"

"I understand why this is troubling you," Nerd said. "I just witnessed a victim for the first time myself. This whole epidemic is horrid! Do you have a restrained specimen that I can observe?"

"Yes! Sadly it is—or was—our captain. We have him in our medical bay. Please follow me."

Nerd and his crew followed Lieutenant Braxton through the hallways of the space freighter. The ship shook uncontrollably for a moment…then stopped.

"Strange," Nerd said to himself. "We're currently located in empty space. There's nothing around that should've done that…"

Nerd was so distracted that he did not notice the other infected crew members lying around the spacecraft's halls. Henry and Sophia, however, were quite shaken over the sights they saw. They all looked just as bad as the one they had seen locked up in the Nebula lab. It was upsetting, but there was nothing they could do.

Finally, all of them reached the medical room. This time the victim was tied to a medical bed, and his jaw was restrained with a muzzle. But Nerd wasn't interested in his face. He quickly went up to the victim's neck. His eyes grew wide as his suspicions were confirmed—yet again, there was a small dot-shaped scar.

Thoughts began to flood Nerd's mind as all the pieces of the mystery started to come together like a puzzle. His heart began pounding as both fear and excitement rushed through him like never before. He was excited that he was about to solve what was happening, but he was fearful and disturbed, because his conclusion was not a pleasant one at all.

Nerd's mind began to replay backwards. He recalled the freighter shaking, the distortion in the stars, and Sophia's panic upon seeing something in an air vent.

"Sophia!" He said. "I need to know what you thought you saw back at Nebula."

"What?" Sophia responded.

"You thought you saw something when we were examining the crime scene. You were looking up at the ceiling at one of the ship's air vents. I asked you what was wrong, and you didn't want to say… I need to know. It's critical that I know."

Sophia thought back to the event that Nerd was talking about and recalled what she saw. She didn't want to say anything before, as it triggered painful memories of her own past, but she could tell that it was urgent that she reveal what she saw. She took a deep breath and pushed herself to explain the image that upset her.

"You're going to think that I'm crazy, everyone else did, but for a second, I could've sworn I saw two glowing green eyes staring back at me."

Instantly, Nerd's excitement was overpowered by fear.

"No," he groaned out loud. "Please, not him."

Nerd had solved the case, but by no means was that a good thing, because now he knew how much danger the galaxy was in.

Fear soon turned into panic as Nerd quickly reached for his communicator. He called the central commander, who responded instantly.

"Central Commander!" he said in a panicked voice. "I know what happened to the victims of the galactic plague! They were not killed by a virus."

"What?" The central commander responded. "What are you talking about?"

"The victims were not killed by a virus but by a man. Commander…they were murdered!"

CHAPTER 14 GREEN EYES

Earth date: February 22nd, 2010
Time: 240
Location: The *Iron Heart*

Sophia was unable to fall back to sleep. She had woken up 30 minutes ago, and it was evident that her mind would not shut down.

She remembered how deeply she had wanted to go on another action-filled mission and how disappointed she felt when she found out they were simply attempting to track down a disease, but this? This was very heavy and unsettling. She could not believe that one person could kill so many people single-handedly, let alone have the heart to go through with it. In her short time on the *Iron Heart*, Sophia had both heard and experienced things that truly made her sick. There were rotten people in the galaxy, people who would slaughter and kill for the most trivial of reasons. She was only grateful that her commander and crewman were not among them.

Sophia was not the only one, however. Even David, the same man who stood up to Dr. Crimson without breaking a sweat, was greatly troubled by the news. So much so that he was unable to tell anyone about who the killer was. He had encountered him before, but that was all David was willing to tell his crew members. He was too upset at the time and Sophia could sense it strongly.

Sophia picked herself up and made her way downstairs. She snuck past the third bay, which was the medical bay. All the guys were sleeping in the hospital beds, snoring up a storm. Thankfully, it was so early she would not have to deal with any of the galactic agents. They were out cold and showing no signs of waking up anytime soon.

Sophia continued through the main level and poured herself a hot cup of coffee. She then made her way to the bridge and was saddened to see her commander still wide awake in the pilot's chair. He was gazing out the front visor and was lost in thought again. It was unlikely he had gotten any sleep, and Sophia wasn't sure when he would or, for that matter, if he ever would.

She sat at the station closest to him and began sipping her coffee. She figured she'd give it a little time before trying to reach him. However, to her surprise, her commander reached out to her.

"I wasn't able to tell you before…but you deserve to know."

"Huh?" Sophia responded. David turned to face Sophia. Dark circles surrounded his bloodshot eyes, confirming

Sophia's concerns that her commander had not gotten any sleep.

"The man who killed all those people…I have seen him before. He…he knows who I am and probably knows more about me than I know about myself."

Sophia was troubled by what David was saying. There was a lot that was still unknown to her, and the more she learned about it, the more horrific it seemed to get. Still, she had to know what was going on. She wanted to know what they were up against before they faced him. So, she asked David to continue filling her in.

"Please tell me what you know about him. You can tell me anything, you know that."

"Very well. As you know, I was part of an organization that took advantage of the weak. Cosmic 5 was a group that promised to only proceed with humane and sensible human experimentation. They promised to do experimentation that was legal and respectful. But I was greatly deceived. Little did I know that my research would lead to the torture, mutilation, and deaths of thousands. The things they did to people still makes me sick! Nothing makes my stomach turn more than what I witnessed in my final days of working there…but it wasn't just a one-sided battle. I managed to get myself wedged between a war. Many of the human experiments stood up to the Cosmic staff and chose to fight back—Hangman, Doll, and the Little Warrior, to name a few. They retaliated, and I couldn't blame them for wanting to kill us, as we had no business doing what we did to them. Although they did murder many innocent people along with the guilty, I still feel for them. I still understand why they reacted the way that they did—all with the exception of one.

Him, the first human experiment ever created on Cosmic 5. One man who went too far, even under the circumstances. Some know him as the Lord of Sorrow, others know him as death itself, but his designation is very simple. His name is Experiment-1, leader of all the Cosmic 5 experiments, and yes, he is the number one criminal on the Deep Cosmos' most wanted list. He is so horrible that he was able to put Crimson in second place."

"Experiment-1? Yes, you mentioned him in your…I mean, I heard him mentioned before, he's just an urban legend, isn't he?"

"Yes, but I honestly thought he was nothing more than a myth, a false legend that was intended to either scare others or for its creator to gain popularity…until I witnessed him face-to-face. He was trying to kill a dear friend of mine, and I intervened. He responded by taunting me about my past, doing everything he could to break me down, and it worked. As a result, I almost lost my life, as I was too discouraged to fight. The scary thing is that I never told him anything about me, yet he still seemed to know where all my weak points were. It's like he had been watching me all my life, and given what I know about him, it wouldn't surprise me if he was."

"That's horrible…but we can take him, right?"

"I don't know. He is fast, smart, strong, and gifted. He's a master of deception and creativity. There are times where I could've sworn I saw him in more than one location at once. His armored suit contains a cloaking device that only reveals the distortion around his body. He possesses a custom sword that can cut through anything; bombs that scream when they explode; vaccines that can kill his victims in horrific ways, which now includes galactic plague. He also has night vision,

and his body self-regenerates instantaneously after it rec-
eives damage, meaning that he can't be killed unless every
trace of him is destroyed at once. To make matters worse, he
obviously has a means of transporting from one side of the
galaxy to the other in a matter of hours, rather than days or
weeks. I don't know what to expect, but I do know this: we
are playing right into his hands, and there is nothing we can
do about it, because he knows what choices we are going to
make. Even if I were to set the ship on another course right
now, I would only be doing what he predicted I would do.
Because he knows people; he knows people better than they
know themselves. Our only hope is if we can somehow
blindside him, and that's going to require someone who is
unpredictable. I don't believe that someone is me."

"David…are you saying we're…destined to die?"

"No, but we most likely will."

"What about trying to reason with him? Is it possible that
he can be reached?"

"No. He is a raging killer, one that enjoys his work. I once
found him standing over the body of a child. When I asked
him why he had done this, he simply told me, 'Life is a game
to me, a game that I intend to win!' He then seemed to vanish
into thin air, showing no remorse for what he had done…so
no, there is no reasoning with him. He delights in his work
too much. I can't tell if he's a cold psychopath like Crimson
or if he has completely lost his mind like Smiley. What I do
know is that those who see his mask rarely live to tell about
it. I am almost thankful to be one of the few."

"I'm thankful you are one of them too. Have you ever seen
his face behind the mask?"

"No…at least, not that I know of. That's the scariest thing about him. He could be anyone. A celebrity, an authority figure, a family member, a friend. Anyone could be him, hiding in plain sight."

"Wow…that is scary."

"May I now ask you a question?"

"Of course you can."

"Back at the freighter, you said that everyone thought you were crazy when you mentioned the two glowing green eyes. Which tells me that you've seen him before. May I ask how long this has been going on for?"

Sophia felt a great deal of discouragement settle over her. She hated talking about the things that led to her family disowning her…but at least she now knew she was not crazy. She figured if she was going to tell anyone about this, David would be the one to talk to.

She took a deep breath and revealed as much as she could emotionally handle.

"I first saw him when I was 14. I left my closet door open one night, and as soon as I turned the lights off to go to sleep, I saw his green eyes watching me in my closet. I screamed and yelled for my parents to come save me, but as soon as my parents ran into my room, he was gone. I don't know how he escaped, but I figured it was nothing more than an illusion that my mind had made up. I was wrong. I kept seeing those eyes off and on throughout my teen years. The worst was when I was by myself. I was walking through the streets of Loss Elton. I was 16, and I had just been kicked out of my house, this time for good. It was midnight, and I had made up my mind that I was going to join the V.T.C., because they recruited young teens to train up to join them. Considering I had no job and had nowhere to go, it seemed like my only chance at survival. I decided to take a shortcut through the dark alleys. I could barely see in front of my face, and as I made it halfway through, I realized that I had made a horrible decision. I began to pick up my pace, hoping to escape before anyone found me…and then it happened. The shadow of a man appeared right in front of me. He began speaking to me, calling me by my own name.”

Sophia stopped, taking a breath and shaking her head as she recited,

“‘Sophia, oh dear Sophia. What a shame nobody cares about you. It must be so hard knowing you will always be alone.’

“He then reached out at me with his hand and stroked my face gently. I was terrified. I wanted to run away…but the fear that he induced paralyzed me. I couldn't run away; I couldn't respond. I begin tearing up because I was so scared…and oddly enough, I think that got him to withdraw his hand. He didn't really seem interested in hurting me. Honestly, I don't think he understood why I was so terrified. This calmed my nerves just enough to get a few words out of my mouth. But only a few.

“‘What do you want from me?’ I asked as my teeth began to chatter.

“It was then that I realized that his withdrawal of his hand was not an indication that he wasn't a creep, and his words still hurt me very deeply to this day.

“‘You are broken beyond repair. I know what that's like, and I'm so sorry, because no matter what you do, you will never be okay. You are beyond hope, and it's all their fault…but I can help you. I can put you back together. I can teach you how to even the scales. I can teach you how true greatness can be achieved. What I want from you, my dear Sophia, is your loyalty, your devotion, and the very heart that beats within your chest. Don't you understand, Sophia; I want your soul! Give it to me, and I will help you. But if you refuse…' His green eyes lit up, and he quickly pulled out a sword. Before I could react, his blade was resting against my throat. "'Then I will put you out of your misery, and you won't have to live as a worthless human being anymore! I will give you time to think about it. If you want to join me, then just say so out loud. I will be watching you very closely, my dear. I will know when you are ready to join. But be warned, my patience has its limits. I will not wait for you forever.'

"As soon as the final word fell from his mouth, he instantly vanished. I never saw him again…until now. I honestly thought that I was crazy. That maybe being disowned by my family drove me to hallucinate, because when I did talk to the V.T.C. doctors about it they convinced me it was all in my head. But now…now I know my life is in danger, just as it was before."

David's eyes grew huge. Already Experiment-1 had done everything in his power to harm one of his closest friends, and now he very well could be seeking to do it again; but, it didn't make sense he would go as far as he had, just to get Sophia's attention. So, David knew there had to be more to this than just her, and somehow, that provided David a little comfort, knowing that Sophia was not the only target he had in mind.

David leaned back in his chair and started rubbing his forehead.

"I'm so sorry," he said to her.

"So am I," Sophia responded. "All of this is my fault."

"No, none of this is your fault. I don't know what monster lurks behind that mask, but I know his intentions can't be good. We must keep fighting him. I'm not going to let him hurt you without a fight. I can't. He's hurt too many people already."

"I know you won't, and please try to remember that I've become a stronger person since then, too. Maybe this is a monster we can overcome together?"

"Maybe. There's only one way to find out, I suppose."

Sophia felt a little discouraged at David's reply. They were clearly overpowered by this one madman, and it was very upsetting, but she had to try to stay determined. David was a brilliant man in her eyes, but he was lacking motivation in this scenario, and although she did not doubt that David would run into the front lines to protect her, she knew he needed her to be the warrior Sophia if they were to both survive, at least for now.

An hour passed, and the other crew members woke up. David put his glasses back on, as he did not want the galactic agents to discover his identity.

Captain Baker was the most alert and awake of the four. Still, he was a bit lost as to where they were headed.

"Where are we going?" he asked.

"We are in route to the planet Obian," Nerd responded. "It is a jungle planet like Zentar, only this one is much more hostile and primitive. Thankfully, we will not be landing on the planet. There is another spacecraft orbiting Obian as we speak, and regrettably, they too lost a crew member to the plague."

"I see. How much longer until we arrive?"

"Only ten minutes, and I'm hoping this will be the last one. I was looking for answers to the virus last time. Now, we're looking for clues to lead us straight to the killer."

The ship reached its destination, and Nerd deactivated the hyperdrive. The ship entered regular space, and the planet was visible in front of them. It was green, vibrant, and beautiful; about the same size as Earth, home of the first human race. However, if everything went to plan, they would not be landing on it, as their mission was simply to board a nearby spacecraft where another murder had taken place.

Nerd activated the ship's scanners to search for the ship and was puzzled when nothing showed up.

"That's odd," he said. "According to the central commander, there should be a spacecraft on this side of the planet."

"Do you suppose something could've happened to them?" Baker asked.

"Unlikely. If their ship was destroyed, I feel confident we'd be picking up some debris on the scan. My sensors are picking up nothing."

While David examined the ship's scanner to make sure it was working properly, Sophia received a text on her communicator. The number was unknown, which wasn't surprising considering she had gotten a new one only a few days ago at space station 1529 and only had a few contacts on it. She opened the message, and it read:

Unknown: Hey! Is this the phone number for Sophia Nelson?

Sophia: Why yes, haha! Who is this? I don't recognize the number.

Unknown: Oh... Just a friend of David Bell's. How are things?

Sophia: Ummm, good, I guess.

Unknown: That's wonderful to hear. Thank you for taking care of the old kid. He has been quite moody lately, and it's nice to know he has a little ray of sunshine in his life now that you're around.

Sophia: Aww, of course :) Nerd has been a huge support to me! I'm glad I could be the same to him.

Unknown: I'm glad the two of you are so close! It makes my job a whole lot easier.

Sophia: Speaking of which, you still haven't told me your name, let alone what your job is. You seem really nice, but it would be a little less creepy if I knew who you were.

Unknown: How rude of me! I tend to be rude at times. I can't really help it, but I'll try to do better. Why don't I say something nice for a change! Things like... I really like the way you're wearing your hair today. Or, your makeup came out perfect today. I really like what you did with the eyeshadow. It makes your face come alive! Is that better?

Sophia: Ah, no, that's really creepy 😵 How did you know how I braided my hair? Wait, is this Nerd or Henry playing a joke on me?

Unknown: And here I was trying to be so nice to you, and look at you, you're upset! Makes me want to cut your face.

Sophia now felt very uncomfortable. If this was a joke, she no longer thought it was funny.

Sophia: Umm...sir, please stop! How are you observing us? Please tell me!

Unknown: David keeps a security camera on his bridge in case he is...murdered or something. So I hacked into it. Looks like you guys are quite confused right now.

Sophia: Yes...

Unknown: Are you losing interest in this conversation? Bah, you're no fun. Fine, I will get to the point. I need to ask you a question. Something that I want you to think about and consider.

Sophia: Okay...

Unknown: Do you want to die? Because I'm going to kill you.

Sophia's heart began to race. She was learning very quickly that her stalker was not a friend at all.

Sophia: I've had enough of this. I refuse to believe you and David are friends, and if you can see me, you know I'm two seconds away from showing my phone to him.

Unknown: So much hostility. I'm going to enjoy watching you die

Sophia: Stop it!

Unknown: By the way, would you like to know my real name?

Sophia: I don't care anymore! You're a creep!

Unknown: I think you may want to know. It's important to me that you know.

Sophia: I'm ending this chat!

Unknown: Let me tell you my name, and then I will let you go.

Sophia: Fine! What is your name?

Unknown: MY NAME IS EXPERIMENT-1, AND MY PATIENCE WITH YOU HAS RUN OUT 💀

Suddenly, the room went dark. The interior lights started flashing, the ship's engines powered down, and the communication screen over by Nerd's computer activated. The sound of a music box started to play; a soft yet grim melody flowed from it. Nerd cringed upon recognition of the morbid tune that played on. *Amelia's music box. How did he get his hands on Amelia's music box?*

Two glowing green eyes were visible on the view screen. Nerd knew they were in danger and at the mercy of his greatest nemesis. He was about to ask what Experiment-1 wanted with them, but Experiment-1 began talking as soon as he hacked into the view screen.

"Greetings," he said in a very calm voice. "My name is Experiment-1, leader of the Cosmic experiments. It has come to my attention that someone on your ship has something that I want…" Experiment-1's voice grew harsher. "Something that I need! And I don't care if I have to bleed it out of him to get it!" Experiment-1's voice became very calm again. "But don't fret. If I get what I want, I will spare your pitiful little lives. If I don't…well, just sit back and relax. Because the road to death can be…most unsettling…"

Suddenly, the ship's engines fired up to maximum thrust. Any crew member that was not sitting fell to the ground, and the G-force began to press heavily against them. Captain Baker picked himself up and panicked when he saw that the ship was heading straight for the planet. Nerd was frantically trying to regain control of the ship, but alas, nothing was working.

"I can't stop it!" Nerd yelled. "He has taken control of the ship. Everyone hang on to something, because it's going to be a rough landing!"

The ship began to burn as it entered the planet's atmosphere, and the ride only got rougher as the *Iron Heart* continued to draw closer and closer to the planet's surface.

Thankfully, the ship's nose began to tip up, and the landing procedure began to activate. The trees of the jungle surrounded most of the surface, but a long, narrow line was visible. It went on for ten miles before dropping off the edge of a large cliff.

"Oh no," Nerd said out loud as he realized that his ship was not slowing down. "He wouldn't…yes…yes, he would."

The crew members were confused about what David was referring to, but they were relieved to see that the narrow line was actually an opening for a runway. In theory, the landing should have been safe. However, it wasn't, and soon the crew began to realize what Nerd was nervous about.

The ship continued at the same blazing speed, showing no signs of letting up. It plunged down and landed hard on the runway. An explosion could be heard as both engines overheated. Thankfully, the thrusters were no more, but the ship's momentum continued. It dragged the ship mile after mile; a loud, high-pitched screeching sound could be heard as the bottom of the *Iron Heart* was dragged across the runway. The crew began to realize the danger they were in, as the cliff's edge was continuing to draw closer. The momentum was beginning to slow down, but only a mile was left, and they were not sure if the ship would stop in time.

The *Iron Heart* was now a quarter of a mile away from the edge. They had now slowed down significantly, but was it enough? They were about to find out.

The ship's momentum was now at a crawl. It was ten feet away from the cliff's edge; then six feet, then three, then one. The nose of the ship began to inch its way over the cliff, and right before the momentum stopped, almost half of the *Iron Heart* protruded over the cliff's edge. A sinking feeling overpowered the crew as gravity began to pull the nose of the ship downward. The bottom of the drop was visible from the ship's visor, but the momentum had completely stopped, and the ship seemed to be balancing itself, ready to fall but not committing itself to it.

"We have a 50-50 chance," Nerd said. "It depends on how much of the ship has passed over the cliff's edge."

The ship teetered on the cliff's edge for a few seconds, which seemed like an eternity to the rest of the crew, but relief soon came to them as gravity began to pull on the back of the ship rather than the front. The ship was now level and safely on the ground.

The crew breathed a huge sigh of relief. Though everyone but Nerd was completely clueless about what had just happened, they were still thrilled to be alive, as the incident was too close for comfort.

Nerd, however, was irritated at what Experiment-1 had done. He pulled a flashlight out of his lab coat and ran out of the bridge as soon as they landed.

A few minutes went by, giving everyone time to regain their composure. The shock was heavy, and even though they were grateful to be alive, uncertainty was a feeling that was now starting to overcome the shock.

Sophia was the first to express curiosity about where Nerd had taken off to. She grabbed a flashlight and left the room, followed by Henry, Baker, Collins, and Howard.

They noticed the door near Nerd's bedroom was open, a room that neither Henry nor Sophia had explored. They could hear tinkering going on inside. So, the five of them decided to walk in.

The room broke off into two little rooms located on the left and right side. Thankfully, they did not need to explore them, as Nerd was examining the ship's computer located at the back of the room. He had opened one of the panels on it and had half his body stuck within it.

"Aha!" he said victoriously. "I found it!" Nerd quickly pulled himself out and revealed a small computer chip in his right hand. "One of Experiment-1's devices. He must have planted it inside the ship's computer when we were docked at Nebula. This is how he was able to hack in and control the ship."

"What?" Captain Baker exclaimed. "He hacked the ship through that? That one little chip?"

"He is very brilliant. This technology is most likely his own. I'm actually not surprised; I just wish I had checked the ship over before. Whenever this guy is involved, you have to prepare for everything."

"What do we do now, bro?" Henry asked.

"I will contact Deep Cosmos. The ship's power circuits have overloaded and both engines have blown. The *Iron Heart* will fly again, but she will need to be repaired first." Nerd reached into his pocket and pulled out his communicator. He began to panic when he was unable to contact the central commander. He tried reaching others on his contact list, but still, nothing. He tried contacting Sophia and Henry. The call went through, meaning they could still contact each other. However, that was not what Nerd wanted to see.

"Guys!" he said to his crew members. "I need you all to see if you can contact someone outside of this planet." Everyone but Sophia tried; she only had Nerd, Henry, and Experiment-1's contact information, two of whom were right by her and one of whom she seriously did not want to call.

The others had the same problem as Nerd did and were only able to reach people that were in the ship with them. Nerd let out a sigh.

"Something is keeping us from contacting anyone outside the planet. We're going to have to find out what it is. If it's the planet's atmosphere, we may be here for a long time."

Nerd ran out of the computer room and made his way downstairs. The other five crew members made their way back into the lobby and waited for their commander. After a few minutes, Nerd made his way back upstairs. He had a drone in one hand and a remote control in the other.

"Follow me, guys!" he said to them. "Let's find out what the trouble is."

Nerd opened the ship's airlock and extended the ramp down to the planet's surface. He then made his way down to the ground. The six of them exited the *Iron Heart* and were refreshed by the sensation of the crisp, sweet air filling their lungs and the warm glow of the planet sun covering their skin. Only Sophia and Nerd had been on a planet that contained such a beautiful atmosphere before. That was Zentar, the other jungle planet, whose inhabitants cared for and provided for the world they lived on.

Nerd activated the drone and sent it away to search the area. The remote control had a view screen on it, so Nerd was able to see where the drone was flying. The drone also had a scanner for him to use. Thankfully, it was picking up a powerful radio signal coming from the north. He piloted his drone towards the signal until a massive structure was visible in front of him. It was a temple, and sure enough, the signal was coming from the very top of the tallest tower. Nerd scanned it, revealing that it was a signal jammer and it was projecting a shield across the planet's atmosphere.

"Bingo!" Nerd said. "It will be a long hike, but if we can destroy that thing, we may have a chance to escape." Nerd flew the drone back and notified his crew about the journey that lay ahead.

"We're going to head north. It will take at least a day to get there and back, but if we run into trouble, it could take a lot longer. Pack anything you will need for the journey. This planet is very dangerous, so make sure you prepare for the worst."

The crew members reentered the *Iron Heart* and gathered their things. Henry Smith was excited to don his new battle armor and the dual-wielding laser pistols he had bought at space station 1529.

"Money well spent!" He said to himself as an arrogant smirk covered his face. He also strapped on the flamethrower and rocket launcher he got from Smiley and made sure he loaded two new rockets inside it. He had everything he needed and was prepared to fight anything that came his way. Sophia, on the other hand, changed into her usual attire, which included her high heels, which she needed to have on her at all times, even on a journey through a jungle planet.

She gathered her sword, bow, and normal arrows she had gotten from their space vacation, as Nerd still had not figured out a way to re-create the shadow arrows.

Half an hour went by before everyone had packed everything they needed. They were ready to head out, eager to destroy whatever was keeping them from escaping the wild planet of Obian.

The six of them made their way through the vast jungle and were amazed at the life that surrounded them. Although the planet was very green, the shapes and patterns of the trees and plant life were very different than anything they had seen before. Some of the trees were so tall they could easily challenge a small skyscraper. There were mushrooms that were at least five stories tall and as wide as an average-sized house; there were bushes whose limbs spread out and spiraled inward like a snail shell. The plant life was not the only thing that was unique about this world, however. The sound of bugs and wild animals filled the air. A few of them were visible, and they were not like anything they had ever encountered before. Despite the fact they were very creepy and alien-looking, they were all thankfully herbivores. Most of the carnivores came out at night, a situation the crew would sadly need to deal with on the way back. Overall, the planet was very beautiful, but a sense of danger still lingered, as if evil was lurking somewhere in the heart of this green world.

The crew continued, and Collins was distracted by a very large, flat plant. It was laid out like a lily pad and seemed to have some sort of saliva gland inside each leaf. In the very middle was a flower that was incredibly beautiful. It glowed with radiant light and was truly desirable.

Collins felt himself being pulled in by the flower's beauty and began to make his way towards it. He was stopped when Nerd caught sight of him doing so. He ran up to Collins and grabbed his arm.

"No!" Nerd yelled. "That's a Venton; it lures its prey in like a Venus flytrap...only it can devour much larger prey than a bug. Its leaves engulf its victim, and it pours acid out of the glands you see on each large leaf. The victim is devoured instantly. Not even a cell survives."

"Ah!" Collins said. "That's no good."

"At least these predators are stationary, and the bait it uses is very noticeable. So just keep your distance from the glowing flowers, they will kill you."

Nerd stepped ahead of the group and continued to lead. It was evident that he was familiar with the planet, even though he claimed he had never been on it personally before. Normally this would raise suspicion, but this was Nerd. He had probably researched every planet in the galaxy and would have somehow found doing so enjoyable, rather than a chore.

The group continued to make their way through the jungle. Minutes soon became hours, and the crew began to feel the effects of their long travel, especially their leader, Nerd.

As noon approached, the temperature rose severely, and Nerd, who was still in his lab coat, was drenched with sweat and was about to collapse from exhaustion.

"I need to stop for a few minutes, guys," he wheezed.

The rest of the away team didn't see any reason to argue, given the fact that they had been on the move nonstop. So, they found a spot to relax for several minutes. Sophia removed her high heels and began rubbing her feet. She was used to walking great distances with them on; she was used to wearing them through nature walks or other activities that were done outdoors, but she wasn't used to all three at once, and for the first time, her feet were sore from walking in them. Henry Smith, on the other hand, was restless. He was longing for some hostile creature to come attack him. He still had not been able to test out his new weaponry, and he desperately wanted a chance to use it.

He took his seat next to Nerd, who was still panting and drenched from head to toe in sweat.

"This blows, man!" He stated. "All we've done so far is walk in a straight line. I need some action!"

"Be careful what you ask for, Henry," Nerd warned. "It may come true."

"Dude! We survived the entire *Wrath* team. I think we can take on this planet!"

"I'm not worried about the planet. I'm worried about...him."

"That creepy stalker guy? Come on, man! He's only one guy...who single-handedly killed millions and managed to hijack our ship without anyone noticing...but still, we can take him!"

"Henry, I need to be honest with you about something. That guy, the one with the glowing green eyes? We...we don't actually stand much of a—" Nerd stopped. He was distracted by the sound of a creature coming through the woods. Judging by the sound of its steps, it had five legs, had a long stride, and was moving towards his crew at a very high speed. "Oh no. Henry! Draw your weapons now!"

David's command was music to Henry's ears. He armed himself with his dual pistols and was ready to kill whatever was coming towards them. Not long after, a five-legged creature came jumping through the foliage. It had a leopard-like body, a roundish head with no neck, a long and relatively wide jaw that nearly hit the ground and could easily eat a human whole, and one big eye located on its forehead. The fifth leg was located where the tail of a wild animal would usually be. The creature was fast and extremely hungry! Henry wasted no time and began firing his dual weapons, alternating them one by one, shot after shot.

The creature fell by Henry's feet, burn wounds all over its body where Henry had shot it.

"Brill, man!" He shouted. "Don't know what that was, but it's dead now!"

"That was a Ja-gore beast," Nerd said to the group. "They are fast, strong, tough, but not invincible. Henry could've put it down with a few shots, but obviously he was really excited to kill it, as you can tell from all the unnecessary blast marks that cover its corpse."

"Should we expect to see these creatures often?" Captain Baker asked.

"Unlikely; they usually hunt in packs. But the fact that this one came alone should mean it was a drifter…unless…"

Nerd stopped. His sensitive ears began picking up the sound of more Ja-gores coming. There were five…ten… twenty… Nerd groaned and realized the significance of the situation they were in.

"Oh no," he said as the ground began to shake

CHAPTER 15
GREEN EYES PART 2

"Everyone load your weapons!" Nerd yelled. "We are about to be attacked from the east side!"

Immediately all the away team formed a line, facing towards the direction that the other creature had come from. They raised their weapons and prepared for a fight. Sophia had to choose between her bow and her sword. She thought about the creature and how she could fit within its jaw. Close contact was not her best option. So, she loaded her bow and hoped that her regular arrows would be strong enough to break the creatures' skin.

The first Ja-gore made its way through the foliage. Then the second, followed by the third. Instantly all three of them fell to the ground, as the team wasted no time getting on the offensive.

Five more Ja-gores made their way through. These got closer but were unable to reach anyone before dropping dead, just as the first wave had before them. Next, ten of them came through at one time, and the away team felt a brief moment of panic, but before the monsters could get anywhere near them, the two in the middle were met with a completed Rubik's cube that landed right by their feet. The Rubik's cube exploded, and all ten of them were sent soaring through the air in flames. Nerd reached into his pocket and began to solve another Rubik's cube; he had prepared for battle this time.

Another wave of five, then seven, then three, then twelve, then two. Wave after wave of the creatures fell, and Nerd could tell by the sound of the stampede that they were almost finished. It was dying down, with no more than ten remaining. However, all ten came at them at once, and Nerd did not have enough time to prepare his third Rubik's cube. The other five members went straight for an all-out attack and were able to drop nine of the ten Ja-gores. But the tenth Ja-gore broke through the line and went straight for Nerd. Nerd was so focused on trying to solve his Rubik's cube he didn't notice the creature lunging at him until the last second. Nerd jumped up and just missed getting swallowed whole by getting enough air to make impact with the creature's snout. The impact with the creature launched Nerd backwards. His head throbbed in pain as it slammed against a large rock.

The blow to the head caused Nerd's vision to blur out for a second, and he was unable to predict the creature's landing pattern. When his vision cleared, it was already too late. The Ja-gore was only inches from Nerd, ready to consume him whole.

Nerd spent his final moment self-reflecting. He hated his life, he hated being who he was, he hated having a mind like his. Despite his gifts, he still felt empty and dead inside. However, at least his life was not in vain. He had encouraged Sophia to find herself and had the honor of watching her regain her confidence and become a strong warrior again. He had helped Henry to take a step away from his life of crime and proved to him that there was some excitement and thrill in fighting for good.

He had helped both individuals to see the potential they had and had no doubt they would continue to flourish even long after the beast had ripped his body to shreds without mercy. It was okay; there was no reason to feel scared. He could die now, knowing that he had made a difference…but something was wrong. He was still alive. The creature had not devoured him.

Nerd opened his eyes and noticed a large snake-like creature wrapped around the Ja-gore beast. The creature immediately snapped the Ja-gore's neck, and the beast let out one final cry before it died. The giant snake creature then unhinged its mouth and began devouring the beast whole. It was a gruesome sight, but it only took a few seconds.

The snake creature was now fattened from its meal, but not for long. It quickly started to regain its shape, as the creature's digestive system seemed to digest the creature in a matter of seconds.

Now the creature's true form was revealed, and Nerd was able to identify it instantly.

Although he was snake-like from the waist down, his torso was very much like that of a human male. He had two arms and a neck. However, that was where his humanoid features ended. His hands were very alien; they had three fingers and a thumb, with a large claw attached to each one. His head was the most interesting part of all. His lower jaw looked a lot like a steam shovel and his scalp was very spiky; he had four eyes that glowed green, but they were shaped differently than Experiment-1's. He had one blue shell located on his forehead. However, Nerd never could figure out what it was for. His skin was very reptilian and was purple in color.

Overall, the creature was very masculine and absolutely massive. But although watching it consume the Ja-gore was a very scarring experience for most, his appearance was harmless, and he didn't give off a vibe of aggression.

Nerd knew that this creature was a Grunt, a native to the planet Obian and considered primitive to most of the advanced races. Grunts were known for their endless appetite and limited vocabulary. Nerd was uncertain if he could make contact, but considering the creature had just saved his life, he figured it was worth a shot!

Nerd walked over to the Grunt and attempted to talk to it.

"Hey!" He said to the creature. "Thank you for assisting me back there! I—" The grunt instantly started making its way towards Nerd with a hungry look. He grabbed Nerd by his left arm and lifted him up with ease. He gave Nerd a lick and instantly rejected Nerd's taste.

"Blah!" the creature said as he threw Nerd ten feet away from him. "Food taste bad. Grunt no like!"

Sophia and Henry ran to their commander to help him off the ground. He was bruised from the fall and was not in a very good mood. However, he attempted to regain his composure, as the creature thankfully did not like the taste of human flash.

"What is that thing?" Sophia asked.

"A Grunt," Nerd responded. "A native to this planet."

"It looks funky, man…" Henry stated. "Reminds me a little too much of modern art."

"It's definitely unusual," Nerd agreed. "Or should I say, he. This is definitely a male of the species. Maybe he can show us to his colony. If we have a place to stay when night falls, it will increase our chances of survival by eighty-nine percent!"

"Wait," Sophia replied. "What do you mean by eighty-nine—"

"Hey, Mr. Grunt! I was just wondering what your name was. I heard you say Grunt before, but most Grunts have names that don't involve their race. What is yours?"

"No!" Grunt responded, drawing himself up with an offended look. "Me Grunt! Grunt me name!"

"Interesting…well, no need to judge. My name is Nerd. Supreme human intelligence."

When Nerd told his name, the large creature burst out into laughter, doubling over as he smacked Nerd on the shoulder repeatedly, "Nerd! You called Nerd! Name make Grunt laugh!" He continued his hysterics, and Nerd suspected, wryly, that if the creature had been capable of tears his face would've been streaming with them.

"Great, even the Grunt is unimpressed."

"Yo, my bro!" Henry said. "My name is Smith, Henry Smith. I was just wondering if you could take us to your village, yo? I'd totally like to see your pad and hang out. You seem pretty cool, bro!"

Grunt made his way over to Henry and seemed very excited.

"Smith! Grunt like Smith. Smith got style, yo!"

Nerd was stunned upon hearing Grunt's words.

"Wait a minute," he said. "Did you just say…style yo? Where did you learn to speak like that? I realize we all have a translator device equipped, which is the only reason we're understanding you now, but Grunts never use human slang unless they have been around a human for a while."

"Humans!" Grunt said. "Humans Grunt's friends."

Nerd breathed a sigh of relief.

"Excellent! Could you lead us to them? We could very much use their assistance right now."

"Take you to them? Yes! Grunt take you to them."

Grunt signaled everyone to follow him. They did so, desperately hoping the primitive being knew what he was talking about.

The crew traveled onward for a few more miles and were relieved when they came across a human settlement. It was small and contained a number of slum-like buildings that seemed to be made from the materials of a wrecked ship. The inhabitants looked beaten, run-down, and very discouraged. However, their faces lit up upon catching sight of Grunt and his new friends.

"Humans," Grunt said. "Grunt bring friends."

The villagers ran to meet the *Iron Heart* crew members. There were only thirteen of them, which was small considering that was the entire population.

The tribe leader was a large, middle-aged man who was wearing an army suit and hat that represented a position of great authority. He was part of the galactic government, which again made Nerd nervous, as he still did not want to be discovered by them.

"Welcome!" The man said. "My name is General Rice. I oversee this settlement. Our ship crash-landed about a year ago, and we were starting to give up on ever escaping from this dreaded planet. Have you come to save us? We were a crew of 32…but as you can see, I lost a lot of good men and women on this dreaded planet."

"Greetings, General Rice," Nerd responded. "My name is Nerd, supreme human intelligence. These are my crew members, Mr. Henry Smith and Miss Sophia Nelson, and a few temporary allies of mine; Captain Tim Baker, Lieutenant Joe Collins, and Mr. Stephen Howard. Sadly, we are trapped on this planet just as you are. However, I do believe there is a way for us to escape."

"I see…well, at this point, we will take any good news we can get. What's your plan for escape?"

"Do you know of a nearby temple? It should be only a few miles north of here."

"Yes. We have not explored it, as we have encountered enough hostility on this world, but I'm listening."

"At the very top of the temple there is a device. It's emitting the frequency that is keeping space signals from leaving the planet's atmosphere. If we can destroy it, I may be able to contact Deep Cosmos. They could send a drop ship to get us out of here."

General Rice breathed a sigh of relief. He was thrilled to hear Nerd's news and was optimistic that he had finally escaped from this dreaded world, something he had waited an entire year for.

"Nerd," he said. "If there is anything I can do to help you, please let me know."

"Right now," Nerd said, "we need food, shelter, and volunteers to explore the temple with us tomorrow. I don't want to risk traveling the jungle at night, so if we could rest up for one day and head out tomorrow morning, that would be perfect!"

While Nerd and General Rice were talking, Grunt had made his way over to a hut that was a little larger than the others.

"Alcanore!" he called out. "Come meet Grunt's new friends!"

A few seconds later, the doorway to the hut opened, and a Renex warrior stepped outside.

Like all Renex, he was tall, standing at around seven feet. His limbs were very long, and his hands and feet were very large. His forehead had many ridges in it; he was bald on the top of his head but had black shoulder-length hair in the back. The creature did not have a human nose but still had two nostrils on his face where a nose would usually be. His jaw was long and had two fangs that stood out in front. The only clothing he wore was a pair of animal hide leggings, and he had a massive spear mounted on his back. The deadly spearhead was heavy and bigger than a human head. It wasn't very long, but Nerd knew a Renex spear could extend when in combat without compromising the weapon's integrity. The strap of his spear's sheath was the only thing covering his bare chest. His skin was a mix of tan and purple, and although the creature was long in stature, he still possessed extraordinary strength, which could be seen in the tone of his muscles and his noticeable ten-pack.

He was an extraordinary sight—a living tank bred to fight in the front lines. He was also very intimidating, considering the Renex were a race dedicated to fighting wars.

The Renex that Grunt had called by the name of Alcanore made his way towards Grunt.

"What is it, my fellow warrior?" Alcanore said to Grunt. "Why have you summoned me?"

"Grunt make new friends!" Grunt replied. "Alcanore meet Grunt's friends!"

Alcanore made his way towards Nerd and the others, a look of fierce judgment burning in his purple eyes. He was obviously the shrewdest of the tribe, and Nerd could tell he was protective of his Grunt friend.

Nerd, feeling very intimidated, attempted to speak to the seven-foot warrior that was standing in front of him.

"Hey," Nerd said. "My name is—"

"Nerd," Alcanore interrupted. "Supreme human intelligence. Stories of your travels have reached even the Renex empire. Though I respect how you are able to defeat opponents using only your wit and mind, I must say that I do not trust people right off the bat. If you intend any harm to Grunt, or anyone in this colony, I swear your last memory will be my spear being driven between your eyes! Got it?"

"Please ignore my chief of security," General Rice interjected hastily. "He's a bit on the blunt side, and a bit paranoid, given what we've been through over the last year. Once you are in his trust, I can assure you that he is quite personable."

"Alcanore?" Sophia said excitedly. "The Alcanore? I have heard so much about you! You were the one who changed the tide of the war for the Renex against the Kelson.

I always longed for the day that I could meet you in person. Please know that I have admired you for a long time. You were a huge inspiration to me when I first joined the V.T.C."

Alcanore did not respond to Sophia's fangirling. He slowly walked away from the others, keeping one eye on Nerd as he returned to his hut.

"Don't take it personally," Rice continued. "It's not you."

"How did one of the most renowned Renex warriors end up with you?" Sophia asked.

"The Renex, Zentar, and humans are all part of the galactic government. Alcanore was assigned to my ship by the Renex to learn about human nature, as our three races don't always understand each other. Alcanore was chosen because his voice is powerful with his people, and he would be able to impart what he learned to the rest of his race. Sadly, only a month after he was assigned to us, we crash-landed here after picking up a distress call on the planet's surface. He has gradually gotten moodier ever since."

"You...received a distress call, too?" Nerd asked.

"Yes, but it was forged, and somehow some stupid virus was downloaded onto our ship. I still don't know what happened. But obviously someone wanted us here."

Nerd placed his hand on his forehead. He knew that their meeting was not coincidence. But why? Why would Experiment-1 want this?

Nerd swallowed his fear and decided not to tell General Rice what was going on, as he didn't want the rest of the tribe to panic. He figured it was best to direct the subject back to Alcanore.

"Grunt seems to be very close to Alcanore," he said. "Is it because they're both alien to your crew?"

"Not quite. Alcanore saved Grunt when he was a child. Grunt is no older than two years of age. Alcanore showed up one night with Grunt in his arms. He wouldn't tell us where he found him or what happened to his family…but man, was he protective of him. The two are a powerful frontline for us though, so as simple-minded as Grunt may be, we are glad that he is on our side."

"I see."

"However, enough about that. As I've said, we lost a good number of our crew members, so a few huts are available. I'll show you to them. We are going to have dinner in the large hut in about three hours. Why don't you join us? I'm sure Alcanore will start to warm up to you after he observes you for a little while in a group setting."

Nerd and his team agreed, and each of them was directed to a hut.

Night began to fall, and Nerd received a text message on his communicator. Figuring it was either Sophia or Henry, he paid no attention to it at first. He was lost in thought and didn't want to be disturbed. However, as his communicator continued to alert him, he decided to take a look, as he was starting to worry that it could be important.

Unknown: Hey, David! Are you enjoying your little stay on Obian? I was most impressed with the way that you fought off those Jagores. My favorite part is where you almost died.
Unknown: David?
Unknown: DAVID!
Unknown: If you want to live, answer me!

Nerd was shocked to be reading what he was reading. He did not recognize the number, but what the person was sending him was very disturbing.

Nerd: Who is this? And how do you know my name? Also, if you threaten me again, I will block your number.

Unknown: You know who I am. We used to work together on the Invader Project, remember?

Nerd's heart began to sink. He knew it was Experiment-1, and he knew his adversary was attempting to get into his head. If he angered his enemy, he knew it would cost someone in the camp their life. So, he decided to keep talking, with hopes that he could amuse Experiment-1 long enough for him to feel satisfied.

Nerd: What do you want?

Unknown: You know what I want.

Nerd: Humor me.

Unknown: The location of the Invader Project. We were so close to unlocking the most powerful weapon in the galaxy. I need it, David, I need it!

Nerd: What do you need it for?

Unknown: To get to the core of Cosmic 5. There's something I need in there.

Nerd: What do you need?

Unknown: I won't tell you. If I tell you, you're going to try to get there before I do.

Nerd: I seriously doubt that.

Unknown: Enough of the small talk. Are you going to tell me or not?

Nerd: Never! The Invader Project is corrupt and unstable. If we release him, he will kill all organic life in the galaxy! That includes you.

Unknown: Not if I persuade him otherwise.

Nerd: I'm not telling you where I put him. It's too dangerous!

A pause ensued, which meant that Experiment-1 had either lost interest or was up to no good. Regrettably, the latter was evident, as he replied a few minutes later.

Unknown: I could say I'm going to kill everyone. But that wouldn't carry as much weight within your heart. So, I'm going to say something that's going to strike you deeper than anything else ever could.

Nerd: What could be worse than saying you're going to kill everyone?

Unknown: If you don't help me...

Nerd: Yes?

Unknown: I'm going to kill Sophia! 💀

Now Nerd was angry. He frantically typed his reply.

Nerd: If you lay one finger on her, I will kill you myself!

Unknown: I struck a nerve! Now I know I have the right pressure point. Enjoy your meal with your friends. Make sure you talk to Sophia a lot and say your goodbyes... She won't be alive for much longer.

Nerd began shaking. A panic attack had been triggered, and he couldn't take it anymore! He began flapping his hands uncontrollably. His heart ached at a level that was paralyzing. His mind began to self-destruct, and reality seemed to just tear itself apart around him. He curled up onto the ground in the fetal position as all his tormenting memories came back to haunt him. This was the true meaning of pain, and Nerd was experiencing it at a level that went far beyond what a normal human was capable of taking.

So often he felt like he was able to make a difference. But now, Nerd felt completely helpless. He was tired of losing people that he loved, especially to horrible men like Experiment-1 or Dr. Crimson, and it was wearing him down; every time he felt comfortable with his life, every time a glimmer of light seemed to find its way towards him, he would lose it before he had a chance to heal, and it was consuming him from the deepest parts of his soul.

His friend was going to die, and he couldn't save her. He couldn't do anything to protect her from the predator with green eyes.

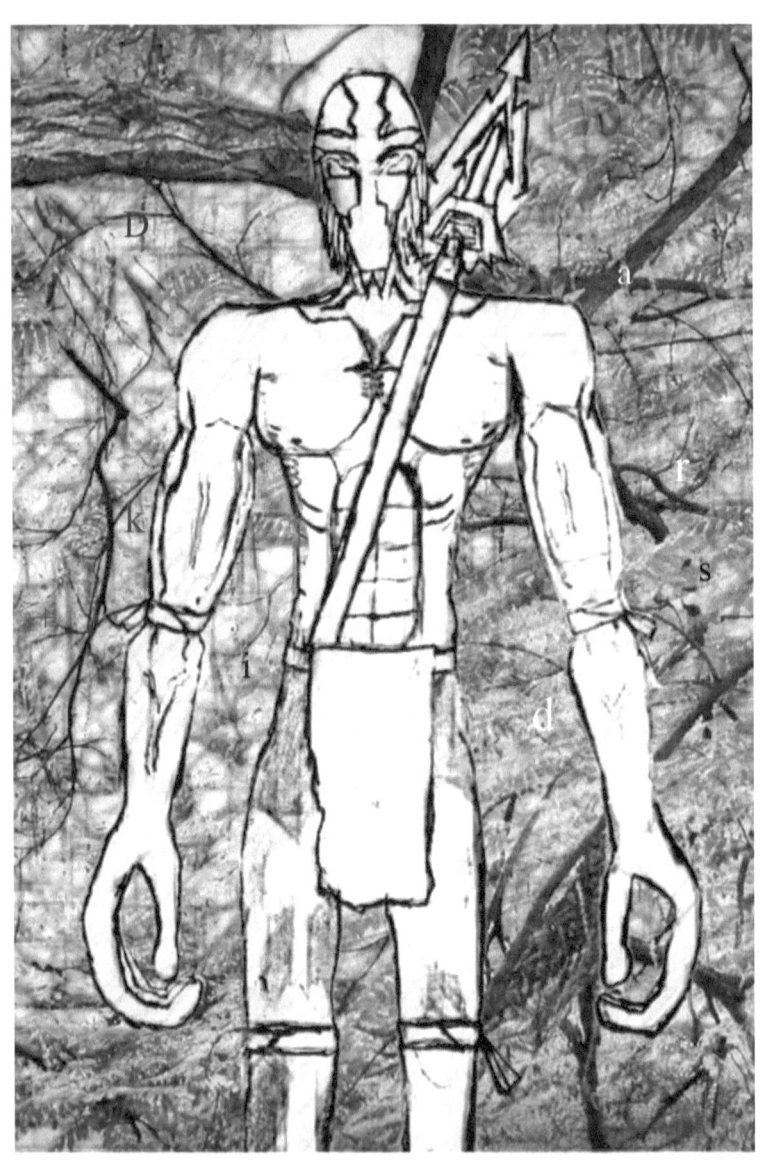

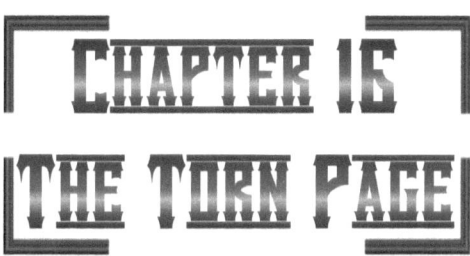

CHAPTER 16
THE TORN PAGE

An hour passed, and Nerd's attack had eased to the point where he could leave his hut. He slowly picked himself up and made his way out, as the time for dinner was approaching. As if his day wasn't bad enough, the first person he saw was Alcanore, who was waiting for him outside. He met him halfway and stopped him dead in his tracks.

"I know who you are, human!" Alcanore said. "You are the most wanted criminal in the galaxy, David Bell."

Nerd was not in the mood to argue. So, he decided to just come clean.

"Yes," he responded. "I am."

"You won't deny the truth; I will at least give you credit for that. Still, that doesn't excuse all the innocent people you—"

"I don't have time for this! There are more serious matters here than you and me."

"You think I don't know that! I know someone is responsible for everything that's happened to us, and although you may be the most wanted, I don't believe you're the worst person out there. You're just the worst person who got caught."

"I didn't kill those people. Dr. Crimson killed those people and paid off the judges to frame me. I don't really care if you believe that or not. But like you, I don't lie. You deserve at least a chance to know the truth. Whether you are open to it or not is your choice. Regardless, my main concern right now is to get these people off this planet alive. And that's what I'm going to do, with or without your support."

Alcanore paused for a moment. He was not foolish enough to take someone's word for something right off the bat. Especially a claim of that magnitude, but he never really liked Crimson, Something about him always seemed suspicious. Not in an awkward or harmless way, but in a way that filled even his brave heart with paralyzing fear.

Alcanore took a breath and continued speaking.

"If you are innocent, don't hurt anyone on my crew. If you don't, you will earn a level of goodwill from me. But if you do decide to harm one of my friends, I swear you will be longing for death like no human has ever longed before!"

"You never go back on your word; this much I do know. I take it that you're going to keep my identity a secret?"

"For now. Don't cross me, and I'll keep it a secret even after we escape from this mess."

Nerd bowed his head in a Renex fashion that showed Alcanore had his respect. He was desperately hoping it would buy him at least a little goodwill from the Renex legend. He then made his way over to the big hut where everyone was gathering, making no further eye contact with Alcanore.

The inside was much more appealing than the hut he was given, at least to the point where he didn't lose his appetite, but it was still far more run-down than what he was used to. There was a long table, set up for 20 people, in the center of it. All the guests had arrived, including Henry and Sophia, who were already seated at the table. Nerd was given the guest of honor seat in the very middle of the table—which was the last seat he wanted, given his social anxiety. However, he was still in a non-confrontational mood, so Nerd just accepted his position.

Alcanore sat in a large seat at the far right of the table. There was also an open spot on the far left side, where Grunt sat. General Rice was on the opposite side of Nerd, at the table's center. Next to him was a man who looked like the town's medic. He had dark skin, green eyes, a short buzzcut for his hair, and looked to be in his early twenties. He seemed to have a very kind way about him, and Nerd didn't feel as threatened around him as the others. He was still too emotionally distraught to really start a conversation or, for that matter, carry one on, but he tried regardless. He knew he may only have a few moments left with Sophia, and he continued to attempt to make small talk with her. At first, she had no problem talking to him, but after a while, she got a little irritated.

"Nerd!" she said to him. "Please let me talk to some of the other table guests. It's not like you're never going to see me again."

"I'm not sure about that…" Nerd responded.

"What? What do you mean by that?"

"…It's nothing. I'm just really nervous talking to people I don't know."

"Well, here's your chance! Gotta break out of your shell sometime."

Nerd began moving his leg up and down nonstop. It was very noticeable, and the table began vibrating with each stomp of his foot. General Rice noticed Nerd was uncomfortable and wasn't communicating with any of the dinner guests but Sophia. He attempted to get Nerd's attention, as many of his tribe members were eager to hear more about him.

"Nerd!" He said. "I want you to meet my chief medical officer, Mr. Tom Brown. He's been a bit of a fan of yours for a while. He wouldn't shut up about you when he read the book that you published last year."

Nerd was distracted and did not respond.

"It's an honor to meet you, sir!" Tom said. "Tales of your space travels have intrigued me since I first entered the medical field. I have been looking forward to this day for a long time…although I thought you had brown hair in your online pictures. I guess it doesn't matter! It is truly an honor to meet you in person."

"Yeah…" Nerd responded, still distracted by his situation. "Nice to meet you too, Dr. Brown."

"Please call me Tom. It's only Dr. Brown when I'm on medical duty."

"Okay."

"Um…so…what do you think of this planet? It is a prison, no doubt. But there is something about the atmosphere that I must say I find intriguing."

"Yeah…"

Tom was very confused and a little discouraged at Nerd's lack of interest. He didn't seem to like him very much, and this was upsetting, given how long he had waited to meet someone he had looked up to for so long. He sighed and went back to eating his Ja-gore meat.

Suddenly, Nerd processed something that General Rice had said before.

"Wait!" He said in a loud voice. "You read my book?"

Tom was completely taken off guard. He paused for a moment, and then answered Nerd's question.

"Yes," Tom said.

"And you understood it?" Nerd asked.

"Yes. 'Knowledge is endless, and we as humans have barely scratched the surface of it. No matter how smart we are, we will always have the ability to learn, and that's okay! Because what good is life if you can't continue to grow?' I was inspired by that statement, because so many intelligent people today act like they have all the answers. Their ego burns inside of them like a fire ready to consume any trace of reason that dares challenge what they teach. You, on the other hand, are arguably one of the smartest humans in this galaxy, and through the entire book, you seem to compare yourself to more of a child, rather than a wise man. It was humbling, but not at a level where it was discouraging. You have proved that we all have much to learn, and always will."

"Impressive. I appreciate that you're willing to take a look at that. I was in a bad place when I wrote it, and I wrote the entire book within a week. I was suffering from depression and was bedridden. So, I had a lot of time on my hands, and when I obsess over a project, I tend to go all out."

"You wrote that in a week? That's insane!"

"I have my gifts…but they come at a price. What about you? What's your story?"

"There's not much of a story for me. I had a simple upbringing within the once beautiful landscapes of Zecarah. I had good parents who raised me to respect the universe and all the wonderful gifts it has to offer. I chose to get into the medical field as a means of helping people and to use my knowledge as a means to prolong life in a galaxy that seeks to devour it. That's about it. I'm really nothing special."

"You seem to have your head screwed on straight. That's rare to find these days, especially in this galaxy. I'm glad you chose the medical field. It is a good feeling when you can help someone to recover."

"Isn't it! It is my dream to ONE DAY BE JUST LIKE YOU. I HAVE LOOKED UP TO YOU FOR SO LONG, AND I HOPE YOU UNDERSTAND HOW MANY PEOPLE FEEL THE SAME WAY.

Nerd grabbed his head with both his hands as the morbid flashback repeated like a broken record through his mind. These exact words were once spoken to him by his friend Ronald, who he had ordered to his death.

Nerd's leg began bouncing up and down again. Everyone was concerned, as they knew he was not doing well, and they didn't know what to say to make it better. Even Alcanore was watching him very carefully, which made Nerd feel even more nervous. But unknown to Nerd, Alcanore was not trying to intimidate him. He was starting to realize that Nerd was more vulnerable than he came across, and for the first time since they met, he felt concerned.

The guests finished dinner and left the big hut. Nerd shot out like a rocket, and Sophia noticed that he was indeed troubled by something. She quickly followed him out and chased him down.

"Nerd!" she said out loud. "Wait! What's wrong? You seem upset about something."

Nerd turned around and faced Sophia. He didn't want to tell her that her life was threatened, as he wanted her to get to sleep that night. However, for all he knew, this could be the last time he ever talked to her. He didn't know what to say. He didn't know what to do. He was at the mercy of a heartless killer, and he was powerless to stop him.

"Sophia…" he responded. "If anything happens to one of us, I just want to let you know that you're wonderful. I don't always know how to express it…but I do feel that way about you."

"I know. I've known for longer than you realize. David…I mean Nerd, there's something I need to tell you, something that's been bothering my conscience for a few days now. It seemed like a good idea at first…but I had no right to do it!"

"What's wrong? What did you do?"

"When you went to what you thought was your court-martial, I…I looked through your diary…and I'm sorry! I shouldn't have done that. But I saw what you wrote about me, and it was very touching. You will never know how much that meant to me…but I'm so sorry. Please don't hate me."

"My diary? Sophia, I already knew you looked through it. I saw it was misplaced, and I began to get paranoid. So, I took some fingerprint scans, and I found your fingerprints on the pages. It was a bit sneaky, and I was upset at first, but I'm over it. I'm at least glad to know that you approve of what I wrote about you."

"You took fingerprint scans? Why?"

"I just had to know if you had done it, that's all. But that doesn't matter right now. I just…I just wanted to say it to you in person. Until I met you, I was a wreck. But you have helped me to get better, and in case anything happens, I want you to know."

A few moments of silence went by, and neither could think of anything else to say. To Sophia's surprise, Nerd walked over to give her a hug. But…it was different this time. He wasn't forcing himself to do it. In fact, he seemed to have a hard time letting go. Sophia knew that there was something wrong, but she couldn't figure out what.

As soon as Nerd let go of her, he smiled and told her that she should get some rest. Sophia nodded her head and made her way to her hut. She turned to face him, as the question that had been floating around in her head for the last few weeks began nagging at her. She needed that final puzzle piece to complete the mystery that was plaguing her.

"Nerd, wait!" she said. "When I read your diary, I noticed there was a page ripped out that expressed your feelings after you…unintentionally killed someone. I was just wondering what that was all about. Why did you feel the need to remove the page?"

Upon hearing Sophia's question, Nerd stopped dead in his tracks. He turned around to face his friend and realized that a moment of truth was about to commence. He wasn't ready for her to know, but given Experiment-1's threat, this could be the only opportunity. Sophia deserved to know; she deserved an explanation as to why he was so apprehensive about taking someone's life, even if it was an accident.

Nerd took a deep breath and walked over to Sophia. He reached into his lab coat pocket and pulled out the ripped page she was looking for.

"If you read this," he said to her, "you will never quite view me the same way again."

"I highly doubt that, sweetie. You're the most noble man I have ever met…even if you are a bit of a dweeb sometimes. But you value life, and I trust you. I know you hate the thought of taking someone else's life."

"It's not that simple. The reason I ripped out the page was so I could keep it close to me, to remind me of what happens when I kill, what thoughts go through my head afterwards, and why I always need to avoid doing so. My emotions are very real, and I need to remember why I can't afford to become anything more than a doctor… Please try to understand."

He handed Sophia the diary page with his trembling right hand. Sophia accepted it but was now a little concerned by how troubled her commander seemed.

"I'm sorry," Nerd continued. "Really, I am so sorry!"

Nerd turned around and swiftly walked away from Sophia. He entered his hut and ducked out of sight. Sophia remembered what the end of the left page said and what the beginning of the right page had quoted. She kept the words in her mind and placed the words on the page that was in her hand in between like a mental puzzle.

"When it happened, when the life faded from my attacker's eyes, I felt— pleasure! An overwhelming sense of satisfaction that I have never experienced before. I killed a predator, someone who sought to harm me. For the first time, I was not the victim. The predator had been slain by my hand, by the hand of its own prey, and it felt so good that I can't keep my mind off it. I have already calculated 1,896 other possible ways in which I could kill again and get that rush! I thirst for it. I thirst for the power…power beyond what I have ever experienced before. I want more. I would do anything to be reunited with it, so much so that I honestly don't even fear the consequences anymore. Every person I have seen since then is but an object to me, a statistic, an opportunity to retrieve that thrill. Though I know it will pass, at the moment, I long to kill again, no matter who I'm able to hunt down…but I know it's wrong. I know it's not me. I know that if I feed my impulse and get the sick thrill I crave, in the end, it will control me. I will be left powerless, empty, and completely dead inside, living as a slave that needs that rush to survive. I know this because I got to see firsthand how it affected Dr. Crimson. The rush was so desirable to him that he would go to any lengths to get his fix. When I think of it that way, I realize that is someone I don't want to be remembered as. True, that drive may help me succeed in punishing the wicked, but I will also hurt the innocent. I know that lust will only grow stronger if I continue to feed it… *—and that is why I will never intentionally kill*

someone. That is why violence will always be a last resort. Because the memories of what I experienced will forever stay with me, and I don't ever want to go through that again! Never...never."

Sophia continued holding the page in front of her, even though she was done reading it. At first her emotions went numb...but then a grim feeling of fear and panic overcame her.

"What?" she said out loud. "No...that isn't David. He would never..."

Sophia couldn't even finish her sentence. She could not believe that all this was buried beneath the man who she felt to be the gentlest person she had ever met. This couldn't be true. David wouldn't feel pleasure from killing a man. He felt miserable about it, she was convinced of it, she was... no...this was the truth. This was reality. This was a key puzzle piece to the mystery of David Bell. He was indeed a good man, who fought bravely to bite down on his impulses, to become as good of a man as he ever could. He didn't want what he was given, and that was a good thing. She needed to remember that. She needed to keep in mind that this was not David's choice. The only choice David had was whether or not to act on the genetic code that he had inherited, whether or not to become the killer that burned within his veins, and thankfully, he chose not to.

On the other hand, David was correct. How could she ever view him the same way again? There was a violent maniac buried deep down within his soul, who had inherited impulses that were downright horrible, and if that killer ever decided to come out, would he actually consider turning on her? Was her life in danger, even though her friend had good intentions? These were questions that Sophia was not ready to answer, nor did she need to answer them just yet. It was terrifying, but she had to give David credit for one thing: he let her see that side of him. He did not try to hide it from her when she asked, and this meant that she could trust David on one thing: he would never lie to her, even when the truth was ugly.

Sophia took a deep breath and began making her way back to her hut, but she stopped dead in her tracks at the sight of Alcanore exiting the hut where they had dinner. Her heart pounded vigorously. This was the perfect distraction to keep her mind off the mess she was now in. Alcanore had barely said one word to her at dinner, but he was going to acknowledge her now. She wasn't going to give him a choice.

She drew her sword and was ready to fight. She charged at him from the side, enough for him to see her attack coming, as she knew better than to sneak up on a Renex from behind.

Alcanore noticed he was being challenged, so he braced himself to fight his opponent. He drew his spear and pressed the button to extend it to its full length. He also armed his energy shield, which looked exactly like the one that Nerd used against Star-Creeper. The giant warrior was ready and armed.

Sophia went in for the first attack, but Alcanore pushed his shield into it. The force was devastating, and Sophia was thrown backwards. She lost her sword in the fall and was completely defenseless.

Alcanore leaped into the air, aimed his spear at Sophia's head, pulled his weapon back to gain momentum for his attack, and dropped it down to finish off his opponent.

Sophia closed her eyes as Alcanore went in for his finishing move…but he stopped his attack right as the tip of the spearhead was half an inch away from the gap between Sophia's eyes. He then drew his spear away and put it back in its sheath, deactivated his shield, and offered his hand to help Sophia up. Sophia accepted and was pulled back to her feet.

"You're a sprinter!" he said to her. "Your speed is impressive, especially considering you're wearing those height extenders on your feet. However, you might not want to go in full force next time you challenge a tank. You're quick, nimble, and agile. Use those abilities to hit and run. I would hate to see you fall to such a rookie strategy in your next battle."

"I'll keep that in mind," Sophia said sarcastically. "Also, they're called high heels, not height extenders."

Alcanore laughed at Sophia's sarcasm.

"You definitely have spirit, and you were smart enough to attack me from the side rather than from behind. If you attacked me from behind, I would've taken that as a threat. But we Renex challenge each other all the time, to keep us alert and on our toes. I am flattered, but next time, give me more of a challenge. I do, however, want to apologize for ignoring you earlier today. It was nothing personal. I don't trust outsiders very often."

"I have looked up to you for a long time. I know I shouldn't have taken it so personally, but I had to get your attention. I hope you understand."

"Don't worry, brave human! I had my heroes growing up too. So, please know that I am glad to hear that you have followed in my footsteps for so long. Now please, go get some rest, for tomorrow, we journey into the temple of Obian."

Alcanore made his way to his hut. Sophia smiled; she felt giddy. Her dream had finally come true—a fight with the most feared warrior in the galaxy. Even if she did lose within the first few seconds, it was worth it. She walked over to her sword and put it in its sheath. She then made her way to her hut and retired for the night.

Nerd was a complete wreck. He had not slept in nearly two days, and it was breaking him down. He needed to get sleep if he was going to pull through tomorrow, but his mind would not shut up. He was worried sick about Sophia and knew that if he went to sleep, he would wake up to find out that his friend was dead.

An hour passed. Then two hours. Then three. Nerd's thinking was getting worse, and he just couldn't pass out. He was stuck awake, and he didn't feel like there was anything he could do. However, as midnight approached, he received another text on his communication device.

Trembling with fear, he quickly grabbed it and read its contents.

Unknown: I won't kill Sophia right off. You can go to sleep now. She will be alive when you wake up.

Nerd: What? Why the change of heart?

Unknown: This is not a change of heart. You're so tense right now that you're never going to get to sleep, and I need your mind to be fully active tomorrow if I'm going to torture you. I will give you my word that she will still be alive when you wake up...but after you two are reunited, it's game on!

Nerd: Thank you.

Unknown: Don't ever thank me again! Your approval makes me feel squeamish! Now go to sleep. We have a long day ahead of us tomorrow.

Although Nerd did not trust Experiment-1, somehow his promise rang true. Whether it was exhaustion or just a rare feeling of certainty that caused the weight to fall off Nerd's chest, even he did not know. But at least he was released from the torture he was formerly in.

He closed his eyes and passed out, and vivid dreams flooded the hallways of his deep and active mind.

CHAPTER 17
THE LORD OF SORROW

"David, where is Ronald? I haven't seen him in days. Isn't he your assistant?"

"Ronald can't be with us anymore."

"What do you mean he can't be with us anymore?"

"He is dead."

"What? No...no! Ronald can't be dead."

"But he is, I'm sorry."

"But how? How did he die?"

"I don't know, Amelia. He was summoned to the level 2 labs, and I just received a report a few hours ago that he passed away. They never told me how, and it doesn't matter. We will find a suitable replacement soon."

"How can you say that! Ronald was your best friend. He always told me he looked up to you."

"That doesn't matter. Grieving won't bring him back. The logical thing is to find a replacement and move on."

"And what about me, David? What if something happens to me? Am I replaceable, just like Ronald?"

"I wouldn't have to replace you. You serve no purpose on my staff."

"What! Are you saying that I mean nothing to you?"

"No, I am not saying that."

"Why do you even keep me around if I serve no purpose?"

"Because...because you don't serve a purpose to my work. You just...serve a purpose to me. That's all..."

"What is that supposed to... Wait, are you saying that you keep me around because you like having me around, and not because I clean the floors, dust the tables, and put your mess away?"

"Yeah."

"There is hope for you yet, David... David, David, David! Wake up, I need you to wake up!"

The moment was interrupted by a voice calling out his name. He woke up to the feeling of a hand on his shoulder. He was disoriented, groggy, and he still hadn't gotten much sleep.

At first, he didn't even know where he was or who was trying to wake him up. But after a few moments went by, he noticed that it was Henry Smith that had been trying to reach him.

"David!" He urged his commander. "I mean…Nerd! You need to wake up now! The killer has struck the village, and most of the citizens are infected with the plague."

"What?" Nerd said as his sleepy eyes flew open, preparing himself for the worst. "Sophia! Is she…"

"Sophia is fine, bro; the killer infected all the huts around hers but thankfully spared her. She's alive, just a bit shaken over what's going on."

Nerd breathed a sigh of relief, then felt discouraged again as the reality of the situation sank in.

"What about Commander Rice and our other temporary crew members?"

"Commander Rice was infected; he is gone. The only survivors are Grunt, Alcanore, Tim, Joe, Stephen, and Tom, the kid you were talking to at dinner. He's the one who found Commander Rice, and Nerd…he saw the killer with his own eyes."

"No! He only spared three of the villagers?"

"I'm afraid so."

"Where is Tom?"

"He's over by the general's hut. The poor kid is going to suffer some extreme PTSD from this. I think you better talk to him; he needs it right now."

"Take me to him and gather the others. We're going to need to get out of here soon."

Henry nodded his head and directed Nerd to the general's hut. The sun was just starting to rise outside, and just enough light was visible for Nerd to see the tragic sight of the galactic plague victims scattered across the village. Moaning, groaning, and monstrous growls filled the air. It was awful, and although Nerd was grateful that Experiment-

1 had kept his word regarding Sophia, he was reminded that although he had shown a brief moment of honor, it would always be followed by a wicked and merciless deed.

The two men made their way to Tom, who was sitting on a log near the general's hut. His head was in his hands, and he was shaking and panting heavily. Nerd asked Henry to get the others so they could meet. Henry agreed and left to get the surviving crew.

Nerd put his hand on Tom's shoulder, hoping to at least get him to talk a little about what he saw.

"Tom," he said. "What happened? What exactly did you see?"

Tom gathered his thoughts and responded to Nerd's question.

"I saw death itself...and it looked me in the eyes and spoke to me."

"I'm so sorry to hear about General Rice. He was a good man, that much I could see, but I need to know what happened. Any info I can get on our killer is greatly needed right now. He's already a step ahead of us, and if things continue, none of us are going to get out of here alive."

Tom took a moment to gather his thoughts. He knew he had to be very specific. Even if he didn't feel that the information he gave was important, there was always a chance that Nerd could find something in his story that he just couldn't. So, he knew he had to be as detailed as possible. He took a deep breath and told Nerd everything he could remember.

"I woke up early this morning. It was still dark outside. I usually don't wake up this early, but I knew something was wrong. I kept hearing sounds outside, like something was swiftly moving around the camp, and I just couldn't get it out of my head.

"I grabbed a flashlight and made my way to the general's hut. He always wakes up early in the morning, and I knew if there was anyone I could talk to, it would be him. I was so focused on the general that I didn't pay any attention to the bodies that were around me. I did hear the moaning and groaning, but I figured it was just the fear and paranoia in my head—the same fear and paranoia that has plagued me for the last year.

"I then made my way inside the commander's hut. The room was pitch black. I grabbed my flashlight and shined it towards the general's desk. My heart began to race as I noticed the horrifying sight that was staring back at me.

There was General Rice, sitting in his chair, barely half alive! Wordless moaning and groaning came from his throat—he was obviously close to being brain dead. But there was something else that stood out. Something that drove more fear into me than anything ever had before.

"A hand was poised above Rice's shoulder. A black, grim-looking hand, holding the syringe that had been driven ruthlessly into the general's neck. I slowly moved the light up, illuminating part of the person behind the general.

"The intruder was wearing a black trench coat. My heart thudded loudly in my ears, and my body froze to the spot like reeds frozen in a pond in the dead of winter. The chill of fear crawled up my spine. I knew I should move, run, but sheer terror held me in its icy grasp. I desperately tried to wrench myself away, my mind silently screaming to get out, but the intruder didn't let me collect myself.

"I was nearly blinded by two blazing, glowing green eyes. Those eyes. The eyes of death itself!

"I gasped, whipping the flashlight up into the face of the intruder with renewed energy. Adrenaline rushed through my veins as the stalker's face was revealed to me.

"It was white, a pale white that seemed to glow with unholy and terrible coldness as the flashlight beamed off it. Black paint was smeared across his mouth, eyes, and forehead; terrible gashes of darkness daubed across that pale skin. The paint seemed to drip from the corners of his mouth, as if the blackness was oozing from him and not painted on. The blackness around his eyes was like a wet mask, leaving trails of black tears streaming down his cheeks—but it wasn't sad. It was horrifying. Ridges of black paint raked across his forehead, three on the right and three on the left, with spikes jaggedly pointing upward. It gave him an angry look. It was a mess. He was a mess; the paint gouged into his skin like claws of buried fury.

"The thought of what happened next, however, sends shivers down my spine. The stalker opened his mouth and spoke. His voice sent chills through my entire body—the sound of him speaking my language, my mother tongue, speaking directly to me, calling my name… I have never heard anything so frightening, and I hope never to hear anything like it again.

"'Tom…' His voice was soft, calm, and bitter. I wanted to cover my ears, but I couldn't move. 'Your intelligence is admirable; you don't have to die. You can still leave this planet in peace.' He paused, letting the reality of his words sink into my skin like poison. 'Tom. Head in the opposite direction of the temple. That will guarantee your safety. I will have a dropship pick you up and bring you to the next space station. I give you my word, if you run from this.' His eyes dropped to the terrible sight of General Rice before him, then he looked back up at me, pinning me with cold truth. 'I won't go after you.'

"Then he was gone, his entire form disappeared from the beam of the flashlight, escaping with such speed I almost thought he had actually disappeared into thin air. I whirled around, suddenly able to move, and whipped the flashlight's beam about the room, desperately searching for the form of the intruder, the stalker, the killer of my crew, but he had run from me. He had deserted me, left me alone with the gruesome body of General Rice, clearly not interested in ending my life as he had done to our leader.

"That's all I know! For whatever reason, he seems to view me as a person rather than his prey. Maybe he views me as a threat, or maybe he has a twisted viewpoint on lives that matter and lives that don't. I don't know. What I do know is that I won't accept his offer. He killed everyone I love, and for that, I want him to pay."

Nerd was very drawn into Tom's description. He knew what it was like to stand up to the nightmare of their galaxy, and what it was like to be emotionally scarred from it.

Nerd placed his hand on his forehead and took a few deep breaths. He didn't really know how to respond. All he knew was…this was very real.

"I'm so sorry," Nerd said.

"Why is he doing this? Why is he toying with us?"

"He's toying with us so that I will give him the key to unlimited power. I know the location of the most dangerous bioweapon in the galaxy. He knows I won't give it to him, because it would mean the end of all organic life, and if he kills everyone anyway, I won't have anything to lose. No…I know what he's going to do. For once I have a lead on his next move."

"And that is?"

"He's going to pluck us out one by one, and each life he takes will drive me one step closer to giving in. I'm faced with a horrible decision. I either let him kill everyone I love or I save everyone I love and let him kill everyone else in existence. That is the amount of pressure I have on me right now, and it's driving me out of my mind!"

Nerd's hands began to shake. He was trying to keep it together, but it was difficult to do so. With each passing moment he came another step closer to a grim and fear-inspired future—one that he did not want to be a part of!

Henry Smith had returned with the surviving members of the village. Sophia, Lieutenant Collins, Mr. Howard, Captain Baker, Grunt, Alcanore, and himself, along with Nerd and Tom, made a crew of nine. The rest were gone, their humanity stripped away for the final hours of their life.

"This honorless tyrant shall pay for what he has done!" Alcanore said in a harsh and angered voice. "If he thinks he can get away with—"

"He knows he can get away with it," Nerd said. "That's why he does it."

"Nerd! You are known for solving problems that most normal humans can't. Surely you must know of a weakness that can be found within this fiend?"

"Other than the fact that he can be distracted…I'm afraid not. The only way to kill him is to destroy every cell, molecule, and trace of DNA in his body. If so much as a single blood cell, skin fragment, or drop of sweat escapes from him, his body will reform and repair itself immediately. He may not be invincible, but he's not far off."

Silence followed Nerd's speech, and Nerd realized he had unintentionally beaten the will out of his team. He rethought the situation and attempted to find something that would give them hope to survive the mess they were in.

"If we're going to survive this, we can't let revenge blind us to the problem that's ahead. We need to get to the top of that tower. If we can destroy whatever device he has built inside to keep us prisoners here, then we have a chance!"

"No!" Alcanore responded. "He must die!"

"And he will. But not today, not by our hand. If that is the main point of our focus, then he has already won. Experiment-1 uses fear and intimidation to toy with his victims before he kills them. But he can also manipulate his victims' anger to blind them before engaging in battle. So, tell me, brave one, what good is your desire to kill him going to do if you're responding in the exact way that he wants you to?"

Alcanore was unable to answer. He wasn't too fond of the human, especially considering his true identity was that of a wanted man, but regardless, he could not argue with him, because he was right. Experiment-1 was attempting to control him. He let out a sigh and nodded his head.

Sophia felt a mild sense of relief overcome her. She was still shaken over the note Nerd had written, but it was obvious that he was doing everything in his power to keep himself controlled. Still, it was hard for her, because up until that point, she truly felt that David was the only person in the galaxy she could trust. Now…she wasn't so sure. It was nice to hear Nerd speak against revenge nonetheless.

Nerd received another message from his communicator and felt his heart race when he noticed it was from Experiment-1 yet again. Only this time, his communicator was downloading something. It was a pic message. Nerd viewed it as soon as it had downloaded and let out a gasp.

"Woah!" Henry said. "What's wrong, bro?"

"It's…from him," Nerd choked out. He then turned his phone over to the surviving crew, and a strong vibe of fear and panic emerged upon seeing the horrid sight.

Their eyes were overwhelmed at the sight of a picture of all of them. It was recently taken, as they were huddled around the general's hut, and a green marker was used to cross out each of their faces. All but one: Nerd. He was going to kill everyone but Nerd.

Suddenly, the grim melody of Amelia's music box could be heard throughout the village, revealing that Experiment-1 was nearby. The sharp notes drifted slowly through the air, coming from all directions, not giving any hint as to where they were coming from. The crew prepared themselves, knowing that their enemy was preparing to strike. An object flew through the air and landed at their feet. It was a green sphere with a sad face painted on it. Nerd instantly recognized it and urged his crew to move away. The crew responded and were glad they did as the object exploded. A loud, piercing scream followed the booming explosion.

Everyone was terrified and in considerable pain as they felt their ears ringing from the loud, excruciating sound.

"It's a fear bomb!" Nerd yelled. "We need to get out of here now!"

As soon as the words fell out of Nerd's mouth, the sky was flooded with ten, twenty, forty, one hundred fear bombs moving in on their position. Nerd pointed to the north and led the surviving crew members out of the village.

A wave of loud, ear-piercing explosions flooded the village like a tidal wave, moving swiftly to their position, devouring anything that stood in their path.

The nine survivors darted forward as fast as their legs would take them. They did everything they could to keep themselves from being devoured by the green wave of fire that was engulfing everything behind them.

They ran until the sound of screams stopped. Nerd looked back and was horrified to see that the entire village was gone.

There was no going back now. They had to move forward to the temple; it was their only chance of escape.

Nerd counted the crew and was relieved to see that they were all still alive. Their hands were clamped over their ears, the sound of the explosions had given them quite the headache. Nerd could hear the ringing in his sensitive ears; it was piercing and nearly drove him to have another panic attack. Still, his crew needed him to keep it together, so he used all his focus to keep himself from falling apart again. He attempted to speak, to direct them, but nearly lost it when he was unable to hear the sound of his own voice. They were temporarily deaf, and dangerously vulnerable, especially if they chose to stay in their current location. So, he signaled with his hands to swiftly move to the north, before Experiment-1 could devour them.

They ran a mile before their hearing started to return. It was very faint, but at least the unbearable ringing had died down. That was the good news. The bad news was Nerd was already winded, which was evident when the first sound his crew heard was his heavy breathing. He was slowing down, but he knew he couldn't stop running, given who was behind them. So, he forced himself through the long three-mile run that remained.

Two miles lay behind them, and Nerd was dying. He was breathing from the deepest part of his lungs, which was painfully audible as the crew members' hearing got better. It was evident that he was going to collapse if he continued.

"We're taking a break," Captain Baker ordered.

"No!" Nerd responded while panting. "We must—"

"We need you if we're going to get out of this in one piece. Just take a few minutes, that's all."

Nerd was too winded to argue, so he took the captain's advice. The crew rested for five minutes, and after an eight-to-one vote, they decided to continue at a walking pace, rather than running, in order to save their energy for whatever lurked within the temple.

"This is dangerous!" Nerd said, still uneasy, considering he was the one who voted to continue running. "We are giving him time to make his next move."

"You yourself said that he will use fear to control his victims," Alcanore pointed out. "We can't be so fearful that we let him push us to our breaking point. Is that not what you were trying to tell me before?"

"I…I suppose I was. Thank you for actually taking my advice to heart. People rarely do."

Alcanore laughed. "Don't be so hard on everyone. You're a blunt individual, but I can take that! Just work on trusting your team and not always acting like you have all the answers. No one has all the answers, not even you. We may not be brilliant at solving crimes or geniuses in the field of science, but we know how to pace ourselves when in battle. We just need you to trust us. I think you can give us that much."

Nerd, surprisingly, laughed in response to Alcanore's words. The creature was very direct and had a strong personality. He was also very honest and to the point, and obviously wasn't scared to swallow his own pride as well as shattering Nerd's. That was okay, so long as he kept it within reasonable boundaries. Alcanore was warming up to him, and that was huge considering how paranoid he was when they first met.

The nine walked another mile without any interference from Experiment-1, but Nerd was not letting his guard down, as he knew their stalker could make a move at any given moment.

The final mile was behind them, and the temple could be seen in between the jungle's foliage. It was massive indeed, and definitely a marvel compared to the rest of the planet. The temple itself was made from granite, but the craftsmanship was beautiful. There were carvings all through the massive structure that showed the many battles the Obian people had fought to take control of the planet. The center tower they would have to climb up was as tall as a skyscraper, reaching above even the jungle tree line. It was a marvel to see but was also a bit of a downer, given the fact they would have to make their way up it. Still, the structure was amazing. Pity that its creators were extinct, as Nerd knew they could have used their insight to get them out of this mess.

The joy was overshadowed by fear, however, as Nerd received another text from his enemy.

"**Unknown:** Did you figure it out yet? Why I brought everyone here?

Nerd: Yes, you're letting me grow attached to these people, just so you can pluck them off one by one. You spent a full year planning this, just so you could get into my head!

Unknown: Bingo! To tell you the truth, I was getting bored with the idea. I didn't think it would work, because you could have solved the problem before you formed any close relationships. So, I gave up for a little while. But then you just had to go and make it easy for me by befriending your two human friends. Especially her. Oh! The pain it would cause you if anything ever happened to her.

Nerd wasn't going to waste any more time. He signaled the crew to head to the ruins but continued to text his nemesis to keep him occupied.

Nerd: You know I will never give you the location of the Invader unit. Even if you kill everyone I love.

Unknown: We will see about that...

Unknown: I bet you're wondering why I am so eager to get what I want. It must be so hard that I am the one mystery you were never able to solve.

Nerd: It seems like a lot of trouble just to get to the center of a space station, and it is frustrating because I know you're harmful to me...but I have a feeling you can relate to that helpless feeling a little more than I can. For some reason, you can't get into the center of Cosmic 5, and that means you feel helpless too.

Unknown: Yes, I do.

Nerd: Then please tell me, why are you doing this! What is in there that could be so important that you would risk the safety of the entire galaxy?

Unknown: As I said, I can't tell you. But I will give you a hint so you can figure it out when I'm ready for you to know the truth.

Nerd: Okay?

Unknown: Galactic plague is not a plague at all. It's a vaccine, a vaccine that I tried to perfect...but the human metabolism could not take it. So, I scrapped the idea, and now I use it as a weapon to strike fear into my opponents.

Unknown: Want to know something else? Years ago, I killed a small child, and I told you that life was a game, a game I intend to win. I lied. Though I did want to have the most kills under my belt, even I find no delight in killing a defenseless kid. It's just not challenging enough. I had a reason for ending his young life, just as I had a reason for attempting to kill Amelia.

Nerd's heart began to race. They were almost at the temple and were about to cross the drawbridge leading them over a moat that was dug around it. Nerd just needed to keep his enemy talking a little longer before they would be safe.

Nerd: I'm intrigued! Please tell me more.

Unknown: That's all you're going to get from me right now. I know the only reason you're talking to me is because you think it's buying you time. But I have spared your companions' lives for a little while so the numbness of what you dealt with before could wear off! Turn around and look up ^^^

Nerd did just as Experiment-1 asked and panicked when he noticed him stalking them at the end of the tree line. He was clinging to the side of one of the tall trees, only twenty feet in the air. As soon as Nerd spotted him, he jumped off the tree, drew his sword, and darted towards Captain Baker.

"Everyone!" Nerd shouted. "Head to the ruins, now!"

But before anyone could respond, Experiment-1 had reached Captain Baker. He jumped through the air with his sword in his hands and sliced through the top of Baker's head. Captain Baker was split down the middle and was killed instantly. There was no blood, however, as Experiment-1's blade had emitted some sort of energy and had cauterized his victim. This explained why his blade was able to cut through anything, giving him even more power than they had previously given him credit for.

Sophia saw this as an opportunity, as she had remembered what happened between her and Drake. She drew her sword and ran after Experiment-1. The two blades made contact, and excitement filled Sophia's heart when her theory proved correct. Her blade absorbed the energy from Experiment-1's weapon.

"No!" Nerd shouted. "Do not engage him. He will—"

"I know what I'm doing!" she replied. "Trust me, just get everyone inside the temple."

Sophia engaged Experiment-1 with full force, holding back nothing, Sparks flew as the two fought valiantly; they seemed to match each other in both wit and skill.

The only advantage that Experiment-1 had on her was that he was left-handed, which made his attacks a little harder to predict. But she didn't need to defeat him with her blade, she just needed to outlast him.

Finally, her blade was throbbing with green energy, and Sophia was ready to strike. She took a step back and thrust her blade out so that it would not make contact with Experiment-1's blade, hoping that she could engulf all of Experiment-1.

She felt a strong feeling of hope overcome her as Experiment-1's entire body was covered by the blast. He yelled in fury as his body and armor vaporized right in front of her.

Sophia raised her sword in a victory pose, but that victory was short-lived as she saw a mere strand of hair making its way to the ground.

Sophia was mortified to see a human body starting to reform in front of her, and before its head could reveal itself, it vanished!

"What?" Sophia said as her feeling of hope was crushed right in front of her.

As soon as she got the words out of her mouth, an arm and fist materialized three feet in front of her. It punched her in the face, and Sophia was sent back, landing hard on the bridge behind her.

Nerd wasted no time. He ran up to her and picked her up before their enemy could regroup and deliver a killing blow to her. He swiftly headed back and met the others, who were inside the first room of the temple. It was blocked off by another door that could only be opened by solving the room's puzzle.

Nerd put Sophia down and walked over to the temple entrance to see if Experiment-1 was stalking him. All he could see was a wooden lever next to the entrance and the distorted figure of a man walking towards it. Nerd began to step backwards and was prepared to fight, but the fight did not happen. Instead, the distortion made its way to the lever. The lever moved its way down, and the granite entrance door closed in front of them. Green neon crystals lit up as soon as the sunlight was gone, giving the surviving crew members a trace of vision.

However, this may have been the only good news. They were trapped, forced into a prison Experiment-1 had purposely led them into. Again, he was one step ahead of everyone else. Again, everything had fallen in his favor.

An overpowering feeling of dread seemed to overcome them all. Each one began to accept the fact that they were trapped by the will of a merciless killer, and that it was only a matter of time before they would be next.

CHAPTER 18 THE TEMPLE

Nerd gently put Sophia down. She was groggy and confused as to what had just happened. The blow was very powerful, and Nerd was worried that she may lose sight in her left eye. It was red and already starting to swell up.

"Remind me to take a look at that when we get back," Nerd said to her. "If we get back."

"I'm sorry, Nerd," Sophia responded, her tone expressing how disappointed she was in herself.

"Don't be; you almost had him. But his self-regeneration ability definitely makes him hard to beat."

"I remember you said his armored suit had the ability to cloak, but I was able to destroy his suit, and he still seemed to vanish into thin air while his body was regenerating. How?"

"I don't know how. All I know is that he can camouflage himself with his surroundings. At first, I thought it was his suit, but it looks like I was wrong. The good news is, suit or not, his cloaking ability only works if he moves slowly. As you noticed, his arm was visible when he took a shot at you, which tells me that his body needs time to change colors as he moves. At least he won't be able to run or attack us while cloaked. Eventually, he will need to come out of the shadows if he wants to continue pursuing us."

"And when he does," Joe interrupted, "we will skin him alive for what he has done!"

"Easy there, Joe," Nerd cautioned. "Don't let him get into your head."

"He killed our captain! Don't tell me to take it easy!"

Nerd attempted to soften his demeanor, as he did feel crushed over the life that was lost, though he hardly knew him. But his face remained cold due to the overpowering stress he was under.

"Yes," he said in a blunt voice. "I'm so sorry about your captain."

Joe Collins began making his way towards Nerd. He was going to punch him in the face, but Tom grabbed him and urged him to stand down.

"You're not the only one who's lost people, Collins!" he said. "Save your anger for Experiment-1. You're going to need it…trust me." After Collins had restrained himself, Tom turned around to face Alcanore, who was standing in the corner of the room with his arms crossed. "Do you think you can break open the door to the next room?"

"Ha!" he said. "I think I can make it happen. Everyone stand aside!"

Alcanore made his way to the door. He drew his spear and thrust it at the doorway. He was stunned to see that his attack had no effect on it at all. This was strange, as his spear was able to break granite. This structure must be built out of something a little bit more durable than they had previously thought. Still, he continued, with hopes that he could break through.

He thrust his spear a second time, but alas, nothing. He thrust it a third time but was still unable to even chip the doorway. Finally, he lost patience and attacked it with all his might.

After wearing himself down, Alcanore ceased his attack, realizing that it was foolish to waste his strength.

"Well, that blows!" Henry stated. "Anyone else got any ideas?"

Nerd analyzed his surroundings. The room was precisely 30 by 50 feet. It had four pillars inside to support the ceiling, which was around two stories high. The door was located on a platform, with a granite stairway leading up to it. The platform was one story high. There were four Grunt-like statues located in each corner of the room near the ceiling. Their mouths were closed, but Nerd got an unsettling feeling that somehow the statues' mouths could indeed open. Every 30 seconds, the neon crystal lights would grow dim for precisely one second. The room would go pitch black and then return to its original state. While this creeped everyone out at first, over time they got used to the pattern.

The doorway was isolated and had no switch or object near it that could be used to force it open. The only thing nearby was a few words located at the top. Nerd had never seen words in that format before, and he was unable to decipher what they meant.

He pulled out his communicator and scanned them, hoping that the artificial intelligence contained something in its database to decipher it.

Tom also scanned the doorway itself to see if there were any weaknesses to be found, but there were none. The only thing that seemed interesting was that the doorway was heavily insulated. It would make no sound when the door opened or closed. This design seemed to be completely pointless, and for the life of him Tom couldn't figure out why the architects would do this. He told Nerd his findings anyway, hoping he could use the info to work out how to get to the next room.

Henry Smith, on the other hand, was getting bored with being stuck in the room. He leaned on the doorway and let out a sigh.

"What about you, Grunt?" he asked. "Got any bright ideas?"

"Grunt happy!" he responded. "Grunt with friends!"

"Sorry I asked."

Nerd looked closer at the statues. Something was noticeably off. Initially their heads were pointing upward. They seemed to be paying no attention to the people in the room. Now the heads were pointing down and were looking right at them.

Nerd could not tell if he was paranoid or if there was something truly wrong. But after the neon lights went out again, Nerd realized that his fear was well founded. The statues were moving each time the lights grew dim, and now their mouths were open. Lava dripped from each mouth and made its way to the room's floor.

"We should all head up!" Nerd said, his tone urgent, ushering the crew up the stairs and hoping it would buy them some time.

Everyone obeyed and gathered together. Nerd did a headcount and panicked when he realized Henry Smith was not with them.

"Where did he go?" he asked.

"He was here a few seconds ago," Mr. Howard replied. "I saw him talking to Grunt."

"Grunt! Where is Henry?"

"Grunt see Henry!" Grunt replied. "Lights go out, Grunt no see Henry!"

"Well, that was helpful," Mr. Howard said sarcastically.

Nerd received an alert on his communication device. It had finished scanning the doorway. He was optimistic when he saw it had deciphered what the words said:

"When darkness falls, you will have but a moment to sprint ahead."

Nerd knew he had only a minute before the lava reached them. He quickly analyzed everything he knew about the room. The door was insulated, meaning it would make no sound when it opened and closed. Henry was leaning on the doorway when he was talking to Grunt but vanished when the lights went out, meaning Henry was already in the next room.

The lights flashed off and on again and Nerd smiled. It was an easy solution.

"Everyone!" he said. "Get as close as you can to the door, and as soon as the lights go out, run forward. We're only going to get one shot at this!"

"I don't understand," Lieutenant Collins replied. "We're just going to run straight into the door?"

"If you've got any better ideas, now's the time to voice them. Because in fifteen seconds, we're all going to melt slowly in a pool of boiling lava."

No one had any better ideas. So, all seven of them gathered as close as they could to the door. The crew lined up, three by three; Sophia, Alcanore, and Grunt in the front; Collins, Howard, and Tom in the middle; and Nerd stood solo in the very back.

Five seconds remained, and Nerd urged his friends to prepare themselves. The lights went out, and the members sprinted forward, and…they continued to run forward. Nothing was stopping them. They could see a light at the end of a long hallway, so they kept running until they reached the location where the light was. Henry Smith was at the end of it, where another large door could be seen.

"Henry!" Sophia yelled. "What happened to you? I was worried."

"I don't know, sis." Henry shrugged. "I was leaning on the door, and the next thing I knew, my weight was carrying me back. I was in another room that was dark. But I saw the light at the end of the hallway, and I figured I'd make my way towards it, and now here I am!"

Everyone looked at Nerd and wanted an explanation. He smirked and filled them in on what had happened.

"It was all just a puzzle, really," Nerd said. "Every time the lights went out, the door opened. Which is why the designers went through such trouble to insulate the door itself. We couldn't hear it, but it would open for a second and then close when the lights switched back on. I worked it out when my scanner deciphered the words on top of the door. 'When darkness falls, you will have but a moment to sprint ahead.' Knowing that Henry had disappeared when he was leaning on the door, I knew that we had to sprint forward the minute the lights went out. I'm glad we all got through…the lava would have consumed anyone who didn't."

"Which would've been you," Alcanore pointed out. "That's why you took the back. Well done, you have earned some respect, but only some."

Nerd chuckled. At this point, he was going to take any goodwill he could from Alcanore. He was relieved to know the he at least wasn't on the warrior's bad side. But wow, was this big guy taking baby steps in his path to trust.

After shifting his thought pattern, Nerd examined the next door and noticed that there were words on top of it like the last. He scanned them before taking note of the lever on the right-hand side. He waited to decipher the code before taking his next action.

The communicator alerted him that the code had been deciphered, and it read:

Only the strong will survive.

Nerd relayed the message to his crew. Alcanore, Henry, Grunt, and Sophia were thrilled at the news and made it clear that they were eager to fight.

Nerd pulled the lever and the door opened. The crew made their way into the next room. It was massive, about four stories high, with a perimeter of about 600 by 1,000 feet. There were four massive statues of guardians. Nerd recognized them as the race that built the temple and was thankful that they were not fighting them. The statues were over two stories tall. Each of them held a sword that was ten feet long, and they were holding them out towards the center of the room.

In the room's center was a blue circle painted into the granite floor, and it seemed to be the spot that the designers wanted them to go to next. Nerd usually would've proceeded with caution, but the three other doors in the room were blocked off, and they needed to trigger whatever was happening next.

"It is likely that the enemy will come through one of those doors when we step in the center," Nerd said as he pulled out one of his Rubik's cubes. "Prepare for the worst!"

Everyone gathered in the circle and drew their weapons. They heard a click as soon as they made contact with the circle. They knew a battle was soon to follow and focused intensely on the three doors far in the distance.

They waited, and waited, and waited, and...nothing. Nothing happened. The crew members became restless and irritated as they realized how foolish they looked just standing around in the circle, waiting to fight something that wasn't there.

"What's next, bruh?" Henry asked. "I ain't standing here forever."

"I don't understand," Nerd responded. "We heard a click when we stood on the circle. This should have activated the next challenge."

Nerd attempted to rethink his strategy but was interrupted when he heard something moving above them. He slowly looked up and was astonished to see that the statues had lifted their swords and were about to use them on himself and his friends.

"Everyone!" Nerd yelled. "Get off the circle, now!"

The four swords dropped, making a loud crashing sound as soon as they hit. Fortunately, everyone had scattered before they were sliced. Nerd and Tom went to the right; Alcanore and Grunt went to the left; Mr. Howard and Lieutenant Collins went straight ahead; and Henry and Sophia went behind them. They lured the guardians away from each other, and each team took one.

Howard and Collins armed their laser rifles and started firing upon the giant guardian. But to no avail, as its stone armor was too powerful for the rifles to pierce. Henry Smith had the same problem, and he realized his blasters were not going to do any good. Sophia considered firing a few arrows, but after seeing Henry's lasers do nothing, she realized her arrows were useless against them.

Grunt attempted to find a weak point to wrap himself around, thinking he could crush a part of the guardian with his strength, but he was not able to find one. Alcanore, on the other hand, tried to outwit his nemesis by allowing it to attack him. The guardian lifted his sword to attack and dropped it hard on the ground. Alcanore then ran up the giant villain and made his way to his enemy's neck. He then drove his weapon into it with all his might. But his spear only took a small chunk off the enemy's rocklike armor.

Nerd and Tom attempted to use their knowledge to find a weakness within one of the guards, but that got them nowhere at all. Nerd did, however, scan them and was relieved to see that the stone they were made of was not the same as the stone of the door. It was destructible, but they needed something with a little more power to destroy it.

Nerd solved one of his Rubik's cubes and threw it at the monster. It exploded on its chest, and a good amount of rock was blown out of it. But Nerd realized that they had accomplished nothing, as their enemies' armor was very thick, and he had only managed to create a giant hole inside of it.

One of the guardians took a swing at Henry Smith. Henry activated his left grappling hook and pulled himself up to the ceiling in the nick of time. He was up there, out of reach of his enemies, but his friends were still trapped down there, and he knew he needed to do something.

The guardian was distracted by Sophia and was about to make a move on her. Henry aimed his rocket launcher at his enemy's neck, hoping that something would happen to turn things in their favor. He pressed the launch button with his foot, hoped for the best, and watched as the rocket flew towards its target. The rocket made contact, and the stone around the monster's neck disintegrated.

There were robotic parts underneath that moved the neck around, revealing that the creatures were androids. Grunt took note of this instantly and darted towards the enemy Henry and Sophia were fighting. He slithered his way up and wrapped himself around the android's neck. He crushed it with his strength, and everyone was thrilled to see their enemy had fallen to the ground.

The guardian's body soon stopped moving.

Henry fired his last rocket at the guardian attacking Alcanore. He made contact again, and the guardian's armor exploded around its neck.

Alcanore waited for the guardian to attack and repeated the process of running up its own sword. He ran up his enemy's arm, over its shoulder, and thrashed his sword against the robotic neck. Again, the android's head fell to the ground, and it was no longer a threat to them.

Two more guardians remained, and Henry realized they were still in a predicament, since he was out of rockets.

"Sorry, guys!" Henry said as he lowered himself to the ground. "That's all I got."

Nerd realized that his Rubik's cube could indeed destroy the neck of the guardian they were facing. There was only one problem: he was down to his last one, and there were two guardians still left.

"Save it!" Sophia yelled as she ran up to them to join the battle. "I can handle this!"

The guardian attacked her, and like Alcanore had done before her, ran up her attacker's sword, but this time she waited. she stood perched on her enemy's shoulder, placed an arrow in her bow and shot it at the other guardian. The guardian realized it was attacked and turned to see Sophia on the other guardian's shoulder. He lifted his blade in a slanted formation and swung it at her. Sophia leapt off just before she was hit, and the blade made contact with the other guard's neck. Its stone armor disintegrated, and Howard and

Collins refocused their fire on the weakened guardian. Its neck exploded, and like the others, it fell to the ground.

There was only one guardian left, and Nerd wasted no time. He threw his last Rubik's cube at the guardian's neck, and after it exploded, Howard and Collins immediately opened fire yet again. The final guardian fell, and the crew were no longer threatened by the temple's defenses.

The eight survivors stood in complete shock at what they had just accomplished. True, they had depleted their heavy artillery to defeat them, but it was a glorious victory nonetheless.

Nerd heard sounds coming from the right, left, and behind him. The doors were opening, but he wasn't completely sure which one to take. He noticed that there were words on top of all three of them. He scanned them, hoping that he could get a clear idea of where to head next.

Surprisingly, things conveniently took a turn in their favor. The door in the back clearly said:

Tower of Legends.

While the other two checked out the left and right wing, Nerd breathed a sigh of relief upon realizing there would not be another challenge in this room.

"This way!" he said to his crew.

All eight left the room and made their way to the Tower of Legends. They were now in another hallway that led to a fourth door. It was relatively thin and cramped, but it didn't look like there were any nasty surprises waiting for them this time. The only thing they noticed was a box-shaped hole cut into the structure's granite walls. There was a breeze flowing through it, meaning that it was some sort of ancient air vent that the tribe had invented. This was not surprising, considering that this race's ingenuity was advanced.

Nerd scanned what was written above the door yet again, and his device was able to decipher it.

Maze

"Well!" Nerd said. "As long as we take it slow and keep an eye out for any traps, we should be golden."

"Knowing the way things have gone for us," Sophia predicted, "it will be flooded with things that want to kill us... but given what we just accomplished, I'm sure we can handle it."

Nerd pulled the lever, and the eight crew members made their way out, not paying any attention to the two glowing green eyes that were stalking them from the air vent behind.

CHAPTER 19
THE STALKER WITHIN

The away team pushed forward through the twists and turns of the maze and were thrilled to find that nothing had tried to kill them just yet. Navigating was difficult, and Nerd couldn't help that much, considering he was so bad at directions. But they kept navigating through it nonetheless, hoping that things would stay as peaceful as they were.

They came to an opening that looked like a small doorway inside the maze's wall. It was pitch black inside, and Nerd did not feel safe entering it. So, he ordered his crew to stand back as he passed by it to make sure it wasn't a trap.

He felt a draft as he walked by the entrance and realized it was part of the air vents that were scattered around the maze and building. Perhaps some sort of maintenance entrance? He wasn't sure, but at least it seemed harmless, and that was good news.

"Come on, guys," he said to his crew. "It's just a maintenance room."

Alcanore wasted no time. He strutted by and was safely across. Sophia followed right behind, and Grunt behind her. Tom and Mr. Howard soon followed, making Henry and Joe the last two. Henry walked by safely, but as he passed the entrance, he saw the image of a man wearing a black hooded trench coat, the same man that Sophia had nearly defeated outside.

Henry knew something was wrong, so he turned quickly to face Lieutenant Collins.

"Wait!" he said as he lifted his hand in front of him, urging Collins to stop, but it was too late. Collins was already making his way across the entrance. A green fear bomb dropped right into Collins' hands, a granite door slammed down over the doorway to the entrance, and before Collins knew what hit him, the bomb exploded, vaporizing him.

The explosion nearly engulfed Henry, who was only a few feet in front of Lieutenant Collins when the bomb exploded. He was driven ten feet back, to where the other crew were standing, and suffered several burns on his face and hands. Fortunately, he did not suffer any permanent damage.

Nerd's emotions had finally surfaced. He angrily ran to the room where Experiment-1 had killed his crew member. He began pounding the granite door with all his might.

"Coward!" he yelled. "You're terrified of your own prey. That's why you hide before you take your victims."

"Easy, human!" Alcanore yelled. "Don't encourage him to fight us; it will only make things worse."

"This isn't about strategy anymore, this is about life! These are human beings he is snuffing out. He has no right to take them as he pleases!"

Nerd began panting in frustration. He wasn't fond of Collins, but he didn't deserve to die; none of the people on this planet deserved to die. Still, although he had snapped at Alcanore, he knew he was right. The more Experiment-1 was challenged, the more danger his crew members would be in. He was not going to scare the killer away, nor would he be able to reason with him. All he could do was get his crew to the top of the temple tower before it was too late.

Nerd looked at Mr. Howard, who was shaken over what had just happened. He had watched both his crew members and friends die in front of him, and this caused Nerd's heart to ache. But he didn't have time to comfort the last member of the galactic squad. He knew Mr. Howard would be next, as Experiment-1 was blatantly going for the people he was least attached to first, in an attempt to weaken Nerd before he made a big move. This gave Nerd and advantage, knowing who his next victim would be.

"He's obviously in the building here with us," Nerd said to the other six. "We must keep our guard up at all times. The moment we let our guard down…that is when he will make his next move."

"Agreed," Henry replied. "I'm not one to let a little action bother me…but this, this is real. Still, I am a little surprised that he is able to navigate through the temple so easily. It's like he has been here before. Also, he was wearing his black trench coat and mask again. Didn't Sophia destroy that when she attacked him?"

"She did. But remember, all this started a year ago when he lured in the galactic crew. It is likely that he has had time to rig this place since he first got here and supply himself with whatever he needs. I'm sure he considered the possibility that his clothes and mask would be destroyed in combat. As twisted as Experiment-1 is, he is not dumb."

Nerd could sense his crew's anxiety rise after he had spoken. The fact that the killer was manipulating the temple was very disturbing to them. They felt like lab rats trapped in a maze—a maze rigged by a madman who wouldn't hesitate to kill—but they had been prepared for the possibility that he would make his way into the temple as well. So, they moved on, hoping they wouldn't have any more visits from the Lord of Sorrow.

The surviving seven had reached the end of the maze and were grateful to see that the next door simply had a lever to open it. This time the sign above translated to:

Speed

Nerd opened the door, desperately hoping that no nasty surprises awaited them on the other side.

They were relieved when the door opened into a long hallway, revealing no traps or life-threatening contraptions. The hallway went on for about 100 yards. Two doors could be seen at the end of it, and it looked like it would be an easy stroll to the next room. All seven members ran inside, and as soon as they did, the door closed behind them. The ceiling began to lower, and Nerd realized he should've practiced what he preached when he told his crew to stay alert at all times.

"Quick, everyone!" he yelled. "Run to the end of the hallway. The ceiling isn't lowering over there!"

All seven crew members ran as fast as they could through the long, narrow corridor. Henry was the first to arrive at the safe point, followed by Nerd, followed by Sophia, followed by Alcanore, followed by Grunt, followed by Mr. Howard. Tom, on the other hand, lost his footing and fell only a few feet from the exit. The ceiling was only six feet from crushing him, and Nerd acted fast. He ran back inside the hallway and picked up his friend, crouching, as the ceiling was now only five feet from the bottom. He threw Tom ahead of him before he had to get on the floor to crawl. Tom fell to safety, but Nerd only had his hands out, and the ceiling was only a foot and a half on top of him.

Alcanore pushed everyone out of the way, grabbed both of Nerd's hands, and with all his strength he pulled him out right before the ceiling could crush him.

Nerd was badly scraped up, but amazingly he had survived the ordeal.

"Thank you, my friend," Nerd said to Alcanore. "There was no way I would have survived that."

"Don't thank me," Alcanore responded. "You went out of your way to save Tom; it would have been dishonorable for a Renex warrior to have stood by and done nothing."

Nerd breathed a sigh of relief. Alcanore's attitude towards him was continuing to soften, even if he didn't want to admit it. And moving forward, Nerd wanted the big man to have his back, rather than looking for an excuse to stab it.

Nerd refocused and examined the room they were now in. There were now two doorways in front of them: one that went straight ahead and another that veered off to the left. Nerd scanned the words above both doors and noticed that the tower would be straight ahead.

The other room spelled out:

Temptation

Nerd did not know what to expect from this, but it sounded hostile, and he wanted no part in it. Mr. Howard, on the other hand, did not know about the translation, and he caught sight of Captain Baker and Joe Collins, who were waving to him from the middle of the room.

"Captain!" he shouted out. "Mr. Collins. You're both alive!"

Mr. Howard ran into the room, which got Nerd's attention. He was about to call out to Mr. Howard and urge him to stop, but Nerd hesitated when he saw Amelia, standing there by herself. She was calling out to him, begging him to come into the room.

"This isn't right," Nerd said. "Amelia has been dead for over a year." Nerd turned to the others. "Do any of you see a little girl in there with blonde pigtails?"

"No," Sophia said. "I see my parents…and they're apologizing to me, asking me to come home."

"That's impossible!" Tom said. "I see my crew, General Rice, and everyone that monster slaughtered."

"And I see a large golden statue of me!" Henry added. "It's got huge muscles, and he's locked in a front double bicep pose… It's the most beautiful thing I have ever seen!"

"The room spelled out 'temptation,'" Nerd said. "It's showing us whatever our heart desires!" Nerd focused his attention on Mr. Howard, who had almost reached the source of the hallucinations that the crew were experiencing. "No, Mr. Howard! It's an Obian crystal. They drive a person into seeing whatever their heart desires. You're walking into a trap; turn back now!"

But it was too late. Mr. Howard had already reached the room's center. He reached out to shake what he thought was his captain's hand, but as soon as he made contact, the door behind him closed, and he was cut off from the rest of the group.

Captain Baker and Lieutenant Collins vanished, and a large purple crystal took their place. But the disappointment that Mr. Howard felt was nothing compared to the fear that followed, as he noticed the skeletal remains of the former victims who had failed this test before him scattered around the floor.

Mr. Howard looked up; there were iron bars on the ceiling of the room, with an iron door in the center of it. He could hear the sound of stone doors opening above the caged celling, and at first, he could not figure out what was going on above him. But his questions were soon answered, as water began gushing in, filling the small room at an alarming rate.

The door was about 30 feet high, but it wouldn't take long for him to reach, as five feet of water had filled the room in under ten seconds. Mr. Howard was soon lifted off the ground and swam as he made his way closer to the door. Now 20 feet of water filled the room.

Mr. Howard knew that he had to keep himself in the middle of the room if he stood a chance, so he used all his strength to swim towards the room's center, but the harsh flow of the water kept pulling him away from it.

It wasn't long before Mr. Howard was able to reach the door handle. He grabbed the handle with his right hand, grabbed an iron bar with the other, and attempted to open the door.

No! The door is locked! Mr. Howard could not believe it. After he had fought so hard to stay alive. But he was not about to give up. He continued to wiggle the door handle in a hopeless attempt to make something happen. The water level soon rose above the barred ceiling, and Mr. Howard took one final breath of air before he was completely submerged. He continued to work on opening the iron door, but he was unable to.

Finally, after being trapped for 40 seconds, he realized that escape was impossible. He let go of the door handle and iron bar. He could feel his consciousness fade, as a deep sleep was about to overtake him. A deep sleep he would never wake up from.

Mr. Howard was finally at peace with the thought, but just as he was about to give up, the sight of the iron doorway opening caught his eye, and a dark hand made its way towards him. Mr. Howard reached out and grabbed the hand, and felt his body being pulled from his watery grave. As soon as he had emerged from the water, he felt himself being thrown over his savior's shoulder, and he was now being carried away from the room. The sound of water rushing could no longer be heard, meaning that the room was no longer filling up with water. *Just enough to drown the victims trapped on the other side of the iron cage,* he thought to himself.

As soon as Mr. Howard was out of the room, his savior dropped him on the hard ground and shut the Temptation room's door. Mr. Howard coughed and gagged, as he had been holding his breath for well over a minute. He then opened his eyes and looked at the man who had saved his life. The room was dark, and Mr. Howard could only make out the man's shadow. He didn't know who it was, nor did he care at this point.

The man took Mr. Howard's gun and began looking it over. He seemed interested in it but had made no hostile motions upon acquiring it. It really didn't matter anyway. The man had saved his life. He took a deep breath and did his best to speak to the man.

"Thank you," he said to the man in a raspy voice. Mr. Howard's gratitude suddenly turned to fear when the man's eyes started glowing with green energy. It was Experiment-1. "You!" he blurted in a harsher tone than before. "It's you! You're the one who killed my friends!"

"Yes," Experiment-1 agreed.

"And you enjoyed it!"

"No, I did not. But it had to be done."

Mr. Howard was very confused.

"Why should I trust you? Why should your words mean anything to me?"

"You shouldn't trust me. I am your enemy, and you are standing in my way."

"Then why did you go out of your way to save me?"

"It's a rule I have, a rule I keep close to my heart. I will never stand by and watch someone drown. It's a dreadful way to go, and my conscience won't allow it."

"I see. I guess there is a little light left in you after all…even if it's very faint."

"Yes…I suppose there is."

Not a moment after he spoke these words, he took Mr. Howard's gun, aimed it at his head, and shot him in the face.

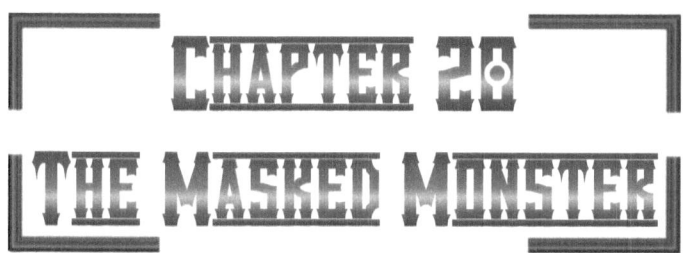

CHAPTER 20
THE MASKED MONSTER

Nerd was desperately trying to find a way to unlock the door where his companion had been taken, but there was nothing he could do. Mr. Howard was on his own, and given the severity of the tests that they had encountered before, he was likely in grave danger.

Tom analyzed the situation and concluded that there would be a better chance of finding Mr. Howard if they continued their journey.

"I'm sure the rooms connect eventually," Tom said. "Let's move on. Howard has probably left the room and journeyed through the temple by now."

Nerd was going to argue his point, as he knew danger lurked in the room Mr. Howard was locked in, but before he could get the words out, he was interrupted by another text from Experiment-1.

Unknown: **Worried about your friend, I see?**
Unknown: **Well, out of the goodness of my heart, I would like to inform you that you no longer have to worry about him.**
Unknown: **Because he's dead! I killed him!** 💀

Nerd's hands began to tremble. He punched the granite door and growled in both pain and anger.

"Easy, brave human!" Alcanore said. "If you break your hand, you will have a difficult time getting out of here in one piece."

"He killed Mr. Howard!" Nerd said.

"What? Wait…have the two of you been texting?"

"Yes, he can text anyone he wants. I don't know how he does it, but it's getting on my last nerve! I was hoping to slow him down or distract him. He is going to get angry if I don't reply…but I'm done. I won't be acknowledging him anymore."

Alcanore looked at Nerd with a renewed sense of paranoia. He was uncomfortable with the fact he and Experiment-1 were conversing. Especially considering the killer seemed to know where they were all the time. Still…if legend were true, it was in the stalker's nature to make a power-play like this. Alcanore chose not to call Nerd out on it, but he would keep a closer eye on him, as he was beforehand.

With the news of Mr. Howard's death, Nerd saw no reason to wait around. He signaled his team to follow him through the other door and led them to the next room.

The surviving six members made their way into the room. It contained a rotating stairway that made its way up the tall tower, curling around the perimeter. Sadly, it didn't have any rails to stop anyone from falling off the sides. It went so high that they couldn't see the top. Nerd was amazed, but he also felt sick at the idea of walking all the way up. Still, they had reached the tower of legends, meaning their journey was almost over.

Nerd began the long journey upstairs, and the others followed. Flight after flight they walked up, until the ground was no longer visible.

Forty minutes had passed when the top of the stairway came into view. This was good news, considering that they were exhausted from the long trek upwards. Everyone, with the exception of Grunt, was panting heavily. Sweat was rushing out of their pores like a stream, the stench getting stronger and stronger with every step they took. A few of the members had become lightheaded; Tom had gotten so disoriented from exhaustion that he nearly lost his footing and fell down the long drop. Thankfully, Henry was able to grab him before that happened.

"Whoever designed this should die!" Sophia snapped.

"Agreed!" Nerd responded, still panting from exhaustion.

The stairs were only four feet wide, meaning that there was not a whole lot of room for error. Each member went one by one. Nerd was in the front, Sophia was behind him, next was Henry, Tom after, then Alcanore, leaving Grunt in the back.

The journey was quiet and uneventful at first, but fear soon returned, as Experiment-1's voice could be heard from the top of the stairs.

"Well done," he said to them. "You're still alive…for now. I must admit, you did well surviving the challenges. If it wasn't for me, none of you would be dead right now. Well, maybe Mr. Howard, but he was too stupid to live anyway."

"Ignore him," Nerd commanded. "He is just trying to discourage us; don't let him get into your head."

"Very good, David! Again, you show me you have potential. Sadly, I plan on doing more than discouraging you. I plan on crushing one of your very souls! The big one, Alcanore, he has a weakness. Do you know what that is?"

"Keep going! Don't let him break you."

"He feels compassion for the weak, the frail, the ones who can't take care of themselves. Why do you think he is so protective of his little Grunt friend?"

"Nerd!" Alcanore shouted. "Make him shut up!"

"Do you know why he is so protective? It is because he failed to protect someone who was dear to him. Or rather, a small handful of someone's. He let them die, and it torments him day in and day out."

"Stay strong, Alcanore," Nerd said in a bold voice. "We are almost out of this."

"I couldn't even begin to imagine the pain he would feel if he were to fail yet again. If something were to happen to Grunt, I have to assume it would have irreversible effects. Maybe it would even drive him to lose his will to live…meaning that whoever could succeed in killing Grunt would succeed in breaking the most fearless of legends ever to step foot in your galaxy."

Nerd felt his heart accelerate. He knew Experiment-1 was about to strike again, and this time, he was going to hit hard.

"Don't do this!" Nerd yelled. "He has barely had a chance to live!"

"And that someone will be me!" Experiment-1 said, ignoring Nerd's response. "In exactly three minutes and 5.2 seconds, your Grunt friend will no longer be with you. This room has a security feature, in case any unwanted guest were to attempt to make it to the top of the tower—a feature that I am about to activate."

Suddenly, sounds could be heard from the bottom of the room, and the more they went on, the louder they got.

"Don't worry." Experiment-1 continued. "The impact should only hurt for a second. The fall, however, will be…most terrifying."

It wasn't long before the crew noticed where the sounds were coming from. Each stair in the stairway leading up to them was retracting within the wall, and it was moving towards their position at an alarming rate. They knew they were in danger and needed to move quickly.

"We've got to get moving now!" Nerd shouted.

The team made their way up flight after flight. The stairway continuing to retract behind them. They were already exhausted from the long walk up, but a life-or-death situation gave them renewed energy, at least enough to get to the top.

Nerd was relieved to see that they were on their final flight of stairs, and before the stairway could retract, Nerd had made it to the top. Sophia was right behind him, and so was Henry. Tom, however, had fallen behind, slowing Alcanore and Grunt down, as they didn't want to risk knocking him off by passing him.

Nerd panicked when he saw how close the retracting stairs were getting to them. He wasn't sure if all three of them would make it in time.

The three made it up to the top right as the final stairs were about to retract. Tom made it to the top just in the nick of time, but Alcanore and Grunt fell as the stairs were removed from underneath their feet.

Henry Smith walked over to the edge and fired his grappling hook at the two that were falling. He fired his other at the wall behind him, as he knew the weight alone would pull him down with them.

Alcanore saw the hook coming towards him. He grabbed Grunt with his right hand and the hook with his left. It worked, but the weight of the two creatures was too much for Henry's grappling hook. The impact broke both retractors, and he was not able to lift the two up automatically. Instead, Nerd, Sophia, and Tom all began to pull the two up themselves, slowly but surely.

Nerd panicked again when he saw that the cable supporting Alcanore and Grunt was starting to break. Each steel wire was snapping piece by piece.

Alcanore and Grunt both noticed this, and Grunt was no longer going to hide behind his primitive mask. He had done the math, and he knew that both could not survive.

"Cable break before Grunt and best friend make it up top," he said to Alcanore. "Grunt no let that happen. Alcanore live, Alcanore live life without Grunt!"

"We'll be fine!" Alcanore insisted.

Grunt, however, knew they couldn't possibly both get up in time. Weight needed to be shed. He reached over with his other hand and loosened Alcanore's grip.

"Bye bye!" He said.

"Grunt, no!" But it was too late. Grunt fell into the tower's abyss, vanishing into the darkness that covered the hard ground below. A loud thump that sounded very much like a balloon popping echoed up the walls…and then silence. It was over. Alcanore's best friend was now dead.

The three were able to get Alcanore to the top. The cord snapped right as they were lifting him up, proving Grunt's theory correct.

Nerd timed the events that had just taken place in his head. The moment of Grunt's death had taken precisely three minutes and 5.2 seconds on the dot. *That creep did it; he predicted all of this!*

The three hugged the old warrior as he growled and gritted his razor-sharp teeth.

"I don't care what you tell me, Nerd," he said. "If I see that honorless pig again, he's going to pay for what he's done!"

"I won't try to stop you," Nerd said. "Trust me…this time I understand. Do to him as you will."

"Nerd," Tom interrupted. "I know this is not the time…but I heard Experiment-1 call you David. Is that your real name?"

Nerd didn't even care at this point if he was discovered, but he couldn't risk discouraging Tom. He needed him to continue fighting. "I will explain everything once we are off this planet," Nerd said to him. "You have my word."

The surviving five looked at the final room. The door was left open and there were no words above it. After catching their breath, they continued onward to finish their journey.

The room had one sign with two arrows: one pointing to a stairway leading up, the other pointing to the left. Nerd's communicator deciphered that up was the very top of the tower, and the side entered the training room, where only the strongest warriors could train.

"We're almost there!" Nerd said. "Just keep your guard up. We know he's—"

The crystal lights began to flicker on and off, and it was difficult for them to see what was going on. Only a few seconds after this had started, Sophia's scream could be heard loud and clear. Nerd knew their enemy was now going to make a move on her. He tried to find his friend, but he was unable to comprehend what was going on with all the flashing lights.

After ten seconds of flashing, the crystal lights finally went back to normal. Sophia was gone, nowhere to be seen or heard. Henry, on the other hand, had fallen to the ground. He had a black eye, and it was evident that he and the killer had gotten into a quick fight.

"Oh, David…" Experiment-1's voice sang, echoing through the left side of the room. "You must be so terrified right now. Your perfect little angel is gone. Where did she go? What horrible things am I going to do to her now? She's at my mercy, David. I can do whatever I want to her, and the most wonderful part about it is…IT'S ALL YOUR FAULT!"

"If you have done anything to hurt her," Nerd ground out, "I swear—!"

"If you want to save your friend, meet me on the far end of the training room. If you choose to destroy the device before saving her, I swear she will be most disfigured by the time you find her..."

Henry staggered back to his feet, with Alcanore and Tom looking on in amazement.

"What happened?" Tom asked.

"I tried to save her," Henry responded. "I saw him enter the room, so I stood in between him and Sophia, but he was too quick. He decked me in the eye and threw me to the ground before I could even react."

"Wait! You were able to see him through all that? How?"

"One advantage of living such a wild life—I'm used to strobe lights. There isn't a nightclub around that doesn't have them. This was no different to me. I would brag...but I failed to protect Sophia, and now that creep has her!"

Henry was clearly shaken, but for Nerd, the incident hit home on a much more intense level. His face was red with anger, and for the first time, Henry saw a side of him that was eager to kill. However, despite his emotional state, Nerd considered the situation carefully. He knew it was pointless to take everyone with him, as Experiment-1 would only pick them off one by one as he had before. Instead, he decided to go with a different strategy, one that the Lord of Sorrow had most likely overlooked in his impulsive capture of Sophia.

"Henry, Tom, Alcanore," he said. "You three take out the device. I will take on Experiment-1 alone."

"No!" Alcanore protested. "You're no match for him! We will—"

"I've outsmarted him many times before. Trust me, I know what I'm doing. The fewer people around me that he has the chance to kill, the better. Besides, after I save Sophia, he will no doubt be on our tail. That will be your chance to fight him."

Alcanore didn't like it, but he knew Nerd was right. They needed to keep the strategy going if they were to win. Besides, as powerful as Experiment-1 was, he was still only one man. Splitting up would make them a harder target.

The three men agreed and began winding their way up the stairs. Nerd disappeared into the left corridor, which led into the expert training room. Henry and Alcanore were so far ahead that they didn't notice the absence of Tom, who had slipped away and decided to follow Nerd into the left corridor.

He can't take that thing on by himself. I must help him.
With that thought, Tom darted quickly through the corridor, ready to fight beside the legend he looked up to.

Remember, David. I will be here for you. My voice will always guide you through the torment and pain.

Nerd kept these words deep within his heart. He was uncertain as to how his plan was going to work. It was true, he always seemed to come out on top whenever he faced off with his biggest rival; but, his rival had gotten the better of him in the past as well, and each time, it cost him dearly.

The room was dark and dimly lit. Nerd knew his stalker had done this on purpose as a way of continuing to control his fear as he got deeper and deeper into his head. It was an unsettling feeling, but he had to admit, there was an adrenaline rush that went with it. He had been fighting the Lord of Sorrow for so long that a part of him enjoyed it, even when the stakes were high.

Nerd walked into a split in the room that went two ways. To his left was a long hallway. To his right was a narrow room that was covered in vines. A Venton plant was protruding from the ground. Presumably it was used for some sort of training exercise for the elite. They had a dirt square built into the floor so it could grow on this level. But something was different about this one. Its flower had been cut off. This made it very dangerous, as it was almost unnoticeable when mixed in with all the vines.

Nerd decided it was best to stay away from that room, so he chose to go left through the long hallway, hoping it would lead to his destination.

Nerd made his way through the hallway, which ended in another training room. There was a lever at the end of the hallway, which was used to activate another granite door that would seal a section of the room off if need be.

Nerd knew he was making his way closer to the center of the barracks, which gave him a considerable rush, knowing that he was making progress. The adrenaline rush was soon overpowered by sentiment as the sound of Amelia's music box filtered down the corridor.

Nerd continued down the hallway, getting closer and closer to the tower's center. Before he could get there, he noticed a light shining where the music was coming from. Sure enough, there was Amelia's music box, sitting in the pool of light, playing the same unsettling song that had followed him on this mission.

He walked over to it slowly, keeping his wits about him, knowing that it was probably a trap. But he was ready; he was ready to make his move.

"You remember," Experiment-1's voice said from behind him. "Don't you?" Nerd quickly turned around to face where the voice was coming from, but there was no one there. He then turned around to face the music box, but it was gone.

Nerd started to clench his fist. He knew Experiment-1 was toying with him, and his anger grew deeper and deeper by the second.

"Did you ever wonder why I was so obsessed with Amelia?" he asked.

"No," Nerd snarled in a bitter tone. "And I don't want to!"

"Of course you don't. Because everything must always be about you!"

"You're one to talk."

"You have no business judging me! If only you knew what I've been through, David! If only you knew what drove me to take these measures to save myself…maybe then you would understand."

"Maybe, but unlikely. I know why you killed people at Cosmic 5. Although I don't condone your actions, I did understand, because what we did to you was truly evil. But you, you have taken it to a level that even my mind can't comprehend! I may appear cold, but you know that's not the real me. You know I feel compassion. That's why I tried to help your people when I found out what Crimson was doing to them. That's why I tried to help you! Don't you understand? I never wanted to fight you. I was put in a situation where I had to act. You were going to kill my friend.

I saw a problem, and I took care of it...and as a result, I opposed you."

"Then the way I see it, you and I are no different. I too was put in a situation, and I handled it...I handled it with vengeance!"

"You and I are nothing alike! Now give me back my friend. Your beef is with me, so take it out on me! You have no reason to hurt her."

"Oh, don't worry, David. I want you to see her. Go to the room to your right, then into the hallway to the left. It will take you to the center of the advanced training complex. Don't disappoint me, David. I've been waiting a long time to see you face-to-face again...or more accurately, mask to mask."

Nerd followed Experiment-1's directions and headed to the center of the training facility. Sure enough, there was Sophia, alive and well. She was chained to a training dummy. Her mouth was muzzled the same way as when the two had first met. She was naturally scared, but her eyes did not look as terrified as last time. She still had fight in her; his enemy was not able to break her.

Nerd wanted to run up and free her instantly, but he walked over to her cautiously, knowing that it was a trap.

Nerd could hear footsteps behind him. He quickly turned around and saw Tom standing by the entrance.

"Oh, thank goodness!" Tom said. "You're both alive. I was worried."

"Tom!" Nerd shouted. "Leave the room immediately! He's—"

But it was too late. The Lord of Sorrow was behind him. He drove a vaccine shot into Tom's neck, a vaccine that was filled with galactic plague.

"Nerd!" Tom said as his brain began to die. "It was an honor to…"

"You didn't have to die," Experiment-1 said as Tom's body began to mutate in front of Nerd and Sophia. "Had you simply done as I instructed, I would've honored my agreement to let you leave this world. A mind like yours deserved to live! But you just had to go and mess it up by allying yourself with him, and for that…you're going to pay!"

Experiment-1 removed his vaccine, and Tom fell to the ground, beyond help.

"No!" Nerd said as he charged at Experiment-1. "You have taken this way too far!"

Nerd took a swing at Experiment-1, but the Lord of Sorrow was easily able to dodge it. After dodging several punches, he drew his sword and slashed it across Nerd's chest. Nerd was cut and burned from his left shoulder to the right side of his stomach. He screamed in pain, and Nerd was horrified by the smell of his own burning flesh flooding through his nostrils. The blow drove Nerd to tears, but thankfully only the tip of the sword hit, meaning the blow wasn't fatal.

Experiment-1 then drove the sword into Nerd's left leg. He pulled it out and instantly went for his right arm. Again, he stuck it through Nerd's tricep.

Nerd whipped out a stimulant shot and injected himself with it. He knew it wouldn't take away all his pain, but the wounds in his arm and leg were serious and Nerd might have to amputate them both if he didn't boost his immune system in time.

In a desperate attempt to save himself, Nerd charged at his attacker with a full-strength punch. Experiment-1 dodged his punch, grabbed his fist in midair with his right hand, dragging Nerd over to one of the granite walls, and placing his left hand on the back of Nerds head, he drove the other man's forehead into the granite with full force. Once, twice, three times he smashed Nerd's head into the granite wall. Nerd fell to the ground, his vision blurry from the impact he had taken. He was still awake able to observe what was going on.

He saw the music box that used to belong to his old friend fall from Experiment-1's coat. Experiment-1 seemed to panic for a moment and lost focus on what he was doing. He quickly picked it back up and put it in the left pocket of his trench coat. For whatever reason, he was very protective of it, and Nerd couldn't figure out why. It didn't matter at this moment because he was currently unable to fight Experiment-1. He was too disoriented and weak to outwit him or outsmart him, let alone outlast him.

"So, David," Experiment 1 said. "It looks like I came out on top this time. But I must say, I'm a little confused. Where are the rest of your…"

Suddenly Experiment-1 realized what was happening. He checked the screen built into his left gauntlet and was furious when he saw that the other two had made it to the top of the tower.

"You!" he said in a harsh voice. "You worthless parasite! Now, because of your ignorance, your friend is going to die screaming!"

He walked over to Sophia and pulled out a vaccine. He was about to inject it into her but stopped for a brief moment and turned around to look at Nerd, thoughtfully looking at the syringe.

"I've been working on a new vaccine," he continued. "I was so hoping it would help me to discover what I've been looking for. But so far, every test subject has rejected the vaccine. Pressure slowly starts building up within them. Their intestines start to burst, and then right before they die, their insides start to dissolve. It is a long and gruesome death, and so far, no one's been able to survive it. But I've altered a few things, and perhaps this time it will do what I intended…but trust me, it will most likely kill her like it did the others. Sophia is going to die, and you will have to live the rest of your life knowing that it could've been prevented. All you had to do was give me what I wanted."

Nerd watched in horror as Experiment-1 waved the vaccine in front of Sophia. Insane laughter started falling from his mouth. He was enjoying this. He was eager to make Nerd pay for resisting him.

Sophia was terrified, but not in the same way that she was back when the two had first met. She was alone back then, trapped in a room with a psychopath who wanted to cut her open. This time, there was someone in the room with her who actually wanted her alive…and somehow this made it worse. She didn't know what Nerd was going to do without her. She still wanted to be there for him just as the Observer had asked of her, but there was nothing more she could do, not like this. Their enemy had won; she was going to lose her life, and Nerd was going to be traumatized beyond any hope of recovery.

Nerd knew this as well and had finally given up. He felt reality flee from him. His mind began to enter a state where only the deepest of thinking could exist. Only the deepest part of him could exist. The core…

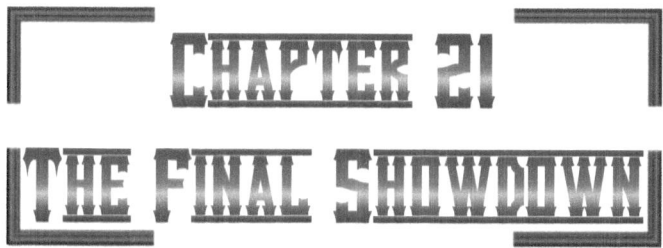

CHAPTER 21
THE FINAL SHOWDOWN

Henry and Alcanore had finally made their way to the top. The room was massive; its ceiling was at least ten stories above them. But despite its extraordinary size, the room was surprisingly well lit. There was a giant mural painted on the walls that surrounded them, a mural that caught both men's attention.

The painting depicted a horrifying scene. Bodies were piled up by the thousands, and the few people who were alive were clearly screaming, terrified for their lives. Behind each living person was a flow of red energy. At the very tip of each flow, there was a three-fingered claw, crooked in a position that looked as if it was about to snatch the life out of every person crying for help. The flows of energy snaked around the room until they met in the very center, located in the back. The energy, the destruction, the chaos, was all coming from the cybernetic grip of one being; or more accurately, a machine.

The antagonist depicted at the center of the mural was a large Invader unit, a mechanical life form known for its unforgiving nature towards organic life. But this one was different; he was a specific model that neither of them had ever seen before. His style was vintage; he looked like a robot straight out of a 1940s Earth sci-fi film. The lower part of his head was very boxy, and the top of his skull was the shape of a dome. There were three antennas on top: two that started on the right and left side of his face and one that was grounded in the very top center point of his head. All three stretched about a foot upwards, giving him the illusion of wearing a large crown. His face was designed in the form of a fearsome scowl that seemed to be biting down on the rage that flowed from his fingertips, consuming the innocent life that surrounded him. His eyes were droopy, and like his mouth, red energy seemed to radiate from them. Both of his hands were lifted, and all the energy that seemed to be sucking the life out of the planet's inhabitants was flowing from the fingertips of his two cybernetic hands. They were his puppets, attached to strings of death.

Above the Invader unit was his name, written in the language of the Obian people. Henry translated it with his communicator, and it simply came up:

Invader

"Tell us something we don't know," Henry said. "Anyone who has explored the galaxy knows that is an Invader unit."

"I don't think that's just any Invader unit," Alcanore replied. "It's *the* Invader unit, the first of all the Invaders. Henry, I think this is what Experiment-1 is after."

"What? What do you mean by *the* Invader unit?"

"I'm sure most of you humans don't follow our galaxy's history like we of the Renex empire, but there was a time when the Invaders used to be the dominant race. It was all thanks to one…him, the first Invader to ever set foot in the galaxy. I could spend hours telling his tale, but right now we don't have time. We need to take out that device before Experiment-1 comes back!"

Henry nodded his head, but not before taking a panoramic picture of the scene with his communicator, which irritated Alcanore greatly.

The device was located in the very center of the giant mural, just under the Invader's feet. It was about three stories tall, circular, and was spinning around in a clockwise formation.

Alcanore turned to Henry and smiled as best as his features would allow him.

"You shoot at the top!" he said to Henry. "I will attack the bottom, and for goodness' sake don't hit me!"

"Hey, hey, I'm Henry Smith," Henry replied as Alcanore darted for the machine. "I make no promises."

Henry opened fire on the top of the machine, Alcanore attacked the bottom, and both felt a great sense of pride when the device went up in flames.

"We have defeated our enemy!" Alcanore said. "Quick, do you know someone to call that can get us off this planet?"

Henry Smith gave an arrogant smirk upon hearing his friend's question. He reached into his pocket and pulled out his communicator.

"I know just the people that can help us," he said as he made a space call.

"David," Amelia asked. "Why are you always so…sad?"

David could not believe his eyes. He was in a white room that glowed so bright that it almost blinded him. Everything was quiet, disturbingly quiet. Yet, at the same time, it felt warm, cheery, and comfortable. David looked up to see the vibrant blue eyes of a ten-year-old girl looking back at him. She was smiling, thrilled to see him. He never understood why she cared about him so much, but it didn't matter. All that mattered was…no, this was all wrong. She was dead. This was all a fantasy made up by his mind. He was about to watch his friend die, and he felt so helpless that his mind went to a place where he wouldn't have to suffer. Insanity, the perfect insanity.

David walked away from Amelia and sat down with his back turned to her. But Amelia followed him and sat next to him.

"What's wrong?" she asked

"You're not real," he said flatly. "I'm at the end of my rope, and my mind is doing this to me to protect itself. You are not really here, you're…"

David began to tear up. This was all so frustrating to him. He had fought so hard to do the right thing, and in the end, he still lost everything. Just as he always lost everything.

Amelia reached out to grab his hands.

"I will always be a part of you, David," she said to him. "Is that not what you promised me?"

"Yes…it is…" David replied.

"Then trust me, David. You kept part of me alive in you, and right now you need that part to help you through this. What's wrong? Why are you crying? Why are you so sad? It makes me feel sad."

"Experiment-1 is going to kill Sophia, a girl I care very much about, and there's nothing I can do to stop him."

"That big fat meanie that used to chase me? David, you have beaten him before."

"But he always comes back, and he always kills when he does. How many innocent people must die because of him, and why does he do it? For whose sake? It's wrong, it's sick, and it makes me feel helpless, because he always finds a way to get into my head. I have tried so hard to keep him out, but he always finds a way back in! Amelia…I can't beat him."

"Maybe you need to think more like him."

"What do you mean by that? That sounds like a horrible idea."

"I don't mean you should do the things that he does, but you've been doing things your own way this entire time. You're so scared that he's going to get inside your head. You've done everything to keep him out. Have you thought about what makes him scared? What makes him angry?

"I don't understand."

"You forget, David; behind the mask of that monster is just another man. A man who is mean, yes! But he is still just a man."

Something clicked in Nerd's head. He now knew what Amelia was trying to tell him.

"I need to get inside his head. I need to attack his insecurities…but then what? He's still invincible. What good will attacking his sanity do if I can't defeat him physically?"

"Please look back on your memories. I will help you with the first thing. Experiment-1 is not invincible; he can still die if all the DNA molecules in his body are destroyed, correct?"

"Correct."

"Now I want you to think back to what you have seen on this journey."

Nerd thought back to all the dangers they had faced…but one stood out among the rest.

"The Venton plant. I told Collins that it devours every cell instantly."

"Bingo! And what is hiding across the long hallway at the top of the tower that you are in?"

"A Venton, and its flower has been severed, making it harder to spot… But he's still too observant; he will know."

"Think, David. What is Experiment-1's only weakness?"

"His own obsessive mind, I suppose. When he's fixated on something, he only sees that objective, and he will walk through anyone or anything to get to it. I need to make myself his next objective!"

Amelia smiled at Nerd. She clapped her hands in delight.

"Good job, David! Now go, save your friend, and make that mean old man go away!"

Suddenly, reality returned to Nerd. His mind had solved the problem, but he needed to act fast.

Experiment-1 had raised the vaccine needle and was about to drive it into Sophia's neck. He abruptly stopped when he felt a hand reach into his left coat pocket and whirled around to see Nerd with the music box in hand.

"You!" Experiment-1 yelled. "If you think what I'm doing to her now is torture, your mind can't possibly comprehend what I'm going to do to her next! Give that back to me now, or I swear your little human friend will know the meaning of true pain!"

"Nope!" Nerd replied. "Not feeling it."

Experiment-1 drew his sword and slowly made his way towards Nerd.

"You'll be drowning in a sea of red by the time I am through with you!" He said as the black, soulless eye sockets of his mask lit up with green radiation.

"You will have to catch me first!" Nerd responded in a very goofy voice. He ran out of the room and was thrilled to hear his enemy close behind him. He ran through the rooms and hallways until he found the long hallway that led to the room with the Venton. He could hear Experiment-1 closing in and knew he needed to buy some time, so he grabbed the lever that was used to lock the center level and pulled it downwards. The door quickly began to close, and Nerd was just able to barrel roll his way in before the door completely sealed off the room. He smiled when he heard the sound of Experiment-1 crashing into the large granite door that was separating them. The monster was definitely fixated on him, and this was causing his judgment to fade. David knew this only bought him a few seconds, however, and he ran down the long hallway as fast as he could until he came to the room with the Venton plant. He could hear the granite door opening behind him. Acting quickly, he grabbed the vines and pulled himself over the plant and into the very back of the room.

As soon as he turned to face the entrance, he jumped at the sight of Experiment-1 waiting in the doorway. Green flames danced in his eyes, burning with such power Nerd could feel the heat of them licking his pale skin. The monster was panting in rage, and his grip on his sword was weakening. It was evident that he was trembling, and for the first time since they had become enemies, Experiment-1 truly looked scared, but this did not make him defenseless; if anything, it only fueled his anger, making him more of a threat than ever. This became evident as soon as the silence was broken by his harsh, angry voice.

"I need that, David!" Experiment-1 said. "Do you really think that you're the only one who lost someone special? The only one who had someone important taken away? That music box is the only glimmer of light I have left, and now I'm going to take it from your disfigured corpse!"

He took his sword and cut through the vines and began inching his way closer to his prey. Nerd looked down and noticed the Venton was only a foot away from him, meaning that Experiment-1 would have to get close if this was to work.

Experiment-1 took another swing, clearing the vines and closing in on Nerd's position. He was now only a few feet away and was ready to make his finishing move.

"You started your life as an abused child," he said as he cleared another row of vines. "You had no friends, no loved ones, and you lived most of your life alone." Experiment-1 took another swing, clearing the final section of vines that separated the two. His eyes grew even brighter. He was ready to end things, and this excited him greatly. "And now, you will die…alone…"

Experiment-1 lifted his sword, moved forward until he was about a foot in front of Nerd, and thrust it at the defenseless human in front of him, but as soon as the blade was about to pierce Nerd's skin, the leaves of the Venton plant snapped shut and completely engulfed him. Experiment-1 screamed as the plant latched closed. He was devoured and dissolved instantly.

The leaves of the plant relaxed into their former position only seconds later, and Experiment-1 was nowhere to be seen. Nothing had survived; not even a strand of hair made it through the plant's feast.

Nerd took a moment to process what had happened, while his sight adjusted to the sudden absence of the blinding light of Experiment-1's glowing eyes. His rival and greatest enemy was now dead. He would never try to hurt anyone he cared about again. But in doing so, he knew he would never solve the greatest mystery in his life, and that was the identity of the man behind the mask of the monster.

But that wasn't the worst of it. He could feel the adrenaline and dopamine flowing through his brain. *No! Not now, I DON'T WANT TO DEAL WITH THIS NOW!* He tried to fight it, but it was too late. His mind craved the chemicals that were flowing through it, and he thirsted for more!

His surroundings began to darken as they did before. His heart thudded violently, beating at an alarming rate. His emotions powered down, while his brain began to calculate his next move. *I NEED MORE!* he thought to himself. *I NEED*— Nerd felt guilt shoot through him as the image of Sophia's face filled his mind. *No*...*No. I can't become this. I can't do this to her. I can't do this to anyone in my crew. They look up to me, they care about me, they...* Nerd's lust to kill began to ebb. Something was different than last time. He had a tool he didn't have before. He...actually cared about someone, and somehow, that was allowing his conscience to fight back against his impulses, even at a time when his obsessive mind wanted to take control. He was a doctor, not a soldier, and that was a line he refused to cross.

"Sophia," he said. "I need to free Sophia!" He placed the music box in one of his lab coat pockets, jumped over the plant that had just consumed his enemy, and made his way back to the room that Sophia was trapped in. He could feel the effects of his lust for taking lives wearing off with every step that echoed through the narrow hallways of the barracks, as if that morbid obsession was being washed away, cleansed from the deepest parts of him.

After a minute of running, Nerd reached the room he was looking for and caught sight of Sophia. He swiftly made his way to her, unhinged her restraints, and this time he remembered to remove the muzzle that was around her mouth. She instantly gave him a hug, and Nerd didn't fight it, as he had been worried sick over her safety for the last two days.

"I thought you were finished!" She said to Nerd.

"For a second," he said to Sophia, "I thought you were too. But it's okay now. He won't be hurting us ever again. He's gone...this time for good."

Sophia was stunned. She could not believe that Nerd had just defeated the number one man on the Deep Cosmos most wanted list. A man that was very close to being invincible. But again, she knew that he never lied. So, it had to be true. Nerd was a true force to be reckoned with.

She gazed deeply into Nerd's blue eyes, expecting to see the high that he had mentioned in his diary...but it wasn't there, for the lust had now completely faded. The only thing she could see in his eyes was the concern that he had for her, and the joy of knowing that she was okay and still a part of his life.

She gave him a punch on the shoulder and then hugged him again.

"I'm so proud of you, David," she said. "I knew you had it in you. Thank you...for everything."

Sophia didn't notice that her words had brought Nerd to tears. Bittersweet tears, because they were the same words that Amelia had spoken to him long ago...

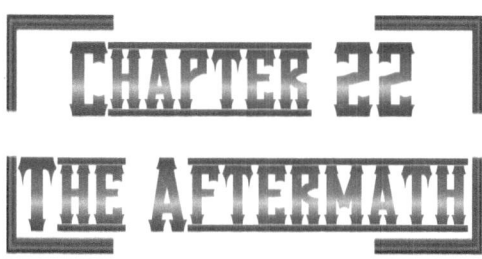

CHAPTER 22
THE AFTERMATH

Earth date: February 24th, 2010
Time: 600
Location: The freighter *Thug Life*

Nerd was rather irritated with his friend Henry Smith, who had not chosen particularly wisely when he called for help. The surviving four members were now on a thug's freighter, and the conditions were quite intense.

"Really, Henry?" Nerd said to him. "Out of all the people you could've called, you picked them?"

"Hey, hey, I'm Henry Smith!" Henry replied. "If you wanted to pick who gave us a ride off Obian, then you should have made the call yourself! But these are my kind of people.

I actually used to be in their gang long ago. But don't worry, that ship has long sailed."

Nerd did not feel relieved. The group members were constantly getting into fights. The music was screeching in Nerd's sensitive ears. The place smelled like a brand of illegal substance that Nerd wanted nothing to do with, and a few of them had already attempted to beat Nerd up, though he was saved by Smith each time.

The smells, textures, sounds, and sights just didn't sit well with him at all. Still, he had gotten his two closest crew members home safe, and even managed to save one member of the other crew. Right now, that was all that mattered.

Nerd noticed one of the thugs hitting on Sophia. She was clearly very uncomfortable, but he still wouldn't leave her alone.

"Yo, Henry," Nerd said in his best attempt at a gangster accent, which he failed at miserably. "I gotta go take care of something."

"Be my guest, bruh!" Henry responded. "Just watch yo' back. These guys can get a little carried away at times."

Nerd made his way over to Sophia and interrupted what was going on.

"Hey, girl!" He said to her. "I need to talk to you. Could we chat for a moment?"

"Yes!" Sophia said gratefully. She grabbed his hand, and the two darted away from the creepy thug and walked over to one of the freighter's large windows.

"Oh, my goodness!" Sophia said. "Thank you so much! I kept telling him I wasn't interested, but he wouldn't stop hitting on me!"

"Welcome to the thug life, I guess," Nerd joked. "But of course! I may be a bit of a weakling, but I will always look after my friends. Always!"

Sophia smiled. She then looked out the giant window and was mesmerized by the blue energy of hyperspace flowing outside.

"Was it everything you wanted?" Nerd asked.

"And more," Sophia replied.

"Then you're still interested in staying with us for a bit longer?"

Sophia punched Nerd in the shoulder at his response.

"Of course I am, you big goober! A little psychotic danger and nearly being murdered by an insane serial killer isn't going to scare me away. You're stuck with me!"

"Good! Then I look forward to many more adventures and near-death situations together."

Sophia chuckled at Nerd's response. The suspense was high on the last mission, and it would continue to be so as they moved forward, but she was eager to face these challenges and knew that somehow, in the end, they would pull through. She smiled and went back to gazing at the hyperspace energy.

"I wouldn't have it any other way!" She replied with confidence.

The moment was interrupted by Henry Smith, who had discovered an article on his communicator he needed to share. He ran towards David and Sophia excitedly and stuck the screen of his communicator right in front of David's face.

"Look, bruh!" he said. "We made the headlines!"

Nerd pushed the communicator screen away to a distance where he could read it. It was the front page of the *Galactic*

Times, and to his surprise, the news was actually good for once.

"'Deep Cosmos agent Nerd and his band of freedom fighters execute justice on the insane killer known as Experiment-1, creator of the galactic plague virus. Nerd's reputation continues to grow in a positive light, as he has once again saves the galaxy from a life-threatening epidemic. We at the *Galactic Times* would like to thank this hero and his team for risking their lives to put an end to this madman's reign of terror! Our hearts go out to the lives who were lost, who fought bravely to overcome this madness. Their funeral services will be held at the center of station 1529, Earth date March 1st, 2010.

"'The galaxy can sleep soundly tonight, knowing that Experiment-1 will never be able to harm the innocent again. May Deep Cosmos continue to prosper and give our galaxy the hope that it so desperately needs right now.'"

"How about that, bro!" Henry crowed. "We are heroes now! I think our exposure has gone up since this mission."

"Indeed, it has," Nerd agreed. "Still…what's this about me slaying Experiment-1? That's not quite how it happened."

"This is the media, bro. They need to sell their story, and the fact that he was killed by a plant doesn't quite cut it. Just be thankful they got the other facts right."

"Yeah, I can't argue with that. Thanks for sharing. It's nice that we gave the galaxy hope." Nerd went back to gazing at the hyperspace energy outside the ship. "I did it, Aiden," he murmured quietly to himself. "I continued your legacy."

Both David and Sophia continued to gaze outside. Henry could sense the gears turning in their heads, and he didn't like it one bit.

"You guys need to stop getting lost in thought," he said to them. "It's bad for ya."

"Honestly, this is the first time I've had a chance to process what's happened," Nerd admitted. "It's amazing… but horrible at the same time."

"True, a lot of good lives were lost. Still, I feel you spend a little too much time in your head."

Nerd did not answer. He noticed Alcanore sitting in a corner by himself, not engaging in conversation with anyone. Henry noticed as well and decided to change the subject.

"You gonna talk to him, bro?" He asked.

"I need to," Nerd responded. "Even if he's not interested, he at least deserves to have that lifeline."

"There ya go! Give it a shot, man; he needs it right now."

Nerd nodded his head in agreement and then made his way up to Alcanore. His heart was pounding in his chest, as he didn't really know what to say, but he walked over to him anyway, hoping his social awkwardness would not get the better of him.

"Hey, dude," Nerd said nervously. "Mind if I take a seat?"

Alcanore did not answer but signaled Nerd to sit next to him. Nerd did so, his right leg moving up and down as it always did when he felt nervous.

"I just wanted to check up on you," Nerd started. "How is Alcanore?"

Alcanore let out a sigh.

"It's rough," he said. "I lost everyone back there, including my best friend…"

"I know. It's terrible. I'm sorry about Grunt. He died most bravely…but it still hurts."

"My people will sing songs about him. This I swear. Still, it could've been avoided. Experiment-1 didn't need to take it as far as he did."

"None of it had to happen. It just sickens me. It sickens me that someone would take such an innocent life. But that's the thing about Experiment-1. I may have defeated him, but even dead, he's always going to drive me out of my mind. I still don't know who the man was behind that mask. I still don't know why he killed so many people. He claimed he did it for a reason, but what reason could he have to commit genocide on such an unprecedented scale? I just don't know. I guess I'll never know. He's right—he is the one mystery in this universe that I was never able to solve. I defeated him, but I could never solve him, and I never will."

Alcanore turned his head and looked Nerd dead in the eye. "Tell me how he died!"

"I have to be honest, it was quick and painless. He was eaten by a Venton plant. It was the only thing I could think of. I know you wanted to go after him yourself, but he was going to hurt Sophia, and I reacted in a way that I usually don't."

"You survived. You were put in an unwinnable situation, yet you still found a way to get you and your friend home safe. I don't hold that against you. You did what you had to do…and what a glorious victory it was! The galaxy will fear you now."

"Honestly, I hope I never have to do anything like that again. I'm not a killer. I'm a doctor. I will always be a doctor, because I have to be…because after Experiment-1 was dead,

I felt something that still upsets me when I think of it, and I don't want to ever feel that way again!"

"Remorse?"

"Pleasure, at a level that's inhuman. If I feed it, I know I'm going to end up just like him, and that is something I cannot afford to do. Besides, as soon as the rush died, I only felt emptier than before. I've spent my life trying to save people, and yesterday I was forced to kill one, a living human being…and as wicked as he was, no rush is ever going to cover up the mental damage I have suffered from it. I don't want this! It's not who I want to be."

Alcanore was stunned at Nerd's response. It was evident that he wasn't kidding. He was speaking in a way that revealed what was in his heart. It was not the Renex way to feel compassion for the enemy, but it seemed like Nerd did. Even when it was pleasurable, he couldn't bear the thought that he had hurt one of the worst men in the galaxy. Although his people may have been misguided to consider that a weakness, it proved his innocence. He could not have committed the crime he was accused of. He just didn't have it in him. Which made his next decision a lot easier.

"Nerd," he said hesitantly, "I would like to join your—"

"Yes!" Nerd interrupted.

"What?"

"You may join my crew! You'll get paid the standard salary, but I'll make sure your first check includes a bonus, given the fact that we've got a HUGE paycheck coming in from Deep Cosmos! Taking down their most wanted man really pays well."

Alcanore laughed at Nerd's response. He was definitely an odd person, even by his race's standards, but he could tell

Nerd wanted to be his friend in the worst way, which meant a lot right now, considering he no longer had any.

Nerd stood up and asked Alcanore to join them. Alcanore did so, and the four friends stood together side by side. The ship exited hyperspace, and the stars came into view.

Henry gave a smirk and pushed himself to make a sentimental statement.

"They are beautiful," Henry said, regarding the stars. "I can't argue with that."

"And as soon as my ship is repaired," Nerd added, "we're going to explore them! One by one."

"Ha! Like that's going to happen. Still, I'm up to visit a few more. Where to next, Commander?"

Nerd looked at a black void where the stars were not visible. It was barren and unexplored. He pointed to it and informed his crew of their next destination.

Their journey had ended, but a new one would soon begin; a journey where new friends and enemies would be made. Where memories would be written and adventure would be lived. Until time itself came to its close, they would be diving into the very heart of the unknown. Plummeting into the darkest corners of space. Striving to unravel the greatest mysteries of the Deep Cosmos.

ACKNOWLEDGMENTS

Thank you so much for joining me on this wild and twisted adventure! I hope you enjoyed your reading experience as much as I enjoyed writing it. As you can probably tell, there were many questions left unanswered. This was intentional, as this book is indeed part of a series, and I plan to include puzzle pieces within each book. This will include the motives—and perhaps, one day, the identity—of Experiment-1. Please stay tuned for the next installment of the *Deep Cosmos* series!

To those who may be suffering from mental illness or depression, please know that I understand the battle all too well. I have proceeded with caution in the way this sensitive topic has been portrayed in my books, and I hope that the message that I intended to send came through in my writing, 'Never give up, no matter how dark, twisted, or hopeless your situation may seem.' Because no matter how low you may feel, know that you are worth fighting for, and you are capable of over-coming whatever it is you may be fighting deep inside. Just as the Characters in my story overcame there's over time. However, if anything I wrote pushes my readers to think more destructively, to self-harm or feel that life is no longer worth living, please feel free to reach out to me, or someone that you love and trust. If it is brought to my attention that something in my books is dangerous to my readers, it could very well affect and change the way I approach mental illness in my future writings.

With all that being said, thank you so much for reading, and staying strong until the very end. You have sur-vived…the Deep Cosmos.

This novel would not exist without the actions of the following.

My editor, Emily Nemchick. She is a professional copyeditor who was kind enough to fix my manuscript for me. She is detailed, easy to work with, and very affordable. Check out her work at emilynemchickediting.com

My dear friend E. A. Catinia, for modeling for Sophia and proofreading my manuscript. She is a talented artist, writer, and proofreader. Please check out her Instagram page @baronessamenagerieandart

About the author

Project Kyle is a self-published author from New England known for his obsession with psychology, mystery, and sci-Fi. He started his author journey as a Wattpad author, but after taking 1st place in three writing contests, and 2nd in two, Kyle branched out into the publishing world. His mission? To keep readers guessing while providing them with an adventurous and unique tale they won't find anywhere else.

An interview with Project Kyle

1. What drew you to the world of writing?

I have always had story ideas sense I was a kid, but I decided I wanted to write when I was 18. I started out with a book called "The forgotten galaxy." Which was a sci-fi story about a late teenager who discovered an ancient gateway to a world known as Zecarah. The planet was post-apocalyptic, and he had to solve what had happened to this once thriving world. Sadly, I was a perfectionist back then, so I never got any further than four chapters.

2. Do you think you'll finish the story?

Possibly, it needs a good rewrite, but I may get back into it as it takes place in the same universe as Deep Cosmos.

3. You said you were interested in writing since you were young. Did you have a favorite author or genre to read?

At that time, I was more into kids' books like Dr. Seuss. When I became a young teen, I enjoyed novella additions of H.G. Wells and Jules Vern. I've always had a thing for Sci-Fi, but my liking to it grew as I got older.

4. I know you were writing on Wattpad for a while. Do you plan to continue to write on their website?

Absolutely! It's a great place to get feedback from beta readers. I will definitely be posting new work on their site.

5. Nice! Now, I know you've struggled with grammar and spelling, you're pretty open about it; how have you been able to work past that?

It's been a rough challenge to overcome, and I still have a long way to go. I think getting tips and feedback from Whattpad helped me out the most. Also reading and getting feedback from my editor and proofreader that I have taken to heart moving forward. It's helped me to get better, but I still will always have my books professionally edited first.

6. What's your favorite part of writing?

Creating worlds, characters, and ideas that haven't been written yet. I've always enjoyed designing my own universe, and I don't think that is a passion that's going to die anytime soon.

7. Do you have a character in your story who you consider to be your favorite?

I would have to go with the lead protagonist, David Bell. Me and him could definitely be brothers, though he is a lot more intelligent, and a little more socially awkward than myself. We have a lot of the same battles, including our challenges with depression, and autism. I also like how nonchalant he is about standing up to some of the most horrifying situations without breaking a sweat. He is the glue that holds the story together, Voice of reason mixed in with all the insanity so to speak...even though he's not 100% sane himself.

8. How would you say he's grown from the beginning of the novel to the end?

The interested thing about David's character is, I approached character progression very differently with him. Rather than him growing, I have the reader cut deeper and deeper into his mind. To the point where the character you know at the end is a different character that you thought you knew at the beginning. Though he does progress in some ways, such as learning to express his love for his crew and learning to control his lust to kill, the majority of his progression comes from him being pushed past his braking point, giving readers insight into the real him.

9. That's interesting. What made you decide to do that?

I wanted David's character to be mysterious and in-depth. I felt that it fit the Deep Cosmos nature of having a protagonist that the reader would love, but not fully trust. Someone that has good intentions but could turn on his friends at any given point. Although I chose for the goodness to win out in the end of this book, I think it adds a little bit to the eeriness to have that kind of lead, even though he appears to be completely goofy and harmless in the beginning.

10.What would you say is the greatest challenge David has had to overcome so far?

He has faced many obstacles, such as loss, social awkward-ness, and as Experiment-1 briefly brought out, previously being the victim of bullying. However, his greatest challenge to overcome is himself. All the inner battles that he fights day in and day out. The silent battle that no one else sees.

11. What is it you're hoping people understand from David's story?

I think many of us have been pushed to the limit at least once in our life, if not multiple times. Many of us battle with thoughts, or impulses that we may not like. But the message I hope I can send from David's story, is to never give up, and to keep fighting no matter how hopeless your situation may seem. You can be a good person, you can be successful, you can be strong. Even though sometimes it takes time, and we all have to find our own way through the fire and flames